Keith Devine

WILDERNESS OF ICE

A Tibetan Myth Becomes Reality

authorHOUSE®

AuthorHouse™ UK
1663 Liberty Drive
Bloomington, IN 47403 USA
www.authorhouse.co.uk
Phone: 0800.197.4150

Published by AuthorHouse 06/02/2017

ISBN: 978-1-5246-8185-2 (sc)
ISBN: 978-1-5246-8186-9 (hc)
ISBN: 978-1-5246-8184-5 (e)

Print information available on the last page.

Any people depicted in stock imagery provided by Thinkstock are models, and such images are being used for illustrative purposes only. Certain stock imagery © Thinkstock.

This book is printed on acid-free paper.

Because of the dynamic nature of the Internet, any web addresses or links contained in this book may have changed since publication and may no longer be valid. The views expressed in this work are solely those of the author and do not necessarily reflect the views of the publisher, and the publisher hereby disclaims any responsibility for them.

Contents

Preface

Wilderness of Ice is a fictional tale about the yeti legend in Tibet. It is inspired and to a large extent dependent upon a collection of short stories I wrote some years ago called *Nightwatchers*, which received some interest from publishing agents at the time but was generally considered overly complex, as I had tried to link all the stories together. However, there was a thread of common feedback which related to the fact that the individual stories were worthy of expansion, the Tibetan story in particular. Subsequently, I took what was initially the short story version of *Wilderness of Ice* and expanded it into a stand-alone novel, which you are about to read.

Acknowledgements

I would like to express my gratitude and thanks to the following colleagues and friends who made numerous insightful comments and suggestions and provided much needed encouragement: Peter Walmsley, Sandra Habula, Wayne Ashford, and Phil Brabin. Feedback from intelligent readers is truly worth its weight in gold! But I must single out three people to whom I dedicate this book, as follows.

My Mother
Although my mum, because of her age, was unable to read the final version of *Wilderness of Ice* in full, she has encouraged me in my creative writing endeavours throughout my life, for which I am very grateful. Blood will out!

Carl Meewezen MBE
One of the most intelligent individuals you will meet, Carl worked his way diligently through *Wilderness of Ice* and provided value at every stage.

Jane Fransen-Hale
I thank Jane not just for her efforts on this book, but also for times, places, and friendship.

Author's Note

Wilderness of Ice is a combination of historical facts, historical events, and previously published material all interwoven with plots and newly constructed characters to create an overarching fictional work. I have taken a few liberties with the current geography of certain places in Tibet and neither Bran Castle nor Lhasa Temple is as I describe them.

Writing *Wilderness of Ice* has been one of the most difficult tasks I have ever undertaken. It has also been one of the most rewarding. There comes a time for every aspiring author when he wonders if the book on which he has toiled for so long will ever actually be published, so great and so numerous seem the obstacles.

Opening Quotations

I hate all things fiction; there should always be some foundation of fact to weight the airy fabric, some degree of truth to legend, horror and fantasy. Pure invention is but the talent of a liar.

Lord Byron, letter to his publishers, London 1824

I believe that the Aryan race is forged by a combination of ice and fire which originated in Shambhala, a lost Kingdom in the Himalayas; therein might still subsist a creature that is the ancient product of this magnificent fusion.

Heinrich Himmler, telegram to Josef Mengele and Hans Schröder Berchtesgaden, 1937

Chapter 1

Kreuzberg District

Berlin, December 1937

The lemon hue of late evening was fading quickly as the cold sun vanished. Hans Schröder walked through Alexanderplatz, where the towered cathedral was peaked with snow. The street cleaners were out in force, but as fast as they could work, more snow fell. It shone like crystal from the darkening winter sky, which was still covered with lavender and indigo clouds, these succeeded in covering up the first stars of the night.

Alexanderplatz was a traditional square, the front three sides being devoted to the administration headquarters and military barracks of the Nazi Party. The rear section was an SS interrogation block and prison.

On both sides of the cobbled street were tall iron street lamps partially covered in snow, each one radiating gentle pools of orange, flickering in their attempt to light up the whole street.

December 1937 had trapped Berlin in the grip of a deep and intense winter. Schröder pulled the collar of his coat tightly up around his neck and cheeks to try to avoid the burning of the snowfall on his face. The flakes were fine, but the wind was so

1

cutting that the snowflakes stung him like grains of sand. He barely looked up as he picked his way through the narrow maze of streets and alleyways, where the old buildings appeared to lean together in search of warmth.

The movement of cars and his own footsteps seemed abnormally loud, even though he trod cautiously, passing a few parked cars as if looking for his own. He paused under an ornate archway that was the forefront to a small courtyard. Inside, a few stone steps led up to an imposing Gothic building guarded by a uniformed sentry, who at first appeared as a purple silhouette in the doorway.

Schröder narrowed his eyes, expelling his breath like a grey flame into the wintry air. He was approaching tonight's meeting with more loathing than usual.

Above the archway, mounted in stone, was a disc of white with a red background. In its centre stood a hooked black cross: the Hakenkreuz. Borrowed from ancient times, the same shape could be found in the ruins of Troy and Iraq and in the ancient temples of India and Vietnam. In Germany, it was the symbol of the new government: the Third Reich. But the swastika itself had not yet been born as the mighty and terrifying emblem it was to become in just a few short years.

Behind Schröder, children made sudden sorties on their bicycles, leaving trails in the thick skein of uncleared snow as they disappeared into the gas-feathered shadows ahead.

Schröder looked at his watch and then moved with purpose from the tangle of streets into the courtyard proper. Parked outside was a custom-built Mercedes Cabriolet with a black leather interior, featuring a raised back to accommodate a parade platform, sirens, and a shortwave radio. The lower part of the car was virtually buried in snow and would need to be freed by shovels in the morning.

The sentry unbarred the heavy oak door and pushed it open for him, saluting as Schröder went through. He was clearly expected.

As the guard closed the door behind him, Schröder found himself in a small entrance hall with a single door hanging ajar. He pushed it open, the creaking of the hinges loud in his ears.

He peered into the gloom beyond and could see an iridescent light, but nothing else other than a spiralling staircase. The bannister arced like flowing water, with the same smoothness as it must have been done on the architect's sketch. It appeared to float over the wide stairwell with spectral ease. On closer inspection, Schröder saw that it was supported with inordinately ornate wrought-iron balustrades that seemed to grow from the stairs and then spread upward.

He started to climb the staircase warily. The corridor that faced him at the top was long, silent, and shadowy and seemed rich with textures and different shades of light. Above him was a decorative archway upon which was a wooden plaque. It stated in gold leaf lettering, "Corridor of Cryptozoology".

As a zoologist, Schröder knew well enough that this was a pseudoscientific term. The prefix *crypto* is Greek and means "hidden" or "secret", specifically in relation to an animal whose existence cryptozoologists believe has been suggested but not discovered or documented by the scientific community or by direct evidence. The term had entered the modern lexicon outside of the pseudo-sciences. According to adherents, cryptids often appeared in folklore and mythology, which fact led to stories and unfounded beliefs about their existence.

Schröder felt uneasy as he started to walk along this corridor. Above were high bowed windows where a little flecked moonlight filtered in through sections of smeared glass that hadn't yet been covered fully by the snow.

The walls were dark red with pictures depicting creatures of feverish speculation: the Lamia, who was a mistress of Zeus and a child-eating demon from Greek mythology; the Kraken, a sea monster from Scandinavian myths; the Loch Ness monster from Scotland; the unicorn from Patagonia; Sasquatch from the north-western forests of America; the giant ape monster of the Virunga Mountains in Zambia; the Jamaican voodoo Mothman; and lastly, the Tibetan yeti, a mythological humanoid beast that supposedly still terrorised the high points of the Himalayas.

At the end of the corridor, through a partial opening of what seemed to be the only door, Schröder glimpsed light. He noticed movement and some murmuring voices. He approached with some trepidation, as this was not a place where one was invited often. Pausing momentarily, he cursed lightly under his breath. The engraved brass plate on the door simply read, "Heinrich Himmler, SS Protection Squadron".

He knocked on the door once, entering without waiting for a response.

Inside was a plush and sprawling room, high-ceilinged with gnarled oak beams. But it was slightly over decorated with fancy wallpaper, Picasso reproductions, and table lights made from wine bottles that threw pools of light over polished surfaces. There was a tall mahogany set of drawers by the window, each draw slightly open as if it had been riffled through. In the middle of the room, with a chair on either side, stood a wide trunk. It was not wooden and red like the army removal boxes but a similar shape, and made of black metal. And it had Himmler's name in neat gold letters on the front. A red blaze crackled over logs in the stone fireplace, above which hung an oil painting of Versailles.

Himmler scraped back his chair and rose to his feet abruptly, lifting his short stature from behind a large walnut escritoire, where an old-fashioned brass lamp with a yellow glass shade had been adjusted to bring the light close upon the leather writing top to illuminate a map. The map had been fully opened and, along with Himmler, was being inspected by two silent and rather sinister-looking men in dark suits. These men stood close together. For a moment, their shadows, beyond the desk light, almost seemed merged into one.

With a very short military haircut and moustache, crisp-shirted beneath his splendid Hugo Boss–designed black Gestapo uniform, adorned in the lapel with a large ornamental dark-gold-on-black-enamel swastika, Himmler moved forward languidly. His eyes, behind the wire-rimmed glasses, were pale and blue like the mountain sky; their clearness, at times, offered the impression that he looked into one's very soul. Thus he succeeded in establishing a personal link with everyone he met. But anyone who got close to him knew that Himmler was innately insecure and awkward - but not when he liked someone. In that case, his eyes lost that tissue-thin facade and could often seem warm and humorous. Behind his grandiose projection seemed a shyness and diffidence of manner.

"Herr Doktor." Himmler greeted Schröder with an infectious superior smile. There was a click of heels and the traditional salute.

Schröder reciprocated, and then they shook hands. Schröder swallowed, nervous and wary of Himmler, just as everyone was.

Himmler opened a silver cigarette case, took out a small cigar, and lit it with a yellow flare. He blew out a mouthful of smoke in an impatient gesture that might have been mistaken for repressed anger. Knowing Schröder didn't smoke, he asked, "A Pernod or cognac? Or maybe a glass of wine, Hans?"

Schröder relaxed a modicum, as this was a definite sign that he was not here because of some perceived act of disloyalty to the SS, which he joined under protest in 1933. He would claim, much later, to have been an unwilling recruit to the organisation and that the SS was a step necessary to secure safety and advancement for him and his family. He had worried about the accusation of disloyalty as he walked across Alexanderplatz. Thankfully, there was no look of displeasure on Himmler's face.

"Red wine would be splendid, Heinrich. Thank you."

Schröder was a known drinker. Some of the time, he drank for the sheer glow of it, and at other times, with SS associates and grand bureaucrats, for more palpable results. Like few others, though, he was capable of staying canny whilst drinking - and of keeping his head clear.

Himmler waved a hand for him to sit on one side of the metal trunk as, from a crystal decanter, he poured two glasses of claret with precise delicacy. He handed one to Schröder.

"It is not Château Laffite Rothschild," he said jokingly. "In fact, not a vintage of which I expect very much at all." Himmler smiled benignly. "It is from Sicily, so closer to olive oil." He laughed again. "But our country's time of wealth and power is coming, my friend. We are forging a new Europe."

He seemed to draw on a knowledge of future intentions.

Both men raised a glass to the Führer and took a sip of wine. "Rather good," Schröder said, agreeing that it was no vintage.

Himmler lifted the cigar and made a sucking sound as he dragged a deep puff of smoke into his lungs. Then, as he exhaled, he leaned forward on the trunk, following which there was a short silence. "To business," Himmler announced with brittle assurance, his voice gruff with the smoke's expectorant, which added to the grand illusory image that he tried to project of himself.

He clicked his fingers and one of the two dark-suited shadows brought the map over from the walnut desk and placed it on the shiny metallic top of the trunk. Himmler's head was angled over it like a hungry bird, with his spectacles perched on the brow of his nose. The men retreated to sit together in the emptiest corner of the room once again.

Schröder rested his chin upon clasped hands and glanced towards the window on the far side of the room, where an ominous black cloud, pregnant with snow, was sweeping over Berlin, casting weird and sinister shadows across the skyline.

He suddenly felt a certain icy pang quicken the rhythm of his blood. Looking at the map, he asked directly, "What did you want to talk to me about, Heinrich?" His tone was perfunctory but polite as he imagined a host of dreadful answers. He had expected to see a map of Europe, but instead, spread out on the trunk top, was a chart of the Far East. His look was one of intermingled despondency and curiosity.

A certain glassy smile flitted across Himmler's lips as he waved a hand across the map. "Dach der Ende" ("Roof of the World"), he said. Then he spoke in a thin voice, in the manner of a lecturer addressing a public meeting.

"You are aware of the work of our promising young geneticist Josef Mengele?" Schröder nodded wordlessly and felt a further chill of concern, faint dewdrops of sweat starting to glisten on his forehead as he thought that Mengele's Nuclein wizardry was nothing more than science fiction.

"We believe that his work – his hypothesis, if you will – although testable, will in time revolutionise the world's understanding of Nuclein, our comprehension of the nature of the beast and how we Aryans may evolve further up the evolutionary chain at a faster rate than Mother Nature might otherwise allow." He drew on his cigar. "To be in possession of such knowledge and power would galvanise our dominant supremacy." He was emphatic in his tone, breathing out a plume of light blue smoke, content that the crucial dictum had been deposited.

"I see." Schröder looked mildly askance at him. With a darkening suspicion, he dabbed at his forehead gently with a handkerchief. His face clouded; there was unhappiness impressed on his countenance. He was slightly purple-nosed, as the oxygen which by right belonged to his veins had for years gone to feed the sharp blue flame of liquor. And so it continued to do so that evening.

He lapsed into silence and waited for Himmler to volunteer further information. His heart beat raised a fraction as he took a considered sip of wine, his eyes gently searching the hawk like face before him.

Himmler waited in his guarded way, meeting Schröder with an unchecked stare, a vinous light in his eyes.

"I was with the Führer and Mengele in Berchtesgaden last month. We have agreed extra funding for Mengele's work, and," Himmler bared his teeth in a somewhat mirthless smile, waving a casual hand towards his SS colleague, "we want you to assist him in much the same way that you assisted the palaeontologist Ralph von Koenigswald two years ago in Hong Kong." His face contained a look of veneration, and in his voice there was a tone of triumph.

"Your report on hominid fossils caught the eye of the press and was quite inspirational." This was said with genuine admiration.

Schröder considered this and felt further heaviness like a dropping stone in his throat, falling and spilling ripples through his stomach. He gave an enigmatic smile. "But Heinrich." His shoulders slumped a fraction. "I am a doctor of zoology. I know nothing about human Nuclein. I am not a geneticist. How could I possibly assist Josef?" Schröder's lament was indignant, almost affronted. His question coalesced intrigue and approaching dread, but it also contained a trace of defiance.

9

Himmler considered this and made a pattern on his face, curling his moist lips into an intended sneer. He continued with an air of nonchalance.

"Your analysis of dragon's teeth in the limestone caves of Hong Kong last year, and the conclusion that it belonged to a giant extinct reptile that was a 'new species' to zoology, was superb. You also found a very odd oversized skull with a brain cavity in excess of ours in those caves in the hills above Kowloon Harbour, did you not?" His eyes were sparkling as if he were telling some marvellous tale.

Schröder went to speak, but Himmler wasn't in listening mode. "And what about the lobe-finned coelacanth, the ocean reptile thought to have been extinct over sixty million years ago?" He paused. "Did you not catch one off the Eastern Cape province of South Africa only last year to prove the 'no longer alive' theorists wrong?!"

Schröder nodded in the affirmative and said rather feebly, "I did but ..." The words froze on his tongue, the sinking stone and dryness of the throat suddenly becoming worse as Himmler raised his hand to cut him short once again.

"And other scientists have stumbled upon new species in this century. The okapi, an African forest giraffe, was only discovered in 1901. And this set me thinking, Hans." Himmler drew deeply on the cigar before crushing orange embers into the ashtray. "Mainstream science, normally unconvinced anyway, might not be the answer in the way Mengele perceives it." He jutted out a finger to emphasise the point.

"Josef at first thought your findings in Hong Kong to be fallacious, casting disdain, I can assure you, but your merit has been well documented, so he has somewhat changed his mind. And he is now also exploring the various aspects of human ancestry with great passion, in particular Vindija Neanderthals, who lived alongside *Homo sapiens* about a million years ago, and the matrilineal linkages – plus other interbreeding and genetic hybrids between humans and some other creatures, in fact any animal unknown to science. But," Himmler was conciliar for a moment and appeared to deflate, "he lacks your expertise in this field, Hans." He made this last statement in a tone halfway between irony and triumph. "And he endlessly goes on about 'good science' and 'bad science', which is wearing thin on both the Führer and me.

"We need to stop guessing about the Aryan race, Hans. Please travel, as I'm about to tell you to, and you will better understand." His voice was silvery and clear. "Go to the root of the legend and get far away from libraries and editorial offices. In these places we can only speculate – often badly!"

Then Himmler became both agitated and enthusiastic, moving like a sleeping cobra from a state of inertia into venomous action. He reached for the carafe and topped up both glasses excitedly, regarding Schröder in a bright and steely way.

"Take the sixth sense – we are no different from any other animal. Animals have a sixth sense and so do we, but the problem with human beings is that most of us are not forced to use it. When you're in situations and you're traumatised to a very high point, you are actually forced to dwell in the sixth sense that we're all born with. And of course in combat or in war itself you're living in those situations. It's continuous.

You become an animal yourself, and by doing so you start tapping into your own sixth sense, so what if …" He hesitated to let the pending question linger in the air. "What if we could develop automatic sixth sense activation to draw on whenever we wanted, as simple as taking an aspirin for a headache? It would dumbfound other humans and give the Aryan race an advantage. We might develop extrasensory perception, have paranormal abilities, and use telepathy. It has been proved by the force of nature that the strong will always prevail and that even in the gentlest stream or the fairest meadow, there is no form of life that doesn't put itself first.

"You work amongst perfect elements, Hans and therefore, politically, you are an idealist. There will always be slaves, although the name may change. What is slavery but the domination of the weak by the strong? How can you make slaves and their master's equal? Or are you fool enough to think that all men are born equal?" Himmler paused for effect.

"It is the nature of the beast that creatures will compete only in proportion to the adaptation of their peers. The world is nothing if not competition. So it is no surprise that the inhabitants of one region should be supplanted by inhabitants from another land. And should those inhabitants prove themselves greater in fitness and power, who knows what the master race might achieve?"

Schröder didn't answer because he didn't know what to say, and was afraid that he might stammer and appear weak. He was aware of his heart thumping in his chest, like a living creature quite separate from himself. He gripped his wine glass white-knuckled and simply said, "so what *are* we trying to achieve?"

Himmler met his eyes with consternation. The remnants of his smile fell away. "It is a strange but unique task we ask of you, Hans, for we have agreed to explore beyond the human species in order for us to create the master race. But even that is not the strangest part of your assignment."

There was no bravado in Himmler's manner, his enthusiasm simple and honest. It was clear that he passionately believed in the master race quest.

A mild irritation flickered in Schröder's eyes as he ran his fingers through his thick greying hair, then taking another mouthful of dark red wine.

Himmler was well known for his strange ideas, legendary in fact. There were rumours that he actively practised the supernatural and had joined a black priesthood, the Shaitan, using the ancient rune script to summon demons, holding séances and exorcisms, and even partly convincing Hitler that these forgotten and largely cursed religions could be reborn to help restore the might of the Fatherland.

On this basis, Schröder hoped that the strangeness of the idea was that of the scientifically based Mengele rather than of Heinrich Himmler. But the next few words destroyed any fragile hope he may have held in that regard.

"There are forces in this world," Himmler stated with a dangerous wheeze, "full of power and sublimity. Man is ignorant of the nature of his own being. Even the idea of his limitations is based on experience of the past. And every slow step of his progress only serves to extend the limited empire." He stopped abruptly and stared fixedly at his SS colleague, letting the implications of his words settle like a shadow conjured up in daylight.

Schröder, feeling awkward about the sudden silence, wondered what to say. "I'm not sure I follow." He frowned, the simple assonance of his voice trailing away like an echo. He looked genuinely puzzled. Himmler smiled consolingly at him and pretended to consider this uncertain statement for a few moments, but it was clear when he spoke that his assertion had been prepared.

"Extinction, or perceived extinction, has its secrets, in libraries, in the ruins of ancient towns, in secret temples and forgotten graves, and high up the flanks of the tallest mountains in the world." He tapped the map. Schröder saw that a circle had been made around an area between China and Tibet close to the foothills of the Western Himalayas. In a pencil someone had written the word *Shambhala*, followed by a question mark.

Another log was thrown onto the fire. Schröder watched as the flames welcomed the wood with a noisy crackle. He then held the glass up to his lips as firelight flickered merrily through the crystal, sending multi coloured shapes across the uneven surface of the map. An apprehensive chill, like wet leaves, clung to his back.

"What is it precisely that you wish me to do?" he questioned more directly now, contemplating further distasteful options.

They spoke in detail for the next hour, consuming another bottle of wine as Himmler shared his fantastical thoughts and ideas, with both of them reading through Mengele's meticulously scribed report on coaxing sequenced Nuclein, which Himmler had thumb-marked on several pages. Mengele had stated that he lacked live human specimens, which made Schröder shudder. In a tiny way, he was suddenly glad that he was not going to be involved in the direct human element of what Mengele had named "the master race biological template".

But surely the task proposed to him was preposterous. Perhaps it would come to nothing, as Himmler always spoke of vague schemes. Maybe this was just another act of caprice on his part. What Schröder could not be quite sure of was whether this was caprice of a blameless mischievous man or the sport of a guilty man taking pleasure in his own immunity and cleverness.

As it unfolded, it was neither.

Himmler proceeded to click through a black-and-white slide show that demonstrated how much preparation had already gone into his assignment. Schröder knew then that escape from responsibility was impossible. He was shown pictures of the vehicles, the weaponry, and the terrain he would traverse. The military lead was to be a Commandant Gerber, but Schröder was to hold overall command on account of his rank and the nature of the expedition. He was to concentrate on the zoological aspects, whereas Gerber's focus was to be security.

The first resting point would be Bran Castle, in the rust-coloured hills of the Borgo Pass in Transylvania.

It was not lost on Schröder that Bran Castle with its Gothic medieval towers was the one time fortress of Vlad the Impaler, who had earned his nickname by sticking Turks onto sharpened poles until their stomachs exploded, the bodies then positioned along the roadside like milestones and left to rot until the stench of decaying flesh became unbearable. Staying in the Stoker-inspired Dracula castle en route would surely be a fitting beginning to the adventure that lay ahead.

It was clear that Himmler was acting largely on his own maniacal thoughts, the longing for something which he didn't understand, a desire like gold lust. But these days he also possessed the necessary authority to make his ideations reality.

Schröder did his best to consider his task professionally, but he looked in perpetual doubt now, his brow etched with deep lines of concern which he could not hide. He swirled the remaining wine around in his glass and then emptied it in a single indulgent gulp.

Himmler looked at him with eyes that held a scuttling spider of a look, something like predatory menace.

"Come now, Hans," he said, his smile broadening to one of genuine pleasure, "you are always complaining about a lack of funding for your line of work, yes?" He paused. "Well, on this expedition you will have plenty of money, supplies, and transport, plus troops and weapons to guard you. You will stay in grand settings on your way, and in Lhasa there is an ancient temple close to the foothills of the Himalayas, which I'm sure you can," he halted, and then laughed like a child slowly understanding a Christmas cracker joke – "occupy!"

Wine-headed as he was, Schröder felt a slight touch of anger. Another sudden burst of anxiety struck his heartbeat. He understood, though, that anger and anxiety were much easier to bear than humiliation.

"We need an alternative hypothesis," Himmler proclaimed, "to understand the origin and nature of the beast!" He was bristling now, stoking the embers of a long-lost yearning, his deep-socketed eyes retaining a menacing look as his shaped eyebrows drew together in thought.

Himmler appeared lost in reverie for a moment. "It is a wondrous jagged land you will visit: verdant hills, open glades, richly wooded forests, and icy waterfalls, but shift your gaze ninety degrees to the east and at the same distance of fifty miles a range of snowy mountains appear on the horizon, stabbing up into the sky, mountains where nothing can live." He clasped his hands with unbridled excitement suddenly. "Or can it?!

"What stays mysterious also stays unexposed," Himmler said profoundly, with a wire-thin smile on his face. "I know my thoughts seem wild and unfair," he admitted with uncharacteristic candour, "but we need you to drag myth into Fatherland reality."

Logs in the fire collapsed and scattered orange embers above the metal guard, like watchfires on an ancient field of battle. The moon through the window emerged from behind a ragged mass of cloud, creating a strange spectral form outlined against the silver of its curve.

"Do you understand, Hans?" Himmler snapped his question like a bullet splintering into rock.

Schröder, making a gesture of assent, issued a sound, not from his throat but more like through his nostrils, the way a horse snorts. And although he didn't commit straight away, he verbally confirmed: "I understand." His voice cracked slightly as he glanced down at the map, doubt lining his face at every point.

Almost as an afterthought, Himmler spoke to him in a low, urgent voice. "Keep this as secret as the grave." His demeanour indicated the level of intended threat. At the same time, Schröder was handed a single sheet of paper embossed with an extravagant crest, which he accepted somewhat listlessly. It was the official endorsement from Hitler, his instructions made clear.

"There can be no survival without due fitness and power," Himmler said. Schröder nodded gravely and stared for a moment with defeated eyes. "Race, blood, and soil is not the art of pure science, which standing alone teaches us no such thing."

They shook hands silently and saluted the Führer again.

As he left the Reichsfuhrer's office, forlorn and without the certitude that all would finish well, Schröder glanced back momentarily at Himmler, who was waving a jovial farewell and wearing a honeyed smile as he said, "To Germany's soul."

Over the next four years, Himmler would develop the SS from a mere thirteen-hundred-man battalion into a million strong paramilitary group and, following Hitler's orders, would establish and control the concentration camps, including taking a particular interest in Auschwitz-Birkenau, where Mengele would finally get his supply of live human specimens. But at the end of 1937, apart from his increasing influence on Hitler, Himmler was simply known to have good organisational skills and for selecting highly competent subordinates.

Schröder prayed that he was not merely going to be someone enlisted to undertake a fragile project linked loosely to his background and one that future historians would criticise him for.

* * *

The snow had abated momentarily and the darkness was unmoving with the iciness of the night. The trees in the square holding no colour, were mere black skeletal arms and fingers, the bones of the trees holding withered leaves, like signposts to winter.

In less than a decade, Alexanderplatz would be the backdrop to Checkpoint Charlie and the governance point of the Berlin Wall, separating east from west. Berlin itself would not be the capital of a unified Germany again for another fifty years.

Schröder, feeling solitary in the side streets, walked home in a sour and thought-churned mood. In spite of the low snow-muffled growl from Berlin Central, higher-pitched sounds carried far, clearly audible on both sides of the roadway, the rumour of the approach of any passenger preceding them by a long time. He half slipped on the ice, held himself upright, and shivered.

As he entered his apartment, a strange air of loneliness and empty space gripped his heart. Schröder lived on the second floor of a nineteenth-century house at the end of Ostbahnhof. The wide French windows in the lounge looked down over the back of a restaurant, which was lit by a clear light. Clouds of steam rolled out of the kitchen and tiptoed stealthily across the cobblestoned lanes, diminishing at every step like shy ghosts.

Above the crooked rooftops, the night fog was still seeping over the city, although the sky was largely cloudless and the lanes lit by unhindered gas light. For a while Schröder fell into a reverie, contemplating what awaited him on the long assignment ahead. Then he glanced at Hitler's letter again. Both rational and irrational fears filled his mind. Reluctant to identify them too closely, he left them unformed on the margins of his mind, yet he knew he would have to face them at some point soon.

Schröder took a hot shower, holding his eyes open under the needles of water until they hurt.

* * *

The following morning, the alarm went off one hour before the creamy flow of dawn. Clouds obscured any sharp distinctions between night and day. Berlin appeared completely silent, no breath of wind, no birdsong, the moon a mere opaque fleck on the horizon.

Schröder's bedroom was impenetrably dark as he passed through into the larger space of the living room, where the walls were lit by a pale light from a single window. That feeble glow revealed bookshelves and a small glass case crammed full of skins of small animals, exhibits carefully sewn and preserved. He crossed the room as if walking through a shallow pool of darkness and peered into the cabinet, catching memories like the rag end of dreams.

Like most people who ended up as zoologists, Schröder had been fascinated by creatures other than humans ever since he was a boy – the mystery of the little universes of life and death existing in hollow trees and earthy burrows; African ranges of the elephant; and the ocean-wide hunting grounds of the killer whale. As a child he was always spotting similarities between human beings and animals.

He pulled back the blinds to the main window overlooking Alexanderplatz.

Fog drifted above the white city walls where the gas lamps glimmered like carbuncles. Through the muffle and smother of these fallen clouds, the procession of the city's life was now starting to roll in slowly through the great arteries of Berlin.

Above the black-purple bulk of the cathedral, the fog was broken up and the odd haggard shaft of beige daylight would glance in between the swirling wreaths, but shortly great wafts of snow floated in the air like dandelion seeds. The sky was pure white once again.

Schröder sat in his local café drinking cups of strong coffee in swift succession, also taking in an early morning schnapps. On his right was a hollow wounded building – a ruined synagogue – its mortuary buildings and half-tumbled walls showing gravestones like teeth in the cruelly exposed mouth of winter. The plaque declaring the name of the last chief rabbi lay smashed in jigsaw pieces in the rubble.

Later that day, in the strange luminescence of a snowy winter dusk, he would be heading east, but not to Moscow, as was commonly the case for SS officers these days. This would be much farther east, in the way that Himmler had described.

Schröder felt the sword of Damocles hovering above his head, or a Babylonian finger simply pointing. But it was true that without the support of Himmler, such expeditions of finding the origins of the Aryan race would have been impossible.

Schröder was not a cryptozoologist, but he had often been thrilled by tales from faraway lands, tales of half-man, half-beast creatures that roam the high peaks or survive in the densest forest and jungles. He wasn't sure he believed in those tales, but neither was he completely ready to dismiss them. Could *something* undiscovered still be out there? But the details of his assignment defied any rational explanation, something that, as a scientist who believed in the triumph of reason over superstition, he considered profoundly disturbing.

What he didn't want, at any cost, was a direct involvement in the master race programme or the additional responsibility to "capture one male and one female alive and bring them back for breeding and use in our weapons division," although he was aware of a recent ambitious and chilling series of experiments to create ape like hybrids in the Soviet Union, including finding volunteers amongst the local population for insemination with ape sperm. Genetic amalgamation was gathering in popularity, as was the biological definition of what actually represented a true species.

But in the short term there was no alternative, so escape from the madness of the escalating and seemingly unrelenting Nazi regime appeared impossible. As a result, Schröder adjusted to the political situation, his mind turning towards proving Himmler's theories about glacial ancestry. Schröder may not have seen Tibet as a sanctuary for a proto-Aryan race in which a priestly caste had created subterranean ice realms, but he did see it as the cradle of humanity.

Schröder's mind spun in different directions. The thrill of being the very first person in the world who might discover something new had always been at the root of why he became a scientist in the first place, but now, as a foremost zoologist and advisor to the joint Oxford–Lausanne, English–Swiss museum of zoology, he would be heading for Tibet as part of a Nazi inspired lunatic quest.

He knew that everyone had to balance risk and reward, but the implications of this were potentially enormous. Without warning, anxiety turned to a glimpse of dismay. And then the unexpected mystery of his situation came home to him anew, and with it a true sense of peril.

Did the Himalayas' most ancient mystery figure in the origin of humankind's creation?

Suddenly his face was gripped with a look of astonishment, as a man swimming in deep water might look up hopefully in search of land. There had always been stories of a strange beast roaming the forests and the ice deserts of Tibet, frightening away human intruders and killing yaks with effortless ease. Could Tibet still be the home of an existent beast? Was Shambhala the prehistoric cradle of humankind?

On that polar morning in Berlin, Schröder faced his task unswervingly. He had no choice but to take on Himmler's special mission. At that point, he relocated his courage and turned his attention to the matter in hand.

He was going in search of the yeti.

Chapter 2

Bran Castle

Transylvania, January 1938

𝔇𝔬𝔤𝔰 𝔥𝔬𝔴𝔩𝔢𝔡 as peasants made their way home from the fields where they had worked the cart horses all day.

Over the castle, the encroaching night was growing heavy, oozing down and uncovering a myriad shapes and shades as it came. Nearer to the horizon, the sky was a milky blue, fragile, hardly able to bear the impending weight of darkness.

Night had slumped on Transylvania. The Gothic towers of Bran Castle, poking up over the valley, were indistinct. This ancient fortress now belonged to King Carol II and was the epitome of his despicable epoch. The old castle stood on a rugged slope, moonlit snowdrifts piling against the jagged walls. The derelict battlements glistened with ice, their ragged outlines blending into the rocks behind.

Slavic knights had built the first wooden castle on the site in the thirteenth century, situating it near Bran and in the immediate vicinity of Brasov. Later, after being burnt to the ground by the Mongols, it became a stone citadel on the mountain pass between Transylvania and Wallachia, and later still, a fictional gateway to the realm of Bram Stoker's Dracula.

Bran Castle, at the entrance to the Borgo mountain valley through which traders had travelled for more than a millennium, became a royal residence within the Kingdom of Romania. But in 1937 the castle was the monarchical home of King Carol, named "the Mad Monarch", who had reigned fiercely and held extreme anti-Semitic views, turning his kingdom into a de facto dictatorship under his sole governing power.

Inside the castle, Carol wandered the plush corridors waiting for his visitors. The castle was a vast structure with turrets, stone steps, imposing doors, steeply twisting staircases, ancient walls, circular rooms in towers, rich tapestries of emerald green and gold hanging on the walls, suits of armour standing guard, swords crossed against various coats of arms, narrow passageways, windows like great slits in thick walls, and an oak drawbridge on iron chains.

At the far end of the ballroom, across two smaller reception rooms, Carol pushed through folding doors with sixteenth-century flower paintings on the panels. A huge portrait of a soldier on a horse dominated the wall facing the stairs, and on all sides of it there were carefully arranged bouquets of fresh flowers. The floor was a complex pattern of black, white, and red marble, arranged in a mixture of shapes.

He ascended a long staircase, heading then through the maze of corridors that weaved their way back towards the front of the castle.

Carol was lord and master of his land. He knew that. In his time he had bent Romanian history, deformed it at will in fact. It was a straight line drawn from Vlad, except today, the stench surrounding Bran was caused by the factories of Cluj and instead of rotting Turkish flesh. In his way, Carol was more feared still, maintaining tyranny year after year by the increasing power and unfathomable loyalty of his secret police force. Romania became an ally and supporter of Adolf Hitler in 1933 and would subsequently fight on the Eastern Front alongside Nazi storm troopers. The castle would also be used as a hospital for wounded soldiers, until being occupied and partially destroyed by the Soviet Union in 1944.

Carol and Vlad were spiritual relations, and both had castles everywhere. Bran was the most splendid in Transylvania, jutting up like something from a cartoon fantasy. And since nobody had ever dared to challenge Vlad's authority, it followed that he, like Carol today, just took over the property. The only difference between the two was that Carol did not indulge in public displays of bloodsucking. His torture and tyranny were undertaken strictly behind closed doors.

The tall and wiry monarch paused at a door along a dark corridor, opening it slowly. The billiards room with its mahogany panelling was unchanged since being furnished to the taste of a nineteenth-century beer baron. Even the antlers and the family portraits remained in position. The windows opened onto the front lawn, but the sky outside was dark, the room lit only by the green shaded lights reflecting from the baize table tops. Carol stood in the doorway motionless for a moment, fidgeting with his silver ring and staring at the tables as if interested in nothing else.

Then he closed the door and continued his walk through the castle.

The enormous dining room with its ornate domed roof was that evening to be seen by the flickering light from three chandeliers. He could hear the thin wind creating draughts in the room through the shutters, tossing the light of the candle to and fro, making it dance in the reflection of the silver cutlery, and allowing the massive paintings to be glimpsed in the darkness beyond the melancholy candlelight. He caught a glimpse of himself in the silverware. Like a vampire who had fed on blood, a warm flush of expectation was rising in his cheeks.

Struggling for a moment to break free from the spell of his own face, Carol walked over to an enormous window. Drawing back the red silk curtains, he stared out.

A swirl of lavender transfigured the sky as the perishing ball of light sank below the horizon, leaving behind a sliver of dark orange. The remaining phosphorescence from the dimming sky danced along the glass windows until it faded completely.

Although he could not see much of it then, he thought of Transylvania as a wonderful part of the world, a sort of Switzerland without the smugness. Though officially part of his Romania, it was a chillingly beautiful mixture of old Teutonic towns, Hungarian turn-of-the-century architecture, and ancient Romanian villages, all set in a countryside which contained everything from dramatic gorges and snowy mountain passes to rolling plains and forests.

Every sound came edgy and distinct; in the silence he heard an owl, the trees moving in the wind, the steady tick of the skeleton clock on the mantelpiece, and movement of burning wood settling in the grate – and then a servant's footfalls along an empty corridor.

The servant came in behind him, bowed, and put plates of cold meat, cheese, and bread on the table. There was a sound of a cork opening and of wine being poured. Carol, not acknowledging the servant, barely glanced at the food and wine.

From the fireplace there came a series of cracks, a bright snake of flame, and a smell of sap as the remnants of a log was enveloped by the fire.

Twenty minutes later, the massed yellow headlights of a convoy of field-green military cars came into sight at the far end of the walled approach to the castle, sweeping snake-like past the Gothic chapel and the folly, and a grotesque tower inspired by the tales of King Arthur, before halting outside the main entrance to the castle. This convoy had travelled that day from Germany, across central Romania, and then through the Transylvanian hillside itself, bringing its passengers from Berlin to Bran.

Guard dogs barked and bayed to announce the arrival as the lightning came suddenly, a brilliant shock of white in the graphite sky, forking silently into the unsuspecting ground, the subsequent thunderous boom calling its warning order, too late as always.

A grey-haired man emerged from the back seat of the leading vehicle. He was clearly in charge, but equally clear was that he was not comfortable in military uniform. Without glancing up at the shadow at the window, he entered the dark interior of the castle.

The rain started to fall in slanting sheets as Carol allowed a slow smile to shape his gaunt face.

Chapter 3

Kowloon Junk Harbour

Hong Kong, August 2007

Seventy-One Years Later

The name Hong Kong derived from the Cantonese *Heung Gawng*, meaning "fragrant harbour", which name was inspired by the scent of sandalwood, piled on the western side of the island on what, since that winter morning in 1841 when British marines clambered ashore and planted the Union Jack claiming Hong Kong for the British Crown, is now called Aberdeen. Beijing subsequently conceded the Kowloon Peninsula and Stonecutters Island to Britain, giving history's largest empire complete control of Victoria Harbour and its numerous trade routes.

The British soon turned the island into a vast bustling market for foreign goods, a cosmopolitan community of Mongol, Chinese, Muscovite, Armenian, Kashmiri, Nepalese, and northern Indian traders. Hong Kong was exporting musk, gold, medicinal plants, and exotic furs to far-flung British Empire markets, in exchange for sugar, saffron, Persian turquoise, European amber, and Mediterranean coral.

Deng stared out from his balcony at the resplendent views of Kowloon Harbour, watching the junks and people going about their business. In the strong rays of the setting sun, a junk's huge lowered sails appeared to be on fire.

Translucent clouds were spreading a sunset-bronzed canopy across the sky, making the western peaks seem painted with watery blood. Above them, wisps of lighter cloud were dipped in lilac, but on the line of the horizon, darkness was submerging the paths between the hills, causing them to appear strange and stark against the philosophical stars.

The twilight fell as if a shade had been placed over the sun, robbing the harbour of its brilliant hues. The skyline was now transformed with the skyscrapers of central Hong Kong and Wan Chai decked out in their neon robes.

Deng liked the fact that the South China Sea had so many moods. Sometimes the water was azure and gleaming; sometimes, a dull turbulent brown. This evening it was a choppy green with a faint haze that blurred the view of the farthest skyscrapers and the loftier peaks behind them, which were tonight dyed maroon in the afterglow of the setting sun. The Kowloon Mountains became sharp jagged silhouettes against the stars.

Deng was fifty-one. His marriage had ended three years ago in acrimonious fashion. Although he no longer saw his estranged wife, Perma, she, ever the model of virtue and fairness, allowed him access to their son, Tashi, a name meaning "auspicious and fortunate". Tashi would be fourteen next month.

Deng often wondered if, over the years, inherited personality traits such as being acutely obdurate resurfaced in the heat of his close personal relationships with women. He had grown sapped and morose at times, and had come to loathe his own taciturn nature with the opposite sex. And yet, when he had met Perma, he was shamelessly, painfully, cravingly in love. It was as though a world of greyness had been lit up by a thousand fiery sparks, but over time, and with a degree of inevitability, he started to sheath his feelings with guarded coldness that then turned to ice.

At first, still being young, excuses could be made for him, but after a while he had to accept that Perma needed a softer pillow to lie on than his heart. He realised then that love was a nagging preoccupation, a feeling that the treasure of life had condensed itself to the diminutive space wherever she was. Love was reared in the wilderness and could not be tamed.

He grimaced to himself, remembering when he had first moved from Lhasa in Tibet to Hong Kong at the age of sixteen, to stay with his uncle. Despite the circumstances of his departure, and amazed though he was that he had been allowed to leave at all, Deng had been given a flamboyant and dignified farewell from the temple with indulgences fit for a prince, being held in his honour in the resplendent Imperial Hall. But he remembered his mother warning him against the inheritance that flowed in his blood.

He attended St Martin's College and then the notable Lugard University, where he earned a degree in oriental studies, specialising in Near Eastern and Far Eastern societies, cultures, languages, and people. He then married and lived with Perma in a small apartment in Kennedy Town for seven years after the birth of Tashi. Now he lived on his own in the Kowloon Harbour complex.

Despite emotional insecurities and his sometimes mettlesome nature, Deng had achieved the career status of a highly respected historian and researcher, rendered famous locally in his chosen field of oriental studies. In fact, personality defects could often work in his favour in business, as they gave him a tenacity of purpose, which the uncongenial call obstinacy.

On first moving to Hong Kong, he felt a near continuous concoction of exhilaration, panic, culture shock, and alienation, but this evolved as the months and years passed, gradually being replaced with a feeling of finally being at peace and at home.

He breathed out a deep audible sigh, restless, and then faced the vexing problem that had been on the margin of his thoughts for several days and which was now overwhelmingly important and could no longer be avoided. His mind was congested with dark contemplation of his father, and he was conscious of an almost physical dread catching at his throat, bringing back to him the intensity of that dark face and those burning embittered eyes. His father was named Tenzin, after the first great leader of the unified Tibet, Tenzin Tubo, who ruled in AD 400, Tenzin meaning "holder of the teaching". Suddenly Deng's heart was beating so hard he could almost feel it through his veins.

His father was a tyrannically cruel and heartless man who created the deep darkness of the vast temple in Lhasa, ruling it with a rod of iron and breeding unmentionable fear. He ruled his own family by the use of an even darker metal. In adulthood, Deng once asked his uncle, Tyi, why he had left the temple, to which his uncle simply replied: "Because your father somehow turned into a monster. No one was ever sure how or why, because he hadn't always been like that, and certainly wasn't raised in that way."

Despite the dark whisperings that Deng's father was also a cannibal, the people at the temple honoured Tenzin as a sage, and feared him as a medieval peasant might fear an evil sorcerer. He had achieved incomparable power. His orders, even the simplest ones, were as terrible as the twisted wisdom of the ancients. Servants, the temple's worker ants, would not pass his threshold for fear that their shadow would stretch out and touch his. Deng remembered his father saying to a servant once, "I will make you squirm in pain like a naked worm."

Everyone, including Deng and his younger brother, Kwei-Lan, shuddered at the very thought of Tenzin. The only time Deng's father seemed calm was when he locked himself in the great study and quietly painted. The study was a room reserved for him alone and used only for his painting. Only trusted servants, such as the young Rinchen, were allowed inside, to mix and prepare paints and, of course, to clean up afterwards.

Deng recalled a memory. When as a child his shameless curiosity could hold out no longer, he pushed the study door furtively ajar, glimpsing the interior of a large room with high ceilings and every conceivable section of space overflowing with his father's work – on the walls, lying on tables, or leaning against various low-hanging tapestries. It seemed to him then, at his tender age, that there were galleries of silken canvases emblazoned with millions of colours in that room, more colours than are sprayed out on a dragon's breath, like a real-life Aladdin's cave or a trove of riches from a fairy tale.

There were piles of books towering on tables and shelves, and by the wide-framed windows was a large telescope, aimed at the heavens. He caught a glimpse then of a slender door, which was bright blue in colour, virtually hidden by a combination of screens and a bulky canvas which leaned against a nearby bookcase.

Deng approached that inner door and reached out a tiny hand to touch the tarnished bronze handle. But just at that moment he heard a scurry of servants passing by in the corridor. Suddenly becoming worried about being caught and punished by his father, he retraced his steps urgently, making sure to close the door of the study behind him, running back to his bedroom confused, and even more afraid than usual. He cried in his bedroom that night, wishing that Kano, his grandfather, was still alive to comfort him. Years later he would wonder how his grandfather, such a gentle and caring man, had managed to create such a monster of a son.

Time, as it turned out, would teach him soon enough.

Searching his earliest memory, Deng realised how capable his father had been of strange humour, which wandered the outreaches of his dark mind, and of unfathomable rages. He still had nightmares about the unnecessary cruelty he and his brother had endured as children and the fact that they witnessed the same treatment meted out to their mother, who disappeared at a young age. A shadow of bitterness and pain passed across Deng's face. The full details surrounding his mother's death remained a mystery. Wavering doubts and distrust were still buried in the deepest part of his mind, resurfacing from time to time when his emotional shield dropped.

Something about what had happened to her and what he and his brother were told did not seem right, but they were too young to do anything about it, and certainly in no position to ask their father for clarity or, worse still, to imply foul play. Their mother was dead and they would never see her again; it was as simple as that. As a young boy Deng would often be plunged into deep tantrums of resentment and frustration, but this only served to earn him a beating, and so he had quickly learned to bury all feelings from the sight of others, and would often lock himself in his room, weeping and shaking.

A shrine to his mother, Mi-Sun, was erected with an ancient pillar of delicate stone and was there for all to see in the *jiaohui*, the Tibetan word for "chapel". There were inscriptions on the pillar and a long strip of faded brass to Mi-Sun's memory. But poisonous tongues like wasp stings murmured throughout the temple walls. Her name seemed to hover on every tongue as the rumours grew darker and more turbulent, uttered in whispered tones of horror such that all of Lhasa seemed dizzy with dread at the thought of Mi-Sun's passing. Now a mature man, Deng often felt exasperation about what might have actually happened to her. His inability to do anything about it had come close to breaking him on several occasions.

Grief was the hardest emotion to express because so much of it is numbness; it is also passive, something one undergoes rather than undertakes. It becomes difficult to locate yourself within it. Deng had nightmares, waking up with tears spilling down his face. And there were times when the work of trying not to think about Mi-Sun seemed to be the only thing he was doing, consuming all his energy. He did everything he could to cauterise the pain, to banish the memories from his mind.

He had loved her with a clear crystal heart, as one loves a mirror that will never tarnish, a gift that never stops giving, or a talisman that forever protects. He could still hear her calm, hushed voice, as soft as the music of flutes. For many years he remained overcome with sadness. And even now, decades later, the thought of his mother's death could still cause him to have palpations. When his mother died, a part of him died too. He had developed a technique to flinch away from the memories, pushing thoughts down and out of sight until blunted by time.

After her death, he discovered that his capacity for love, which had always seemed equivocal, was low, hence his failed marriage, as he could not cope with unfettered love and affection from another human being. He concluded that it was an old story. There was nothing original about pain. Hatred could of course be a comfort; he took such comfort in hating his father.

Deng's mind was a dark space with memories and semi-forgotten nightmares. He felt an old feeling of fear returning, descending on him like a poisonous cloud, running through every corpuscle of his blood, lightening him until he thought he would float. Fear for his brother's safety bubbled up once again in a soft web of filaments. He took up the first page of the letter from his nephew and began to skim down it glassily, as though unable, or unwilling, to read through the full detail. His forehead darkened with resignation as he concluded that, after a maelstrom of conflicting thoughts, he had an overarching obligation to return to Tibet.

For a moment he stared into the impenetrable darkness of the night beyond the windows.

He would leave early the next day on the Kowloon ferry across the Pearl River estuary to Macau, and then hire a sturdy overland vehicle on the other side for the long drive up to the mountain temple, his once childhood home, nestled in the Himalayan hills above the capital city, close to the foothills of Mount Everest.

It would take him three days, so he had located and booked bedding lodges en route.

But that was tomorrow.

Tonight he would try to put it from his mind, as he was looking forward to attending a conference by Lino Crowley, the British-born explorer, who would be talking about his recent adventures and discoveries in the Himalayas. Deng eagerly anticipated the conference, as Crowley, whom he knew well and these days considered a friend, was an acknowledged raconteur and could back up his ability to tell a compelling story with serious and unchallenged achievements in exploration.

Deng turned and crossed over to the door, making sure that his jacket contained his theatre permit, enough money to cover the evening, and his keys. Conscious of his hovering grim mood and his desire to hold it in check, he left hastily, taking the lift to the ground floor of the plush Harbour Vista block, feeling free to concentrate for a short time on something unclouded and comprehensible. Or so he hoped.

It was a thirty-minute walk to the conference hall, but not wishing to rush or be late, he had started out with more than an hour to spare.

* * *

Hong Kong's skyline was that of a more picturesque Manhattan, but at street level the city was evidently Chinese. Even in the Central Region, with its concentration of Western tourists and businessmen, the crowds were as Chinese as those in Canton or Shanghai. Apart from the well-established Indian and Portuguese communities, the population was largely Cantonese, but hundreds of thousands of other people from all parts of distant China and beyond came to this former British colony in search of security and prosperity. Peasants from Shandong and Sichuan were overwhelmed at the style, energy, and ebullience of Hong Kong's remarkable fusion of cultures.

Deng wandered across Man Ming Square into the Tin Hau Temple Complex. The square was overcrowded. The back streets echoed with the ringing of countless bicycle bells, and a throng of people crowded past the stalls. Everywhere was an aroma of spices, incense, and fresh fruit. The bustling atmosphere lifted and stirred his muddy spirits, from the smells and tastes on offer from the food vendors, to the free Cantonese opera performances under the stars, and to the gaggles of fortune tellers and cross-legged merchants in the narrow winding streets. The entire square was clogged with stalls and people, the long dappled lines filled with tourists and locals alike. The tourists would stop to see the stars by night and during the day to observe the dragonflies.

The crowds were a ceaseless thickening flow. Deng, letting the tides of human activity stream around him, exited the square via Sun Street, which ran parallel to Temple Street, where the Night Sun Market extended from Man Ming Lane in the north to Naking Street in the south, dissected in the middle by the Tin Hau Temple Complex. As he turned the corner, an explosion of colourful pillars, roofs, lattice work, local fauna, and soft incense clouds emerged. He faced the Taoist temple, which remained a natural destination for all walks of Hong Kong society – pensioners, business people, parents, students, and young professionals alike. Some came simply to pray, others to determine the future with the traditional Kau Chim bamboo fortune sticks which were shaken out of a box onto the ground and then interpreted by a "qualified" fortune teller.

No matter how many times Deng saw the hexagonal Unicorn Hall, with its carved doors, windows, and intricate zigzag bridges and carp ponds, he still admired the sheer beauty of its complicated composition and colour.

The Crowley conference was being held at the Yau Ma Tei Theatre, the oldest and most respected theatre in West Kowloon, located just off Waterloo Road at the junction with Reclamation Street. Apparently Crowley had tried to hold the conference at the Unicorn Hall itself, but that was one form of public concession that the religious heads of the temple would still not allow.

Deng glanced up at the Kowloon–Canton railway clock tower, which chimed as he passed. It was a landmark of the age of steam. In the 1960s, thousands of people had gathered here beneath the clock to protest against a rail fare increase introduced by the British governor Sir Edmund Brinsley. This erupted into a riot, the first of a series of protests which resulted, ultimately, in colonial reform.

He reached Reclamation Street, weaving his way through the decorous excitement of the Yau Ma Tei fruit market. All the stalls in the market were busy. The traders plucked at him as he walked through, but he pretended not to notice, deliberately avoiding eye contact, before showing his pass to a bored security guard in a cream uniform and a red peaked cap.

The Yau Ma Tei Theatre was actually a perfect setting for the Crowley conference. It was very atmospheric, typical of the territory's archaeology, natural history, ethnography, and local cultures.

Making his way through the narrow admission corridors, Deng noted the colourful lanterns that displayed scenes from Hong Kong's history, which he had personally selected and assembled in his role as director of the Kowloon Museum of Prehistory and head advisor to the Lingnan School of Art. He had also helped on archaeological digs leading to the discovery of geometric rock carvings, and many great wonders, deeds, and events never previously recorded and long since lost, like Hong Kong's ancient coastline, to the memory of the world.

Excavation was not usually Deng's area of expertise, but he enjoyed the unknown expectation in the painstaking shifting of rubble and dust; picking out shattered statues, the fragments and shards of pottery and all the other pieces of an impossible jigsaw; dating strata; and trying to map an infinite number of clues to interpret history out of chaos. Truth, he had to accept, could be an exceedingly mysterious affair; and although he did not know it yet, Crowley's conference was about to prove the point further.

The elaborate wall scenes started with prehistoric Hong Kong, which had supported human life since 4,000 BC, mainly mysterious tribes who were presumed to have travelled from the Pearl River Delta, principally small groups of Neolithic hunter–gatherers and fisher folk. These paintings moved on to include replicas of the dwellings of early AD inhabitants, such as the Tanka boat people and the Puntay, who resided in the walled villages such as Kowloon itself. Even today a few vestiges of their dialect, songs, folk tales, and fashion survived, most visibly the wide-brimmed, black-fringed bamboo hats sported by Hakka women in the New Territories. The moribund era of the Ming dynasty, which was overthrown by the victorious Qing, forcing an evacuation inland, was shown in a single image, accompanied with a narrative plaque and a leaflet if you wanted it.

Then there were two slim elongated paintings, in Bayeux Tapestry form, one depicting a pre–Second World War Nazi discovery in the Kowloon hills of the bone fragment remains of a gigantic ape-like creature that had never before been discovered by science and that caused further consternation and debate about the link between primates, reptiles, and humans. But this specimen had a brain cavity bigger than that of *Homo sapiens*, and undeniable proof through DNA analysis, then known as Nuclein, that it had existed for many millions of years before the human species effectively took over the earth.

Deng had tried to find Doctor Schröder, hoping him to be an elderly retired zoologist who could impart his wisdom and experience, but it turned out that he had committed suicide whilst awaiting trial at the Nuremburg Palace of Justice in 1947, the suicide taking place in a cell less than ten feet square along the dismally lit prison corridor, where Heinrich Himmler and Hermann Göring did the same thing in their respective cells.

The other tapestry was of the century of China's 1911 revolution, the story of early British rule, most notably the First Opium War, opium being the "product" most desired by the Chinese. The British, with a virtually inexhaustible supply of the drug from the poppy fields in India, developed the trade aggressively. Consequently, opium addiction spread out of control in China, and the country's silver resources became perilously drained on account of the lack of a capable workforce. A primitive, chaotic, and lawless settlement soon emerged. The British restored order with the help of the Triads, who, ironically, were originally a patriotic peace keeping mini society, before descending into crime and vice and, effectively becoming the Chinese mafia.

An old newspaper cutting, looking more like a parchment, was framed in thin glass: it simply proclaimed: "The poppy war is over."

There was a gloriously colourful jigsaw effect collage of an old Chinese merchant *lorcha*, the forerunner of the modern day junk.

Many other scenes of vibrant composition and colour filled the dark red walls as Deng proceeded slowly through the narrow corridors: pictures of traditional costumes and beds; a recreation of an arcaded central Hong Kong street from the early British rule in 1884, including a Chinese herbal medicine shop that told its own story through the anonymous voice of its "owner"; a tram from 1913; and World War II film footage, including interviews with Chinese and foreigners taken prisoner by the much despised Japanese.

One section was devoted to the formation of Hong Kong's urban culture, featuring a retro grocery store, a soda fountain, and a cinema decorated in a 1960s avant-garde psychedelic design which had three screenings daily of old Cantonese films and free air conditioning. There was another painting illustrating the famous dockyards of Hong Kong, the everlasting economic artery of the island, but also showing that the farther north you went, the quieter the waterfront became, tourist and pleasure boats being replaced by container barges, lovers and solitary men angling for fish.

The penultimate scene before he went through into the auditorium was of the stately lion dance and twenty-four-hour carnival that took place in the purpose-built extension to the Convention and Exhibition Centre in Wan Chai on 30 June 1997. Deng remembered the event clearly. Chris Patten, the last British governor of Hong Kong, shed a tear while Prince Charles remained outwardly stoic, it being revealed only much later in a leaked extract from his private diary that the latter described the Chinese as "appalling old waxworks". Deng smiled as he remembered how he had first read this in the newspaper and agreed that it was wrong that the territories had returned to China. But they had, and subsequently a curtain fell on a century and a half of British rule. Ten years on, there was no reference on the walls to anything post-1997, and Deng had not been asked to update the display or even to consider the possibility of so doing.

There was just one more frieze to observe, stark and alone as you entered the actual seating area of the theatre. It was a photograph of the Sky Disk, found in an archaeological dig headed by a British historian, Sir Robin Cunningham, on the border between China and Tibet in 1972. The Sky Disk was incalculably old but was thought to date back four thousand years. If, as legend had it, the Disk could predict celestial events, it preceded the beginnings of Greek astronomy by a thousand years.

After many years of ownership battles between China and Tibet, the Sky Disk still resided at the mountain temple in Tibet, where Deng had been born and brought up, and to where he was about to travel back.

* * *

Deng took his seat in the front row of the theatre, glancing gently at his watch. He felt a sudden shiver of delight.

About five minutes later, silence was called for by a man in a white robe standing upright in a lattice-lacquered balcony above the auditorium. He was encircled by a dozen or so coloured lanterns. Trails of fragrant Nag Champa incense swirled around him like whispered curls of memory. The melancholy candle flames flickered and caused shadowy shapes and marks to dance on the walls around him like grey-blue ghosts, from dark, almost black shades to slate sky-blue silk, creating an eerie atmosphere.

Deng observed the faint movement of the thick red curtain, which covered the far right of the stage. Then there was a brief explosion of cinematic flashes, accompanied by a burst camera clicks like a machine gun, as a lady, along with Crowley, emerged from behind the curtain with an air of leisurely indifference to ascending applause.

Deng smiled to himself as Crowley, possessing his usual easy confidence, took his seat in the deep armchair which had been carefully positioned in the centre of the stage, his creased face mirroring that of the harsh terrain he explored.

The lady, wearing a fine tunic of embroidered linen over a plain handsome gown, spoke assuredly to the assembled audience, explaining that the conference was concerned with Mr Crowley's exploration achievements in the wild parts of Tibet and Xian. Deng understood the perils that must have faced Crowley. At that moment, he thought that he would be able, more than most, to put Crowley's achievements into immediate context.

Crowley spoke for just over two hours, making often routine things like finding shelter sound fascinating. But after he had finished describing his various exploits, a Chinese news correspondent posed a direct and surprising question.

"Is it a fact, Mr Crowley," the man said blithely, "that you came across an unrecognisable humanoid creature during your expedition in Xian?" Crowley hesitated and offered no immediate reply, carefully considering this question before even twitching a hand or foot to commit himself, sitting there like a waxwork.

"It wasn't during my Xian expedition," Crowley eventually answered with candid clarity, still unmoving in the armchair. "It was whilst I was in Lhasa." His words created a wave of whispered captivation in the auditorium. "But this is not the point of the conference here this evening," he said tight-lipped, trying to deflect the question.

"But why be so guarded, Mr Crowley? It is not that I doubt you. Quite the reverse. Did you see, perhaps, a yeti?"

Unwillingly then, Crowley answered. "Yes, I did, and I will briefly describe it to you now if you have the time." He tapped his watch in a peremptory fashion as if to emphasise that the conference was officially over, with the publicised subject matter having been adequately covered.

To his disappointment, nobody moved. Instead, a faint stir shimmered around the theatre like a cautious sigh. The audience hummed with a mixture of astonishment and expectation. For a moment the curtains swung open and released a flood of light that both highlighted and hid him at the same time.

Then a shadowed silence fell again and a menacing darkness dropped in the theatre like an extinguisher, apart from the single attentive spotlight which reappeared on Crowley, who looked isolated and vulnerable in his otherwise cosy armchair. A few moments passed, seeming like an eternity, before Crowley slumped back in his chair, recaptured some of his natural confidence, and began talking.

Chapter 4

Crowley's Story

Eastern Himalayas, October 2006

"The peaks in the east slumbered in the fading light. I saw how the last dregs of redness faded from the mountains where the sun had left them. An ochre-coloured dusk was deepening and spreading over the forest floor, and storm clouds were massing above the higher ridges of the milk-white mountains. There was suddenly a flash of light and a clap of thunder.

"Travelling alone on foot meant that I'd sacrificed comfort. I had a sleeping bag, a flashlight, a pocket knife, a waterproof cover, and a camera and as I roamed from village to village looking for additional artefacts and discoveries. I would often find myself semi-stranded as I searched the farther reaches for a spark of fire or wisp of smoke.

"I perched on a dry rock above the riverbank. The bubbling water sounded soothing. A dense forest lay before me. I would need to cross it by sundown. I heaved my rucksack onto my shoulders, noticing that it seemed heavier than it had when I crossed the surging ice-clad waters.

"Then something large and dark stepped into a space thirty feet ahead of the bushes that were littered with china-blue berries. A yak, I thought, becoming excited at the thought of meeting some local mountain people and maybe getting some food and a proper place to sleep that evening, as I could often explore for days without encountering a single soul and losing track of time.

"But the thing stood still.

"Then, noiseless and light-footed, it raced across the forest floor, disappearing, reappearing, slowing down, and then effortlessly climbing the crags with impossible speed, neither branches nor ditches hindering its progress. This was no yak.

"The fast-moving shape dashed behind a curtain of leaves and branches, only to step out into a clearing some ten yards away for a few seconds. It stood upright and for one heartbeat was motionless. Then it turned away and, continuing to walk upright, disappeared into the deepening crimson dusk. I had expected it to make some kind of sound, but there was nothing.

"I stared at the spot long and hard, first amazed and then perplexed, where this creature had stood. I just stood frozen, listening to the silence, my senses as alert as those of a wild animal. Then I crept carefully into the undergrowth from where the creature had emerged, noting everything that moved, every sound that rose above the murmur of the feather-like breeze, every scent different from that of the forest floor. There, in the black mud, I found a gigantic footprint of unknown origin. It was absolutely distinct, the wide toes unmistakable. To check that the imprint was fresh, I touched the soil next to it. My boots did not sink in nearly as deep as had the creature's bare soles.

"Strange and unexplained footprints had been seen before, but I had never encountered one.

"Like all Himalayan explorers, I knew of the yeti legend well enough. It was an ageless mystery. And yet my imaginings may never even have skirted the truth, perhaps never even dared draw close to it.

"I felt a touch of something cold inside me at the horrible thought that such stories might actually be true. I knew large parts of Tibet and the Himalayas well, yet even in those remote places where we explorers go and can survive for months at a time, I had never seen anything resembling such a beast.

* * *

"The name *yeti* derives from the Tibetan phrase *yeh the*, meaning 'that thing'. The fable of such a creature drew strength from the drama of the Himalayan landscape: jagged peaks, glaciers, snowstorms, and howling winter nights. This was a place where storytelling came naturally, and the tradition was flourishing. How often had the Sherpas told me of the yeti, the people it had abducted, the yaks it had killed with a single blow, the enormous footprints it had left behind in the soft earth and fresh snow?

"Stories of mythical beasts rushed down from the mountains and trickled into the surrounding villages. However, I also realised that village people were timorous; they could not see, as I could, that their legend was potentially nothing but an echo of past horror stories handed down from generation to generation, or just a monstrous hoax. So it was impossible to say which of the recounted tales were true or merely fabrication. No one knew where one ended and the other began, but still it was all too easy to be swept up in the eddy of the legend.

"However, I also knew that where there is mystery, there must be logic, as well as terror. In this respect I do remember hearing an enraptured tale from an old woman in a remote village who knew the snowstorms of the high Himalayan passes as well as the fiery sun of the Tibetan steppes. And she told it as if the thing she had seen was a ghoulish image, an apparition of some kind.

"Her story did seem based on a real-life experience, so I again fell into that intoxicating world of speculation. Many other people had strange stories too. One lady, wearing a short coarse dress such as a young peasant girl wears and carrying a bundle of clothes and pottery, said, 'When I lost my way along the mountain paths, I started crying at what I saw, because I am naturally afraid of the wild boars and the evil spirits beyond the realm of the human heart, the lust of men and the ghosts of the dead. But what I saw was far worse.' She bared her teeth to display imaginary fangs.

"As it had with the Loch Ness monster and Sasquatch, the world had some notion of the snowman-like mythological yeti – tall and hairy, and teeth longer than a human finger. Stories have been lapped up by the eager masses, drifting through the worlds of our imagination, endowed with a consciousness similar to our own, but not quite fitting into the chain of evolution that we like to think as purposeful and rational progression, regardless of what supernatural notion set it off in the first place.

"Most southern Tibetans live in small villages, cultivating barley in the deep river valleys, where these legends were turned into folklore, but to outsiders it was like hearing tales from another planet, and for over two millennia.

"It seemed the power of the yeti legend would never wane. Quite the opposite – and whether based on a jumble of eyewitness accounts or on more solid fact – the legend would grow in people's imaginations.

"At dusk I came out of the forest into a clearing. Making my way through the blue-berried bushes, I heard an eerie sound, a shrill whistling. Out of the corner of my eye I saw the outline of an upright silhouette rush between the trees to the edge of the clearing where the low-growing thickets covered the steep slope. The figure hurried forward on two legs, silent and hunched forward, disappearing behind a tree trunk, only to reappear again splashed in moonlight. It turned to look in my direction.

"Again I heard the whistle, this time more of a defensive hiss, one issued with sudden force, and for a second I saw the glass-green eyes and sabre-like teeth. The eyes seemed to pierce like laser-green light into my soul.

"The creature towered menacingly, its face a grey shadow, its body a monstrous outline. Covered in thick fur, it stood upright on two stout legs and had powerful arms that hung down almost to its knees. I estimated it was more than ten feet tall, but its body was vastly thicker and heavier than a man of that size. Even so, it moved with agility and surety towards the edge of the escarpment. No human would have been able to run like that at night. It stopped again beyond the trees by the low-growing thickets, as if to catch its breath, and stood motionless for a moment in the mauve moonlight without looking back. I was too mesmerised to take my binoculars out of my back-pack.

"A heavy stench hung in the air. The creature's calls echoed and then receded. I watched it plunge momentarily into the thicket, and then I saw it rush up the slope on two legs, higher and higher, farther into the deepening night and up into the mountains, until it disappeared and all was still again."

* * *

In the conference hall, Crowley's fluid delivery paused as he broke off from his story.

Deng took a moment to absorb the reaction of the audience, who seemed largely startled into silence, although rumblings of excitement and astonishment were clearly evident – and growing! The conference hall took on a sinister appearance, the low lighting and shadows cast by flickering lanterns producing exaggerated shapes which seemed to move of their own accord.

Crowley continued slowly, explaining how he reached a nearby village and tried to tell a group of men about his encounter.

"They were relatives of some kind, clearly looking out for one another. Survival in scattered villages in high altitudes beneath a harsh unyielding landscape meant family members put aside individual interests to work together and overcome personal conflicts as they endured long winters in close quarters. Their lives revolved around Buddhism, street trading, yaks, and barter.

"I knew Tibetan to ask for some buttermilk and lentil stew and a place to sleep with tolerable ease, but not to describe what I had seen. So I used gestures and fragments of English, pidgin Tibetan, and basic Nepalese and Urdu. Miraculously they understood my tale and knew right away what I was talking about.

"Frantically, I told them all I could. The beast had walked on two legs, looked much more powerful than a man, and was as tall as a step-ladder. It whistled by blowing wind between its tongue and its upper jaw. I tried to imitate this for their benefit. And the stench – I illustrated how overpowering it was by wafting a hand in front of my nose.

"Shortly afterwards, one of the men, a gaunt Tibetan with a mass of feather-like black hair falling across his brow, motioned that I could go with them to their mountain village. I needed to sleep. But for the time being, another cypress log was added to the fire for a brighter light. They continued to throw twigs into the scarlet flare, watching as the flame hissed and spurted, before asking a question. They wanted to know how I had survived the monster.

"I said that the creature had seen me, and certainly wasn't afraid, but just disappeared into the forest. 'It came out of the bushes,' I said. 'Its head was as big as a yak's, but without horns, and with thick fur. It rose on its hind legs, turned, and disappeared. The fur was light coloured, but on its back it was dark red.'"

"'*Chemo*,' one of the men said strangely. Shaking his head, he poured me some more butter tea, this time mixed with a yerba herb and raw mountain alcohol. The man's face was of his world, lined with fissures from a lifetime's exposure to Tibet's fierce summer sun, autumn storms, and cruel winter snow. It was a face burdened, one of cracked mud in a dried out riverbed. His eyes were red and rheumy from the wind, but his mind was certainly vibrant and alive.

"We all raised a cup clasped with both hands, which was Tibetan etiquette for demonstrating trust and friendship with someone you had only just met.

"'Chemo?' I questioned. 'Isn't that a bear?'

"'No, no,' one of my hosts exclaimed, 'certainly that was no bear.' They further explained that *Xiong* was the local word for 'bear' and that the Xiong – sloth, blue and brown alike – lived much farther down the mountain, in the densest parts of the forest, and were never seen in the higher planes of snow and ice, although the brown bear sometimes was. Xiong also have shorter legs, have a white patch shaped like a half-moon on the chest, and are otherwise black. 'Xiong can be dangerous,' said one of my hosts, 'but they are not chemos – and they would stand no chance against them.'

"The man confirmed that the male chemo had an ochre-red back, saying that the females have pale marmalade fur. Both male and female share bright green eyes. They are the most dangerous creatures you will ever meet.

"I had heard nothing that did more to strike a cold dread into my blood. The way they said 'chemo' again indicated to me fear and veneration.

"Either the wandering breezes or perhaps the descent of the sun allowed a sudden coolness to inhabit the clearing. The wind moaned and cut across my back. The other men felt it too, and fidgeted restlessly. One of them reached forward and prodded the fire. A trail of dark yellow sparks rose and then scattered on the breeze, fading away into the purple night.

"Everything suddenly appeared silent. White tufts of cloud floated high above the green canopy of the cedar trees. In the sky above the gorge, which suddenly seemed close enough to touch, a few birds hovered, as if lost.

"Rubbing my sore eyes as the first heavy drops of storm rain began to fall, I gazed apprehensively at the sky. I went then with the men to several huts made of clay and wood, surrounded by a brush enclosure. Makeshift awnings were spread over the huts.

"I gave one of the men a small sum of money. He took it and looked grateful, slipping it into a small crescent shaped leather bag that hung like a dagger from his belt.

"They showed me to the farthest hut, which had a butter fuelled lamp on a small table and a yak-hide rug. The floor was strewn with hay. I stripped down to my underwear, lay down on a mattress of dry leaves, covered myself for warmth with a large blanket of sewn sheepskin, and rested my head on straw-filled pillows. A few minutes later, before my heartbeat and my breathing had even slowed, I composed myself into a church-like stillness and slipped into a dreamless sleep. I could hear the thunder like gun shots reverberating in the hills, but I gave it no heed.

"The next morning, I sat up from my comatose sleep, the scurrying feet of mice across the wooden floor waking me with a start.

"The first light of dawn had deftly touched the sky to the east and peeped in through the window slits. The air smelled of stale smoke, melted fat, and alcohol. And in the fabric of my clothing, I could still smell the obnoxious scent of the chemo.

"I opened the door and stepped out of the semi-gloom into the hazy morning. But the colder weather had announced itself overnight. The mountainside was covered in snow like the amble folds of soft winter clothing, with mist hanging in white wreaths, snuffing out the sun intermittently.

"I drew a grateful breath in the morning coolness as a blast of wind sent what I thought was a bucket clattering across a patch of sunlit dirt. Two grey dogs, large and dangerous, barked fiercely as a scrawny chicken ran for cover. The dogs clearly disliked a stranger in their midst, but suddenly, as familiar faces emerged from the other huts, their fury dissipated and they trotted away, snarling, whining, and snapping at each other. Yaks stood around the enclave, snow speckling their long black fur.

"Two pots stood in the centre of the enclave – a large one of hammered copper for water, and an aluminium one for buttermilk. A woman was churning a large dollop of yak butter mixed with rare spices in a leather urn. She added a small handful of Tibetan rock salt and agitated it all into a regenerating broth. A man by her side was pounding tea leaves in a knee-high cylinder, all the while glancing over at me.

"I noticed that around the tree-enclosed clearing, aside every hut, there were tiny wooden statues. I didn't need to count them to know there were 108 in total, the number of sacred books in the Tibetan Buddhist scripture, the number of beads of a prayer rosary. The outside of each hut was decorated with strips of cloth and held up by drawstrings made of yak hair. Ghost traps and dung scarecrows were set up to protect the animals. Dried fruit was burnt as a sacrifice every morning.

"I then looked more precisely at the bucket, which had made a tin-like sound as it was driven by the wind. It had come to rest by a fallen log stripped of bark, the bark being removed as if by harsh rubbing or by claws. The bucket was covered in moss and weeds but was still clearly recognisable as a Stahlhelm, a German war helmet, distinctive in its coal scuttle shape and with the twin lightning bolt symbols on both sides.

I picked it up and looked at it perplexedly, as though finding an ice cube in a volcano. This could be an interesting discovery. I would need to find a way to take it with me.

"My hosts emerged from another hut, amidst the misty smoke bellowed from the stove gutter of a makeshift chimney. They were followed in single file by some lowland villagers, yak nomads in the main. They struck steel on flint to make an outside fire and gave me some broth for breakfast, poured carefully into a wooden cup, sharing generously with me their meagre food. One young girl came up and asked me, 'In your country, so far away, is the sun larger than it is here?' I smiled at her and answered that it wasn't, saying that the sky, stretched out, would cover all lands and would be a weight that only God could carry.

"By ten o'clock my back-pack was ready. A man with one eye offered to carry it for me. His face was darker than that of the yak nomads, in the land where day and night, summer and winter, set the rhythm for the village worker's life.

"We trekked northward. I followed the one-eyed man into the valley, always slightly behind rather than abreast, and then we made our way westwards up the slopes, leaving the dizzy emptiness and entering a realm of colour.

"At the edge of one desolate mountain pasture were signs of a glade encampment and sheep grazing. The sun emptied down invisible arrows and lay golden over the patches of earth, the underbrush a mossy carpet punctuated by clumps of marrow-leaved ferns that had been flattened by recent snow. To our right, about fifty yards distant, a small river tumbled down the mountainside and filled the valley with the gentle sounds of rushing water.

"The previous night's breezes had chased their tails like kittens and found their way up onto the higher levels. We were in a virtual wilderness. Only the odd ivy-clad wooden tombstone hinted that human life had ever existed in this winter wasteland. A snow leopard had left distinctive prints in the moist ground, and beyond a blanket of snow, a herd of yaks stampeded down the slopes.

"My guide pointed at the ground between two knee-high rocks where the snow-matted grass was flattened and combed downhill as if it had been deliberately ironed.

"'Chemo,' he said assertively.

"I saw immense footprints and tufts of reddish-blonde fur. I bent down and realised that these rocks, weighing several hundred pounds each, had been moved about that very night. 'Chemo?' I asked, somewhat uncertainly, looking up at my guide. He nodded absently and pointed at the rocks.

"'Chemo,' he repeated. 'They lift big rocks, looking for food; and they throw rocks, like this!' He let his right hand hang down and then quickly flicked it backwards. 'They kill sheep, goats, and even yaks, and have the strength of ten Xiong. Even the gigantic brown bear, often the same height, would stand no chance against a chemo.'

"'How does it find enough food in the snow and ice?'

"'Usually they live in the forest foothills, but in the autumn they follow the nomad tribes to the highest mountain meadow and then onto the rim of the Qinghai–Tibet Plateau near Everest, beyond the point that even yaks can climb. They cross glaciers to get from one high valley to the next, and maybe live under the ice itself in deepest winter.'

"I stood in front of the large stones and looked beyond the slope at the rock face that towered up into the lapis lazuli sky. What would such a massive creature feed on at such high altitude?

"'The chemo eats what we eat, goat, yak, barley, fruits, vegetables, roots, and nettles, but he is fundamentally a carnivore. And,' my guide said, pausing carefully, 'the legend has it that human flesh is his favourite.' I momentarily shuddered. 'But basically he lives like we live: he watches, thinks, and then makes a decision. He blinks his eyes when the sunlight is bright, and he rests when it is dark. But the one mystery is the one you've raised – how does it live here so rarely to be seen?'

"My brushes with the chemo, if that is what it was, had changed everything. I had been captivated by yeti tales which the Sherpas had brought with them to Nepal during their long march out of their Tibetan homelands. Finding the yeti would mean locating the source of the legend. Had the legend originated during the Sherpas' trek from Kham to Solo Khumbu, a legacy of their origins? Or was it shared by all Tibetans living in the higher snow country?

"Century after century came stories of a creature that would suddenly appear and then disappear, a creature that through time had taken on increasingly human characteristics. Whether these stories were fantasy, nightmare, or truth was unimportant. After all, legends had moved whole nations and kept them together.

"The terrain that I thought I knew so well now seemed masked in mystery. What had I seen?"

* * *

"Two weeks had passed since my encounter with the strange beast, and I still didn't have answers to the questions whirling around in my head. Determined to learn more, I then travelled to Xian, where on that day the air burned like a red-hot iron in the street.

"Xian is a city of ancient history and remarkable discoveries. It was the starting point of the Silk Road and is home to the Terracotta Army.

"I went to see an old acquaintance of mine, Deshi, whose antiques shop was called the Lantian Man, named after a sub-species of *Homo erectus*. In 1963, the excavation of the remains of various fossils, dating back to at least half a million years before present-day human beings, were uncovered in Xian. There was the discovery of a mandible (jaw bone) and a cranium (skull). Then another specimen of Lantian man was found in Gongwangling, with a cranial capacity somewhat similar to that of its contemporary, the Java man. At the time, these findings were commonly thought to be the discovery of the missing link.

"Deshi was delighted to see me and immediately called for a jug of tea to be brought.

"As usual, his shop was full of a delicious profusion of enticements – exquisitely painted and inlaid caskets, pots of lacquer and Cambodian ink, granite and jade figurines, goblets, swords plied randomly in blocks of decorated stone, strange and beautiful ornaments rich with precious stones, rolls of silk and rice paper, gorgeous chairs carved from rich fragrant woods, paintings, tarnished silver trinkets, and rugs piled on the floor.

"A local newspaper had once described the shop as 'fabulously untidy, rich in treasure and all wondrous things'. It was an accurate description.

"And the art work of the ceiling, which I now remembered from a previous visit a few years earlier: the fading paint depicted the snow-covered mountain torrents in the spring and, near the back of the shop, the full face of the red summer moon. Deshi had a shop sign in Sanskrit, made out of the darkest copper, hanging inside as you entered that stated: 'seize the dawn and capture the dusk.'

"But this time all I said was that I wanted information, despite which Deshi was intent on selling me a *Tsaklis*, small cards of layered stiffened handmade paper or of sized cloth painted on one side and often with a Tibetan syllable, word, or line, or several lines of calligraphy on the reverse, assembled into sets and depicting specific deities and symbols associated with rituals practised in Buddhism. The ritual images usually include empowerment ceremonies, the transmission of teachings, and funerals. The cards' use may be as substitutes for ceremonial items or as visualisation aids.

"I cut short the sales pitch by blurting out: 'what do people in Tibet, Nepal, and eastern China call the being that most Westerners refer to as the yeti?' I cocked my head with a nervous impatience.

"A customer entered the shop with a distinctive ring. A little more heat and late afternoon sun seeped into the dusky shop, motes of dust turning gold in the bright sunlight. A brightly coloured bird inside a gilded cage tweeted and hopped on its perch either in fear or excitement. A dog licked up the non-evaporated residue of water from a bowl and then, panting, returned to lie in the doorway's thin ribbon of shade as dusk released him from the tyranny of the sun.

"'Chemo,' Deshi said quite casually to me then, pronouncing it 'chay-mo', totally unfazed by the question. Failing to acknowledge my sharp interest, he continued his sales pitch of the Tsaklis. The art work was wonderful.

Having confirmed that the yeti and the chemo were one in the same, which I greeted with an excited acclamation, I bought the Tsaklis.

"But the more questions I asked in Xian, the more confused I became. Everyone I talked to confirmed that the yeti and the chemo were one and the same, but all had their own explanation regarding the enigma.

"A women waved pots of flour at me as if exorcising an evil spirit. A spotted white bull lolled about in the middle of the street. Like everyone else, I carefully crept around it as if it were a sleeping predator. Bulls were considered holy and no passer-by would dare disturb it, let alone chase it away.

"Most believed that the chemo was an unknown anthropoid that walked upright. I was being increasingly convinced that the yeti was an animal known to the Himalayan people for many centuries. It might be some kind of mutant bear or gigantic primate, or it might be something superior to all of us, but it was surely not a wild prehistoric man.

"To avoid being driven insane by this mystery, I would have to return to the Tibet, and so I left Xian that evening under a sallow twilight, the heat of the day ebbing as the sun sank to the horizon, kissing the sky a warm peach hue before fading. As it rained, I walked through a foul mud-filled lane and some of the loneliest, dimmest streets I had ever known. The air was still heavy with a sultry heat, the kind with the type of prevailing cat-like intensity which, on the approach of thunder, can affect a person's nature.

Crowley now addressed the audience in a more direct fashion. "My quest became the talk of the Xian," he exclaimed with a grim-set expression, "and soon the streets of were alive with rumours of it. These rumours were often exaggerated. I realised that it was detracting from my explorations, which I had come here to talk about tonight." There was annoyance in his voice now but not in his expression.

His brow darkened and creased as he was drowned in thought. He looked suddenly cold. "That is the end of the conference," he announced offhandedly, thumping the armchair with his right hand, his eloquence exhausted. "I came here tonight to talk about my archaeological finds, not an ancient myth."

Noting the effect these words had on the assembled audience, he stood up abruptly, and then braced his back and shoulders as though standing to attention, feeling like the man in the tale who had just freed a genie from a bottle. Blinded for a moment by the star like flare of camera flashes, he walked swiftly from the stage, unhearing or uncaring of the crowds of people with questions which jostled him in the air and were lost somewhere in the journalistic cacophony. There was no backwards glance from Crowley, his determination to leave now being absolute.

There was a splatter of applause, but a more powerful, deep counter-sound of murmured disappointment rose in the auditorium. It diminished slightly but continued to hum as the audience slowly shredded away, realising that, whether they stayed or not, Crowley was not going to provide them with any further information.

Deng sat for a moment, quite still, reflecting on Crowley's story with a twin conflict, on the one hand being based on his own childhood experience, meaning an inherent fear of the yeti legend, having grown up in the ancient Tibetan temple, and on the other hand, pure scepticism, having lived and worked for twenty five years in Hong Kong, one of the most vibrant and modern cities in the world, separated by a great void from the Tibetan yak herders belief in the existence of the Abominable Snowman. That said, Lino Crowley was no yak herder, and so conflicting thoughts continued to expand and race through Deng's mind in equal measure.

Because of his connections with the theatre and his long-standing friendship with Crowley, Deng's pass gave him backstage access. Although momentarily he considered not using it, he decided that he wanted to see Crowley if he could, and so he duly showed his pass and disappeared behind the red curtain. Crowley's predicament was immediately apparent. At first he seemed much troubled, dabbing his forehead and turning his head from side to side restlessly as though he were trying to break loose from invisible strings. He was surrounded by a throng of frantically milling Chinese people, but this turned out to be just the usual mêlée that followed a production at the theatre. The people encircling him were actually Yau Ma Tei Theatre employees. Deng had never really come to terms with the fact that a large group of people, all speaking Cantonese together, tended to sound like they were in a perpetual argument.

Crowley managed to somehow maintain an ascetic calm. He had that heroic look about him. He was a tall, powerful, and assertive man, accustomed to living in the wild, and someone who might initially appear intimidating, but there was a mildness about his mouth and eyes that proclaimed no devil.

Deng approached respectfully. "How are you, Lino?" he said.

Crowley turned distractedly, but at once his frown of concern lightened and a smile lit up his rugged face.

"Deng!" he said heartily, clasping the proffered hand with delight. He combed the fingers of one hand through his hair as if trying to dismiss a memory, at the same time revealing the distinctive mulberry-coloured birthmark by his temple. "Thank God for a friendly educated face," he said. "Please don't ask me about the chemo!" he deadpanned.

Deng was looking at him sympathetically, but Crowley then quickly added, "At least not right now." Crowley slapped Deng amiably on the shoulder and threw his hands up theatrically, his natural smile broadening to a point where he issued forth a short bark of laughter.

"I won't." Deng laughed. "But we do need to talk," he said. "After your recent exploration achievements, the entrance scenes in the corridors leading to the auditorium alone need updating."

A look passed between them, a fleeting look of equal respect. They were both near the top of their professions, Deng the academic and Crowley the master of painstaking exploration.

"Fabulous idea. Can you meet me in Central tomorrow?" he said with a bubble of excitement.

"I'm afraid not, Lino." Deng wished he could have said yes immediately. "Tomorrow I have to start my travels back to Tibet to visit my nephew in Lhasa. I will be away for about a month." He paused thoughtfully. "But maybe after that?"

"Ah," Crowley said, "I had forgotten that you were brought up at that famous old temple. I have only seen it from the outside. Once, before we knew each other, I had a wary craving to enquire if I could look around and maybe stay the night!"

Deng thought silently, *'Lucky you didn't',* as Crowley continued. "Anytime in the next few months is fine, though. I'm planning to be in and around Hong Kong for" – he paused vaguely but earnestly – "quite a while yet. Anyway, give me a call and we can fix a time and place."

"Will do," Deng said. They shook hands in solicitous fashion before he left the theatre through the exit normally reserved for actors and staff. As Crowley watched him leave, he wondered to himself what it was, if not a genie, that had been uncorked from the bottle. Time, in the event, would show him soon enough.

Outside the theatre, Deng paused, and breathed in the night air. The wind was strong, but the air was lethally muggy and humid. It was as if his whole body were wrapped in warm, wet muslin. But after the closeness and tension of the atmosphere in the theatre, he welcomed the warm breeze, feeling as he walked hurriedly down the street, as weightless as a storm-swept leaf.

On the furthest side of Man Ming Square, he saw a gash in the darkness of milling people and lights, but his mind seemed deserted, silence filling him with a strange fevered joy, like a dark drug. He clutched the keys to his apartment in his right hand like a talisman and considered his options, the rhythm of indecision quickening his heartbeat.

He decided that he would not go straight home, stopping instead at his favourite café, the Dong Lai Shun, which offered only four dishes: a black pearl oyster omelette, a Nepalese curry, dim sum – or "touch of the heart", which was the poetic local name for dumplings – and the traditional Chinese hotpot, but all were well known in the West Kowloon District as being the finest dishes inside the walled city.

Sitting at a small zinc table, he ordered the oyster omelette and a measure of rice wine, and did his best to overcome his building sense of unease at the thought of returning to Tibet and facing his father.

The street where the café was located was once the haunt of dandies, where fortunes had been lost and lives ruined, gambled away with the curl of a lip.

Above a shop on the opposite side of the street, there were two faded signs that had survived from the early nineteenth century. Deng remembered how he had tried to buy them for the museum but the owner would not sell. One read, "Sulphur, Pitch, Beer, or Porter – and Opium!" and the other, which had once been above an Anglo-Chinese bar, proclaimed, "Hong Kong: Combining new energies and old strengths."

His mind was fast shutting out the exterior. He wondered if he wasn't in an opium den himself, trapped in the coils of a smoke borne dream, as for a moment he could not even hear the traffic, and the street fronts seemed virtually untouched by lights. Deng could not see what, if anything, the darkness concealed.

The silence filled him with a strange, fevered joy. There was only the screaming of the hot wind and a signboard rattling at the end of the street, and a gate swinging to and fro on its hinges. Sheets of paper, caught by the wind, were fluttering across the abandoned cobbles. He took a gulp of rice wine and, with the closeness of attention, re-read in full this time the original letter from his nephew, Chu. He sighed heavily, knowing that the reserves of his peace of mind were running perilously low.

Deng's brother, Kwei-Lan, had gone missing. Something untoward had clearly happened. Chu was not receiving any support in looking for him, and at the age of fifteen, he was too young to do anything about it himself.

Deng had no love for his father, but he cared for his brother and his nephew, and he had wondered why Kwei-Lan had not responded to his last few letters. So, despite deep-rooted reservations, he would travel to Lhasa to try to understand the situation more fully and, with a fair wind and hope, find a satisfactory solution, although he knew that his father would be the major and possibly insurmountable barrier. A lurch of misery seized him at that moment.

When very young, before witnessing a degree of violence against his mother, Deng had loved and admired his father the way that any son would. He remembered hearing the temple workers talking about his affability too: "If he fell in the sea, he would charm the waves," was one such comment he had overheard as a child as he sat cross-legged on the marble floor of the Imperial Hall, in whispered awe of his father passing on the teachings of the Tibetan Lama, descended from the founding Buddhists, who had travelled from his monastery in Pangboche on the Nepal–India border to Tibet a thousand years before. He explained that faith maintained a linear cosmology, containing themes of transformation and redemption, as he described Tibetan Buddhism as "too great to be inquired after, too powerful to be learned".

Deng's father also spoke about Ekajati, the highest Buddhist deity of which there was nothing he could not teach; the ruler of the wide realm of the skies; the painter of the universe; the maker of humankind, first formed by mixing clots of blood with clay; the creator of all who raised the heavens above the mountains and who had to cast one eye as sacrifice in order to receive the eye of perspicacity from the goddess of the jewel tree, the tree of life, the tree of wisdom, which was also the giant cypress under which Buddha attained perfect enlightenment and wrote the sacred teachings using the Tibetan alphabet, so logical and elegant. And it was a narrative that would stupefy one with the ways of the world, being infinite and strange, as both the past and the future were bound by a single fate.

Tenzin had explained, magically, how the cypress grew from earth to heaven and was filled with the wish-granting jewels that make up the family of living mentors who had reached immortal life and could share their bliss with everyone; protecting, blessing, helping to open up one's own inner doorway into a land of peace and fulfilment, stating that the jewel-weighted cypress tree opened its loving embrace to all people and promoted happiness, which, apart from in extreme times of crisis, should be one's natural mortal state and birth right.

Deng remembered that particular session in the Imperial Hall well because he had, in the image of untroubled innocence, beamed several smiles at his mother that morning as she sat silently and loyally next to his father, who even then sheltered evil in his heart.

Memories, dark and unbidden, were crowding Deng's mind. It was the last time he would ever see his mother.

* * *

Deng finished his meal. As the plate was collected, he was asked if he wanted another glass of rice wine. He held the refilled metal cup under the shade of the fire-coloured parasol that, at night from afar, seemed like a large orange floating on water.

A cooler breeze moved through the street now. He watched as the wind caressed a piece of paper on the pavement in a circle, like a magnet moving a ball bearing.

Deng hadn't responded to Chu's first letter, which was detailed and graphic. He had delayed in replying to deliberately give his nephew time to change his mind, to communicate that everything was now fine and there was no need for further action or concern.

Deng removed from his inside pocket his nephew's latest letter, which had arrived two days ago. It simply read: "Come now, Uncle Deng – please!!" The wind snatched Chu's letter from Deng's grasp. The letter fluttered into the air and across the streets. By some exercise of mental force, or some inner pain, Deng had thrust himself out of cowardly indecision to a level of clear understanding.

He had no choice but to go.

Deng allowed random memories to invade his head, the wine casting a rosy veil across his thoughts. He was suddenly struggling up out of his mind like a diver emerging from deep water.

After many years of peace and an escape from his permanent childhood fear, he was labouring under a blackness of distress. He could feel the nightmares of the past emerging out of the shadows once again.

* * *

He awoke at seven o'clock the next morning in a startled manner, straightening upright in bed and staring at the window, with traces of perspiration on his face after a night of dreams dominated by monsters as bleak as winter and spectres of the dead roaming the corridors and chambers of an endless interwoven underground structure. The images that permeated his mind had vividness far beyond usual bounds. How he wished he could have one night where he just sank into a deep and dreamless slumber instead of being oppressed by the past and, now, an impending dread of and uncertainty about what awaited him in the near future.

Deng went through into the bathroom with a heavy heart, briefly recalling the rag ends of dreams. A bright shaft of early sunlight fell through the frosted window, illuminating motes of slow-dancing dust and causing the mirror to sparkle. He paused in his shaving, blinded for a moment by the gleam, seeing his face reflected, ardent and harsh. Then he carefully angled the mirror round a fraction to keep the glass from the light.

He had awakened to moonlight; it was bright against his face. His dream had been wild and restless, full of romantic despair, of a time when he loved and trusted Perma, before his jealousy and insecurity destroyed everything. Ten years younger than he, she had a round childish face, all roses and snow. Great braids of blue-black hair swung to her waist. Her body had seemed made of the purest silver, and her wide eyes as profound as the fathoms of the ocean.

The dream fragment Deng recalled revisited a day on Perma's parents' farm and the long lemon skirt she wore in those days, which they had spread over themselves like a blanket. It had seemed to them as if they were lying under a sheet of sun.

They lay there for hours in loving solitude, alone with the plenitude and richness of life, crushing winter flowers beneath them, whilst above them shimmered an impassive sky. Perma's heart felt as though it would never beat apart from his again. He remembered that day that he could do nothing but melt into the softness of her kisses, tasting her velvet touch, so beautiful and loving. And when she slept, she stirred and whispered his name without waking, and her breathing was as gentle as the twilight breeze.

But just as there is no love without a dazzling of the heart, there is no true voluptuousness without the startling wonder and philosophy of beauty. Everything else is, at most, a mechanical function, like hunger or thirst. But happiness can be brittle. And if human beings and circumstances don't destroy it, then it is threatened by the ghosts of the past, more dangerous than the spirits of the dead, who have at least been baptised, have tasted the perplexing muddle of life, and have known what it is like to suffer. So, over time, the safe solitude of love and the nights filled with tranquil power faded and then disappeared completely.

Deng lifted his face sharply from the water in the bowl, confronting it suddenly in the dark depths of the mirror, the bulbs on either side of which lit it harshly. For a second, he did not seem to know himself. The face that met his own was lost in creeping shadow, so that it seemed to him at that moment that it might be anyone's at all. And his searching stagnant mind was occupied once again with disquiet consternation and a growing sense of urgency. He seemed to have no time for anything but memories and regret.

Then he roused from his reverie. In spite of the early hour and not having slept well, he actually felt more physically energised than he had expected. He pulled on his clothes quickly, went through into the kitchen, and prodded the coffee percolator to life, taking a small steaming cup out onto the balcony with the first-edition newspaper.

In the farthest part of the harbour, the early sunlight glinted timidly, turning the flat surface of the water into a carpet of diamond dust. Indigo hills cradled the sea. The moon was still hanging full and hazy beneath a cap of dark cloud washed with rose. On the mainland it was dim and murky in the streets, but the top windows of the skyscrapers were touched pink as the enthusiastic dawn lit up the windows floor by floor, as if an army of descending cleaners were at work in every building.

Hong Kong would soon come to life with the normal intoxicating bustle of the day.

Finished with his coffee and back inside, Deng packed abstractly, pausing before taking a miscellany of items from a delicate wooden chest in the corner of the living room. He had forgotten, but now remembered because of the circumstances, that the chest had been one of his leaving gifts from the temple – the most splendid of them in fact, fashioned from the rarest cedars and gilded with patterns of inlaid silver.

Finished packing, Deng, sitting at the kitchen table, flicked through the *South China Morning Post*, one of the least bad of the Chinese broadsheets, to read a review of last night's conference. The headline on page five read: "Yeti Sighting Confirmed by Famous Explorer." Crowley was apparently furious that his explorations and discoveries were barely mentioned amongst the hysteria and speculation surrounding his yeti sighting, which discussion was published verbatim, along with creative associations to Tibetan and Nepalese superstition.

On the ferry ride over from Kowloon, Deng stood on deck, entangled by solitude, allowing the early sun into his eyes, sunbeams pouring through narrow openings and painting the fringes of the clouds in ripe yellow tones. The cool winds blew into his face. It felt good. He faced the water-clad breeze unflinchingly, hoping it could somehow spring-clean the apprehension from his mind.

The sandy wastes of the peninsula were behind him, and the intricate inlets of the New Territories were to his left. Behind those were vertiginous cliffs dominating small coves and dramatic crags of translucent blue. A vast sheet of ocean water spread out to his right, so wonderfully tranquil and blue that if a stone were to fall into it, it would turn into a sapphire.

With a certain melancholy, Deng was suddenly acutely aware of his own loneliness. On the mainland ahead was the elegant facade of Government House, built by the British in 1850, which had been partially destroyed by the great typhoon of 1906 and, rebuilt, was now hemmed in by modern buildings. In an architectural sense, Hong Kong was a strange mixture of Anglo-Chinese, similar to the Viet-French look in Saigon, which he had travelled to last year to inspect a selection of oriental art works on behalf of the Kowloon museum, some of which dated back to the Nguyen dynasty of AD 700. A deal was never agreed, so the precious artefacts remained in Viet Nam.

Despite Tibet being his childhood home, Deng felt as if he were about to step into an unknown world, burdened and unguarded. He looked beyond the Government House to the dark spire that was the Bank of China building and realised that he was pleased to be travelling, pleased to know that he would soon be in a position to find answers to increasingly overwhelming and enmeshed questions:

What had happened to his brother and why was his nephew so fearful?

Chapter 5

Deng's Story, Part I

Lhasa Temple, Tibet, September 2007

The sun hung over the eastern pines, seeping out of the clouds like blood, as the base of the sky turned crimson in the major surgery of sunrise.

Presently, there was not a crack or blemish on the milky blue enamel. Even the sun, floating in the middle of it, did no more than fuse the immediate surroundings so that gold and ultramarine ran into one another and mingled. Out of the sky, light fell like an avalanche so that everything between the mountains lay motionless.

The river water was flat and opaque. The only suggestion of movement anywhere was in the trace of stem that rose from the surface. The flocks of river birds that stood where the mud of the river bank was hard and shattered with hexagonal cracks were looking colourfully at nothing. A few trees hung down their foliage as if they had given up.

Peasants, men and women both, were watering their crops in the growing heat of the day. The summer season had been kind and produced a rich harvest. The spring preceding it was mild and moist after plenteous early snows, followed by a few compensatory showers to keep the leafage fresh and the buds fruitful. The segmented parcels of arable land were adorned with rows of rice plants.

The workers were bent under their load of water buckets suspended from their shoulders by heavy wooden yokes, looking away from the sun, which cast short cobalt shadows at their feet. They stood over their shadows and looked down river, eyes unblinking.

Other workers hoed weeds or led somnolent water buffalo by their harnesses. Deng looked at the fields with their wild clusters of cherry coloured poppies, the herds of patient cattle coated in a dry mud. He paid no real heed to the bucolic beauty of the raw countryside. Before leaving Salween, Deng stopped for petrol, quietly admiring the skill of the pump attendant, who managed to get the very last drop into the tank, withdrawing the nozzle a fraction of an inch at a time until the metal flap at the top of the tank's stem snapped shut. Deng also asked for several jerry cans to be filled. The pump attendant duly obliged, securing them in the boot of Deng's jeep.

Salween, a hamlet-sized settlement of Lhasa, was, like any remote settlement in the southern Himalayan region of Tibet, being gradually reshaped by modern influences as it scrambled to reinvent itself and place itself on the tourist destination map. There was a long way to go. It remained a hamlet divided in two, half characterised by the old Tibetan architectural style and the other depicting a semblance of modern life with corrugated iron roofs. One saw a little industry on the way in, old yards littered with cannibalised trucks, a few dirt streets lined with shops selling everything from prayer flags to brass-plated incense burners, and unpainted stone houses slowly replacing yak-hair tents.

Behind Salween was the bumpy road which wound parallel to the Tsangpo River and would carry Deng into the hills above Lhasa to the temple. Onwards from there, and cuddled by the vastness of the Himalayas, the ground rose wondrously like a wave and then flattened to form the roof of the world: the Plateau of Tibet.

Stretching his legs and his back, Deng walked to the edge of the dusty filling station and looked out ahead of him at the scene. Basically a city man now, he thought of himself as having more in common with Londoners or New Yorkers than these backward rural folk. And yet Lhasa had been his home for sixteen years, and it was where his brother still chose to live his life.

This thought of Kwei-Lan made Deng anxious suddenly. Gnawing on his lip, he returned to the pump and hastily paid for the petrol, soon directing the jeep back onto the broken road.

* * *

Deng had another hour's drive up through the hills, the road at times becoming dangerously narrow and precipitous. The air was growing noticeably thinner, and it was an awful thinness, a thinness of withering flesh. Lhasa was two thousand metres above sea level, and the Qinghai–Tibet Plateau itself a further six thousand metres higher, where it was perpetual winter and the whole world seemed like a frozen desert. After so long away, Deng would need to quickly acclimatise.

There was an unease lurking within him, building and expanding as he searched for anything that would jog his memory, some infallible sign to show that his destination had been reached as he drove through the bewildering complex of signless dirt roads. He had erased many memories over the years in the name of self-preservation, but they were slowly ebbing back into his consciousness.

The jeep glided up beside an aged farmer who stood at the side of the dusty track by a pastel-coloured farm building. Feet bare, with his faded blue cotton suit rolled up to his knees, with pointed callused ankle bones, and with, showing the tips of his heels, broken shoes, he presented a picture of Tibet that hadn't changed in centuries.

"I'm looking for the temple," Deng said in unpractised Tibetan, suddenly realising how long it had been since he had been back in his homeland.

Lean of feature and quizzical of eyebrow, the farmer pushed up his bamboo sedge hat, looking slightly wary. The furrows in his brow deepened for a moment. Bleached by past summer nights, his suit's faded colour matched the tones of the sky. Then he grinned. An inarticulate sound of amusement issued forth from his mouth, showing the blackened stumps of half a dozen crooked teeth spaced widely in the old jaws.

He nodded his head as a cracked finger pointed up to the road on the far left through the spiky araucaria trees.

Following the finger's direction, Deng's eyes saw a thin squiggle of road which led through a crumbling archway that had once marked the ancient limit of the town, beyond which there was an opening in the greenery where stone steps coiled up to a path that snaked upwards, disappearing into the higher trees.

"Thank you," Deng said, and drove off. In the mirror he could see the old man still nodding, pointing, and continuing to grin toothlessly.

On the road up to the temple, the higher slopes seemed moulded into what looked like cowled monks, with young but hardy cypress trees clinging to their habits in defiance of gravity. Deng felt a terrible agitation again. In a semi-haunted mood, he parked the jeep and then barrelled up a stone-strewn path on foot. As memories crowded in on him, he wished, just this once, that he could glimpse the hidden pattern of the future and be assured that all was going to be fine.

Despite being a little out of breath, he continued his hurried pace, halting on the top step to wipe white beads of sweat from his brow, which dampened his strands of short black hair.

In a dense copse of trees was a gang of golden Sichuan monkeys playing, slightly shrouded in a jaundiced yellow haze, moving and swinging with unconscious elegance. Deng remembered his grandfather teaching him how to identify and differentiate the Sichuan monkey from other similar primates – by their bright blue face, cobalt lips, eyelids like the sea, and silky golden fur that can grow as long as twelve inches in length, with tails as long as a yard.

As they played in the trees outside the temple, they randomly ate the plentiful wild fruit, bush leaves, and burgeons. Their collective crying to communicate with each other was an odd sound for a monkey, like a cat meowing. Deng wondered, momentarily, if this was actually the sound Crowley had heard which he mistook for the yeti.

He passed by the shattered base of a mighty gate. Near him through the trees was the oldest part of the cemetery, with wild bushes covered with china-blue berries, the Himalayan poppy, which grew equally well in summer and winter, and many ancient slabs with pitted symbols visible within the tangle of vegetation as thin skeletons of weeds mounted the leaning and broken tombs. The gate barely gripped a rusty sign which read: "Lha so, lha gyelo" – "Our God is victorious."

A narrow path bisected this area. The other side unveiled a small field of neat stone pile graves, each one with a small Tibetan flag made of wood, denoting Tibetan or Mongol symbols of peace and goodwill. Occasionally one of these stone piles was framed with a low iron fence, separating the important from the less important dead.

Deng knew from his upbringing at the temple that the choice of death ritual depended on how you wanted to be sent to the hereafter and, of course, how much money you had. The bodies of small children and the very poor might be thrown into the river to avoid funeral costs. And many hill people were cremated in the temple's giant wood stoves, big enough to take two bodies at a time. Some were buried in the earth, with a slate headstone and intricate coloured engravings, and many more were buried above ground, as here, under piles of stones. The Shaolin elders and high priests, along with the rulers and founders, who had died in the temple in bygone eras were immortally housed within the great halls of stone, or in the innermost sanctuary of the *jiaohui* – Tibetan for "chapel" – under the finest ornate marble, where magical talismans had been carved into the solid structures.

But there was another ancient method of facilitating travel and preservation in the afterlife which continued to the present day, especially in Tibet and Mongolia. Deng remembered this now with revulsion, having witnessed several examples of it as a child. He let the awful memory wash over him for a moment. It was called the sky burial. This involved the naked dead body being taken into the mountains, broken up, and left for animals and predatory birds, or if not eaten, simply left to nature to decompose into dust like the wings of a dead butterfly.

The function of the sky burial was to dispose of the remains in as generous a way as possible for nature. Prior to the procedure, Buddhist monks would chant a mantra and burn juniper incense and sweet-smelling woods, with the ceremonial activities having been undertaken the previous day. The work of dismembering the body was undertaken by Rogyapas, the Tibetan word for "body breakers". As they went about their work, the Rogyapas would be encouraged to talk and laugh as they broke up the body, as according to Buddhist teaching, this would make it easier for the soul of the deceased to move away from the uncertain mortal plane that existed between life and death.

Sometimes vultures were given the whole body. When only bones remained, these were smashed with mallets, ground up, mixed with tea and yak butter, and fed to the cows and hawks. But sometimes, just sometimes, there were stories about whole bodies disappearing overnight without a trace of bone or flesh remaining, which is certainly not the work of vultures.

Near a red brick wall, Deng paused and bent carefully to examine an ornately coloured marble headstone which had fallen forward slightly. The grave was emblazoned with fantastically attractive flowers of violet, red and yellow, clearly more carefully tendered than many of the other graves.

Pushing the headstone upright and brushing the dirt and cobwebs from the inscription, he read: "Lord of the Temple: Kano 1893–1963". And below that, almost obliterated by the endless seasons, was the epitaph: *"With him lies the secret of the hills."* It was his grandfather's grave.

He remembered now how his grandfather had chosen this specific burial place, rather than that behind the chapel's marble walls to which he would have been entitled. Deng forced memories away. Whatever he had once had here was now irrevocably lost, and there was no point in re-living it. He had not come here to rediscover those memories. He smoothed the moist hair back from his forehead and reared his head determinedly.

The wind sighed through the trees, making them rustle mysteriously. In the waving shadows of the branches by the red-tiled wall, Deng was captivated by a powerful sense of being watched, as though there were hidden eyes behind every windowed front. Straightening up sharply as if a voice had spoken aloud, he thought he saw a glimpse there of a wild and brooding terror in the higher reaches of the temple. The golden monkey gang still played and meowed in the trees, but there was nothing else to be seen or heard.

He did not try to understand the feeling and a moment later it passed.

With quick economical movements Deng began ascending a steep path of winding narrow steps, following them strenuously with a shortening of breath towards the top, and then moving down a gentler slope, which led to the high gates of the temple proper.

The temple was a colossal edifice, something far beyond an architect's skill, with towers of black marble and gateways of gold, hiding a vast austere complex of courtyards, rooms, halls, chapels, gardens, orchards, lakes, and lagoons. It was vaster than anyone could ever imagine, with lower depths to it that one could scarcely fathom, containing miles and miles of unlit stone.

The gleaming tiles and gilded cornices of the high pagoda roofs took his breath away. The trees surrounded the temple like great armies defending their citadel, their armoured trunks reaching out in the air protectively. Deng viewed it all precisely, as if it had been somehow preserved by the very force of his memory.

Against the cloudless gleam of the sky, the temple was like a tapestry on silk. The top presented a many-storied tower to one side and a bell-shaped *dagoba*, a Buddhist relic shrine, to the other. As such the edifice was a strange mixture of two ancient influences.

Only a moment's thoughtful hesitation passed before Deng went through the bronze inlaid gates which were covered with ancient blessings in Tibetan and provided an entrance through to the surrounding walls and parapets, the shadow of the opening gate falling upon his face and cutting off the sunlight, which caused his eyes to dilate for a moment. Beyond the inner courtyard, the temple gardens stretched far away, filled with flowers of every colour, sweet-smelling rare and precious trees, and fountains as cool as the soft masks of snow upon the mountain tops.

The herb garden, shaded along one side by a high hedge, had been Deng's best beloved refuge as a boy during those burning summer days as he watched the ducks and swans gliding across the lake, or the doves flying brilliantly white against the turquoise sky, and the butterflies shimmering above the water like clouds of petals shaken from a many-coloured tree. The fragrances of those days hung like a spell in his memory.

His earliest memory was of being kissed by his mother in the temple gardens. But here, a few years later, he had also seen his mother being flogged by his father with a whip, the strings of the flail made of alternate blue and gold. And he remembered that he'd noticed the marks of the whip scarring her arms – red streaks like rope burns – as she put him to bed that night; her smile becoming one of love, she stroked his cheek in an exquisitely maternal gesture and then ruffled the tangle of his dark hair as if nothing had happened. She bent low so that her cheek rested on his head and cradled him, for a long while, saying nothing at all, eyes wet in the silver wash of the moon.

Moving then through the inner courtyards, Deng's nostrils closed in response to the heavy smell of sandalwood. For a second his eyes narrowed against the mild perfumed smoke, which rose from a multitude of table top sized censer stoves, vessels made for creating incense perfume, some of which were simple earthenware, some of which were metal fire pots, and two others of which were much larger, about a metre tall, intricately carved out of copper. Here the temple was cold and dark – a kind of undersea darkness. He stood motionless, his feet on stone, feeling an immense space around him, reaching out his hand as if to touch the cold air.

With more haste, and suddenly a little apprehensive, Deng passed through to a hallway and then to yet another interlocking rooms, deeper and deeper through the labyrinthine twists and turns of the temple, until at last a small entrance room opened into a low, brightly lit gallery.

A grain of sunlight on tiles flashed into view. He screwed up his eyes against it. The grain enlarged to a brilliant patch and illuminated a lonely portrait.

He stopped to gaze at this portrait, which was covered in part by a thin translucent curtain. Kneeling before it, he reached out gingerly with his finger to touch the painted cheeks, the skull that had been shaven. His mother wore a high blue crown with a snake rising up above her brow; her robes were long and white, and her necklace broad and fashioned from a thousand drops of gold, all strung together into a kind of mesh, adorned with affluent jewels. In her eyes was a terrifying loneliness as deep and eternal as the skies.

He knew this portrait of his mother was in his mind and saturated in the depths of sentimentality, but as he reached out and stroked lightly, the image seemed to flicker before his eyes like a true ghost, a veil of infinite shimmering points rising from the wall and hanging instead upon the air. His mother's lips were bright red and gentle. She seemed even lovelier than he remembered, seeming to reach out to him, holding in her hand a rose petal, a little shrunken and weary, but with its natural yellow still silken bright. It lay in her palm like a golden tear.

Gathering himself, Deng leant forward to kiss his mother's lips. A single tear welled in her clouded eye and hung upon her silken lashes, her glassy almond eyes black, her voice the same beautiful tone he remembered. He tried to gather up the rose petal, but as he did so the hallucination vanished.

A window with a broad stone sill looked back towards the cemetery. On the other side a delicate archway overhung the interior of the temple. His eyes scanned the scene and came to rest on a group of shaven-headed monks, kneeling amidst wooden benches as they prayed. The chant they made was emotional, relaxing yet unnerving, rising and falling; seeming to renew itself each time it began to fade.

At the far end of the gallery, a door opened into a room without walls, held up by thick columns of blue stone and containing the ancient *Keepers of the Flame* obelisk, a Crowley discovery. A small garden was contained within the marble shafts, each flower bed blooming a different contrasting colour, but they were flowers without odour. He found himself next to a wondrously crafted door inlaid with Tibetan designs of indigo and gold. He reached forward and opened it. There was no resistance.

Beyond the room was a space that he vaguely remembered, but it had subtly changed. Along the side of the room there was a wall of glass made from panes of different colours – blues, dark greens, nasturtium oranges and reds – so that the light, like the scent of perfume in the air, was remarkably rich and deep and seemed almost to possess the texture of water. Two slim doors were opened in this wall of glass. Deng saw that beyond them stretched a long semi-outdoor corridor. He heard the bubbling of water. Passing through the doors he saw two small fountains spaced at equal distance along a pathway of marble, with trees and plants on either side, and additional pathways running and disappearing into heavy green shadows.

Finally, another archway led back inside into an enormous room, where magenta walls rose in broad daylight like a sweep of sunset. The doors swung on their hinges with a musical note and were placed in such a manner that you followed the entire musical scale when crossing the pattern of the temple from east to west.

Deng blinked his eyes as they adjusted to the brighter light, shading his eyes more closely. Shapes on the ceiling symbolised the seasons, longevity, and the prerogatives of power. And there, above the central atrium, he was reminded, as were all others who ever entered, of his father's artistic gift.

The giant mural portrayed a distant scene of the temple, with the backdrop of the villages in the foothills adjacent to the forest behind it, and above everything, dominating, omnipotent, as true as life itself, the Himalayan peaks with Everest as their indisputable King. Deng's father had managed to show the smallest details in the shapes, and in the infinite diversity of whites, blues, pinks, and mauves.

In the centre of this vast arena, two combatants faced each other, clad in loose black clothing, as they exercised their way through a complicated series of jumps and kicks. Watching from their raised platform were four elderly monks, their hands buried deep within white cotton robes. Deng recognised one of the men instantly and, at the same time, acknowledged his own change of mood. Although no look of acknowledgement or expression passed between the two men, Deng was aware that he continued to be observed by the penetrating eyes.

On the far side of the hall, a boy entered hastily, sitting down quickly on his heels in the lotus position with the nimbleness of the young. From the opposite side of the arena he gazed across at Deng, his smile widening.

Deng returned the smile lovingly. His nephew had kept in contact regularly over the years, but other than in photographs Deng had only actually seen him as a baby when his brother had visited him in Hong Kong. It was well known that Chu was no longer allowed to leave the temple. And he was not yet old enough to forge an escape plan.

Deng nodded his head admiringly. Chu beamed a boyish grin back at him, his jet-black hair flopping forward across his eyes.

Deng then sat in respectful silence, giving his full attention to the arena as the introductory exercises came to an end. The two combatants bowed and began to circle around one another, hands extended, fingers curled. One of the men lunged forward, aiming a heavy fist at his younger opponent's head. The blow was parried neatly with a raised right arm, while the younger man's left hand jabbed sharply into the older man's side. The latter staggered and almost fell, but he recovered in an instant, returning to the contest with a leaping kick.

The contest in the arena grew more ferocious with each blow and kick. The two men were moving with such frightening speed, parrying, thrusting, blocking, kicking, punching, that they were at times just a blur. The older man's right arm snaked out fiercely, aiming directly for the young man's eyes. With a light twist, sudden and deft as to be almost invisible, he grabbed the extended fingers and used them as a handle to twist his opponent around and deliver a sharp roundhouse kick to the temple. A follow-up knife-hand strike to the collarbone made the older man stagger backwards, clearly hurt this time. An incredible agile kick to the head felled him like a storm-struck tree. He then lay exhausted on the floor, unable to move for a moment.

In a single graceful movement, the young victor turned and bowed to the group of monks, who simply nodded their heads to acknowledge his victory. He then helped his groggy opponent to his feet, who, unsteadily, completed his own formal bow.

With the contest over, Chu was already running around the perimeter of the arena, his sandals padding soundlessly over the tiled floor. He was a gangling lad, not yet quite in command of his limbs, being only fifteen and still a few years away from full growth. Deng opened his arms, wishing their reunion could have been under more pleasant circumstances.

"Uncle Deng, Uncle Deng!"

Chu was overflowing with happiness and emotion. Deng continued to hold him, the boy's head pressed deep into his shoulder. But something was already wrong; the greeting had turned to sudden sadness. Chu's voice choked and was submerged beneath sobbing. He looked up, trying to blink back the tears.

Deng looked round to where his father, Tenzin, had sat amongst the cluster of monks, but he saw that he had gone. Within seconds the hall was empty and silent save for Deng and his nephew and the faint rustle of a broom as a frail Tibetan lady swept studiously over the tiles. She seemed as dry and shrivelled as an ancient monkey.

Deng sat down with the boy for a moment, holding Chu's hands gently as the two spoke in Tibetan. "Your last letter had a touch of desperation Chu, which is why I came here today. Now please, tell me what is wrong. Where is Kwei-Lan?" Deng's eyes were sensitive and kind.

Chu, meeting the eyes, was filled with a kind of sunshine inside, but he still seemed reluctant to speak. He paused and gave a sidelong glance towards the woman, who met his stare fleetingly but did not break her sweeping action.

She was working slowly, attentively, almost reverently. Gradually, she drew closer and closer to where they were sitting. "I'm sorry," Chu began, and then closed his mouth. "I wish things were different." He blinked and was obviously unable to continue. Chu could not shake the ominous feeling the woman's presence gave him. It was as though her shrivelled appearance was an omen, or a warning.

* * *

Chu led Deng across the giant hall to a place where a cracked blue doorway revealed a staircase, winding downwards. The steps, made of crumbling stone, were difficult for Deng to manoeuvre at first as he and his nephew disappeared into the gloom below.

A small corridor took them adjacent to the main courtyard. Deng looked up through the grimy window slits and could see the looping branches of wisteria against the red brick walls, where the caged monkeys played. Above this, the giant cypress tree protected the courtyard like a sentinel, equally beautiful in summer and winter, and above the ancient jewelled tree, the ice blue of the sky was dominated by the stark obtuseness of the mountain peaks.

Pausing for a moment as they reached a narrow landing, Deng faced another stone-clad stairwell, where every step brought a noticeable lowering in temperature. He became breathless at one point, the cold air hurting his lungs, Chu racing too far ahead. "Chu, wait!" There was silence as Deng stood in the darkness, hands pressing against the walls for balance and security. Then Chu reappeared, his worried face swimming forward in the gloom beneath Deng.

"Where are we going, Chu? And why is it so cold?"

91

"I must show you something." Chu ministered for him to follow. "It is cold for good reason, you will see. We are almost there. Take my arm. I'm sorry; I'll go more slowly."

The cold damp air wrapped around Deng like a heavy coat of chain mail as he grabbed hold of Chu's arm and continued to descend the worn sweep of steps.

The little light there was showed their breath like clouds of steam. Odd memories from Deng's childhood floated freely in his mind as he forced himself to remember. His happiest days were when he ran and played in the rich maze of chambers amidst the gardens filled with flowers and fountains. But even these times of natural joy had been mixed with sadness, violence, and terror.

A doorway faced them, beyond which a small room was lit by a flickering ruby light. Deng saw paintings on the walls, frescos in the Mongolian style. He could not be sure, but the paintings seemed to tell some sort of religious story. There was crispness beneath his feet now as he and Chu found themselves on flat ground. The room appeared empty apart from the wall paintings.

On the other side of the room there was another door, sturdier than the first and framed by unadorned blocks of stone. The door reluctantly creaked inwards on rusty hinges as Deng and Chu pushed jointly against it.

The flickering shadows across the stonework grew suddenly higher, and ever deeper red, so that it felt to Deng that he were entering Hades itself.

These were the ice dungeons of the temple, windowless and disused for a thousand years, and emanating from a time when the temple had been a fortress. There were old barrels caked in solid ice, with rusty weapons, other horrific instruments of torture, and coils of chain still hanging from the walls. An iron grate looked downwards onto the remnants of an underground stream which emanated from the plateau, flowed through the forest, and came to rest beneath the temple walls. It once provided the only water supply for the Shaolin monks who had taken refuge at the temple during a time of civil unrest in the city. Now it was just a frozen wasted memory of the past.

Chu was clambering onto a stone plinth. Seemingly oblivious to the cold, he was staring down at a block of solid ice, gesticulating for Deng to join him there.

Lips blue with cold, his body shivering, Deng climbed onto the plinth and stood beside Chu, looking down into the surface of the pale block of ice, inspecting it with puzzlement. An old feeling of horror seeped into the conscious part of his mind, fuelled by Crowley's recent conference, for encased in the ice was a giant footprint, oval in shape, over twelve inches long and very wide, with a protruding big toe, clearly shaped.

Suddenly, Chu burst into a flood of speech. "My father is missing, Uncle Deng. He's disappeared." There was a rising note of urgency in his tone. "He went to the plateau one morning and never returned. A group of workers searched the forest and the edge of the plateau, but when they came back it was without my father."

Chu was as simple and direct as a child, but he could not halt the flurry of words. "They found this and brought it back with them. Now everyone is so afraid. No one will continue the search." There was little colour in his face as he stood with helpless eyes gazing. His voice remained animated, even if the tone indicated that life had recently been painful.

Deng cupped the boy's face with his hands and wiped away the semi-solidifying tears.

"What does your grandfather say?" he asked in a voice low and laboured.

Chu stretched upright, his tension palpable. "He says that my dad is surely dead and that the footprint should be preserved as a warning to everyone to stay away from the high forest near the plateau. He says there are many strange tales of giant creatures inhabiting the wilderness and that we should keep to our own territory, or else risk everything. Do you believe this, Uncle Deng?"

"No," said Deng, with a spoonful of assurance. He was about to expand upon this when he heard a shuffling noise behind him, faint but unmistakable. It made Chu jump and turn sharply. An old man stood at the bottom of the steps and began moving nearer to them, his bony face lit by the flickering red light, a candle held aloft in his shaking hand casting a wash of shadows and shapes against the tortured walls.

"And I am right!" The voice was a stone dropped into the depths, soft but threatening. "Why would anyone seek to disturb a nest of hornets?"

Deng was flushed with unease, a deepening feeling sinking through his heart as he wondered how many years it had been since he'd spoken with his father. He stared once again into those contemptuous tungsten eyes.

Deng stroked back his fringe as if to calm himself and saw then that which he had not observed previously in the combat arena, how taut and sallow the flesh was across his father's skull. Tenzin was far frailer than Deng had expected him to be, the ravages of time adding ballast to the former's face. The last white hair was almost gone; the face, a veritable net of wrinkles.

"You have no reason to come here now," Tenzin said. There was a deliberate jag of bitterness evident in his words, and his voice was like iron nails being dragged over rock. His face flushed a pale crimson. No hint of warmth touched the alabaster skin, yet the face seemed lit by some inner touch of flame.

A spasm of anger flashed across Deng's face. "I have every reason to come here," he said hoarsely, the bubbling anger creating an exactness of words for him as he met his father's stare unblinkingly and jutted out a defiant chin.

"I am here to search for my brother," he added with a snap of righteous indignation. "And maybe you should remind yourself why I had to leave here in the first place." His temper had risen, compelling him to reveal the real heart of his grievance, although, given the option he would not have chosen to rush to the matter. He inclined his slender neck, waiting with mock attentiveness for a response, which did not come.

Tenzin moved forward to the edge of the plinth. The beginnings of harboured aggression flared. A tiny flame was struck in the dark. The flame expanded, forcing away some of the darkness.

"You dare to come here after all these years from your big city life and talk to me about my first born!" Tenzin stared straight into Deng's eyes, vehemence in his voice, his features pointed. Irritation and impatience started to build up like magma underneath an earthquake fault line. The blood suffused Tenzin's face, seeming to drown him and make his eyes bolt. A vein on the side of his head pulsated, and Deng noticed his fist was clenched and white. Deng couldn't be sure, but at that moment he thought he also noticed a different colour flash across his father's dark orbs.

"Kwei-Lan is dead," Tenzin exclaimed firmly. "He liked to visit the plateau and drew solace from the silence and the cold. But the plateau is a dangerous place. When he failed to return, I sent a qualified search party, but they did not find him. And do *you*," he said, emphasising the personal pronoun harshly, "actually think you are *more* qualified to locate him?" Finding the idea suddenly amusing, he let forth a strange, abnormal laugh.

A short silence ensued then. Some of Tenzin's anger seemed to evaporate. "Just let it be," he concluded darkly.

Chu jumped down from the plinth. He was distraught and did not attempt to conceal it. Alarmed, he laid a hand urgently on his grandfather's sleeve. "No, Grandfather, no," he said, wanting to scream. "We *cannot* just let it be. We must search again, please, please …"

Tenzin studied the round resolute face of his teenage grandson, considering his options, and there fell a further silence, bleak and eerie and as cold as the dungeon itself. He was clearly irate but, for the moment, defeated. With visible effort, he managed to control his natural tendencies. He was facing something which was momentarily ungraspable.

A fierce spirit seemed to suddenly leave him. The old man's look softened as he stared curiously at Deng. "It is a full moon," he said, "so there is a banquet tonight in the Imperial Hall. You are of course invited." Then in a changed conciliatory tone, which shaded the fierceness of his looks, he said, "We can talk more then, or afterwards." This tempered the oppression in the dungeon. "Your quarters are ready for you. Ask for anything you desire; it shall be at your disposal."

Deng and Tenzin bowed to each other with the expected traditional courtesy. The fire had left them both. Tenzin's face turned into the wash of the candle flame as his ghostly form drifted towards the staircase, the flickering light illuminating the billowing silk robe as he started to ascend.

"Father." Deng called him back briefly.

"What made the footprint?"

Tenzin lifted the candle, and as he did so, the flame seemed to leap and expand with an orange and golden tongue. The glassy eyes held Deng for a moment, but Tenzin said nothing, the silence rich with unspoken meaning. And then he was gone, the light diminishing gradually as he disappeared up the stairwell.

* * *

The Imperial Hall was located in the very heart of the temple and was, that night, a genuine study of splendour. The high ceilings were carved and gilded; dragons and salamanders were etched on the walls, painted in red and gold. Symbols of good luck and long life adorned every table in amber amulets, and light laughter enveloped the room.

Countless wicker cages hung from the ceiling, each containing a colourful melodic bird, their interlaced whistles making no impact against the loud music, which was in the style of a Cantonese opera, the *Yuet Kek*, one of the oldest dramatic art forms on earth – a rich cacophonous spectacle featuring music, singing, martial arts, acrobatics, and theatre.

Walking down the jade steps, underneath the egocentric sculpture of his father, Deng's shadow appeared green in hue like the green of an underwater plant.

A servant sounded a massive gong. Deng smiled openly in appreciation of the scene of intemperance which faced him. He hadn't known such gratuitous opulence since his childhood, when he had lived at the temple and dreamed of the joys of the future and what it might have in store for him.

Bamboo tables were arranged in a gigantic circle, creating a kind of amphitheatre in which the stately lion dance took place, the thickly embroidered costume of gold and white snaking its way around the circle, while the man who held up the heavy carved head shook the great mane and roared.

A small group of young women danced around in circles. The loveliest one, with a red scarf in her hand, headed the ballet with whimsical beauty, turning her back in exquisite time to the music with a faint swish of her skirt as she walked forward with a pert flounce. Deng drank in the sight of her. He couldn't imagine anything more perfect. He regarded her as a walking work of art. She was taller than the others, and her hair, the colour of deepest night, hung in seven tresses. She skipped like a she-goat and flew like a falcon, entwining the scarf like a crimson snake in her hair. Her cream skirt that swept the ground at the back was short at the front, revealing slim marble legs. When the folds of her skirt rearranged themselves, she gave the illusion of being as delicate as an egg shell.

Her eyes were slightly mischievous, and she smiled shyly as she danced. She was exquisite. Deng tried to observe her in an unobtrusive manner, admiring without leering. Yet his gaze continued to embrace and flatter her. She was well aware of it; her pale flush deepened. So young and unused that Deng could actually believe that her freshness, unlike that of a rose, would remain immune to the tide and the passage of the seasons, like an enduring bloom. There was a hint of sublimity, all youth but with an aspect beyond time, both radiant and grave. She caught his eye briefly and the chill of her beauty was thawed by another smile.

Deng pulled his gaze away reluctantly and threaded his way through the rows of tables, glancing in all directions at the endless trays and platters heaped with exotic foods, some of which must have been imported for the occasion. Large roasted birds, rice of many colours, whole crabs and lobsters, and turtle shells polished to shine, stuffed full of shrimp. But there were also traditional pulses and a multitude of noodle dishes, which Deng had grown up on but now seldom ate. In addition there was a flimsy bamboo table clearly straining under its weight of fish dishes preserved in honey and currants, silver containers of cheese made from yak milk, and salted fig cakes. The freshest vegetables and rare fruits, exquisitely prepared, garnished every dish.

At intervals of about ten feet, high burning torches threw a crazed lemon hue across the stone walls, creating a majestic flickering glow that fell on everything. Suspended from the ceiling was a girl sitting cross-legged in a rattan cage-cradle and playing the doleful *di-daa*, a clarinet-like instrument, accompanied by cymbals and drums from below in support of the lion dance.

A woman met Deng's gaze, startled, both in an abstracted and distant way. She was a graceful middle-aged lady with a heavy sheaf of black hair laced with grey, a bright oval face and purple irises as clear as twilight.

"Master Deng?" she questioned in a haughty agreeable voice, continuing to stare at him with a guarded smile. It had taken her a few seconds to remember his name, following which a blush raised like fire in her face. Never remarkable for her beauty, she was however shrewdly amiable with a pleasant face. She did not ask what he was doing there, but he could tell that she wanted to. She was still smiling, but he saw now that her smile was a deliberate gloss, as cold, smooth, and decorative as a coat of gilt.

Remembering more definitely now that Deng was Tenzin's son, the woman opened her lips to force out a stammered courtesy.

"I wish you well for your stay at the temple, Master Deng." She sounded sincere but looked a little dismayed as her face faded before him like a flower exposed to warm winds and summer rains. She bowed respectfully and then scurried away like an innocent faun into the swarm of the banquet.

Deng remembered her now as the ward assigned to look after his mother. Myriads of unanswered questions were spinning madly through his mind, but he chose not to try to find answers to them now. And he did not know how to articulate the potentially dreadful discussions that might follow.

There were also other faces he recognised: his spiritual teacher and his martial arts grand master, both now very old, who did not seem to recognise him. Deng had no wish to re-open lines of communication with anyone from the temple anyway, although he remembered they had all been present at the mini banquet that had been held for him in the very same place before he had departed the temple for Hong Kong when he was about Chu's age. His intention then was to give up the traditional Tibetan ways forever and, so he thought, never to return.

Deng was trying to locate either his father or Chu, but he could see neither of them as he moved light-footed through the crowd to a low table made from painted ivory, from which he took up a goblet of wine. He bowed to the lady who poured it for him, doing his best, despite the circumstances, to adhere to the proper observance of things within the temple.

The lion dance was followed by fire-eaters and sword swallowers, like a chapter from *The Arabian Nights*. In an endless agile procession, the tumblers completed the circle with genuine zeal.

These were masters of grace and control, clad in purple gis. Their movements were dextrous and flowing as they performed a karate ballet with dreamlike ease. They simulated kicks, jumps, and rolls without making contact, changing them from normal speed to slow motion so as to complete the exhibition like divers walking on the ocean floor.

Just then Deng spotted Chu bobbing and weaving his way through the banquet, like a child at a circus, trying to look everywhere at once. He caught sight of Deng's waving hand, grabbed an apple from a huge bowl of fruit, and zigzagged towards his uncle.

"Are you on a diet, Uncle Deng?" Chu asked breathlessly, with a small spark of mischief in his eyes as he bit into the apple.

Deng laughed softly. "No," he said, "just not hungry right now. But I can see that you are!" Chu gurgled a laugh like a little spring, and took another chunk of apple.

"I've made a decision, Chu," Deng announced abruptly, lowering his head to speak and convey his decision in the fewest possible words. "I'm going to search for Kwei-Lan tomorrow, on the plateau, and I've decided that I'll need you to come with me, to keep me company and to stop me getting lost." He smiled, knowing that Chu didn't know the way either.

Chu's face opened up like a flower and his eyes brightened. Then he made a choking sound, a kind of dry sob, and was weeping, laughing, shaking, and babbling all at once, his tears running into his smile.

"Thank you, Uncle Deng, thank you," he said with genuine gratitude and hope. "You don't know what this means to me. I had wanted someone's word, and I wanted it to be yours. I will help you, and together, under your guidance, we will find my father."

Deng felt like an ancient priest, with Chu his eager acolyte. He knew the odds against their finding anything were heavily stacked, so he wanted to temper the wildness of Chu's untutored enthusiasm, but he did not know how to do so right then. He would deal with it as they travelled and was hopeful that the effort and commitment to search would alone be enough. As always, he would manage everything with his natural cautious balance.

But then he offered an unexpected and impulsive option. "I am more than content to go by myself, if you would prefer to wait at the temple for my return?"

Chu shook his head emphatically. "No." The tears welled in his eyes again, and he said the only words that he could find out of the confusion: "I want to come with you. I must."

Deng's face grew serious for a moment as he contemplated the enormous responsibility of looking after his fifteen-year-old nephew. His lips tightened imperceptibly, but otherwise he betrayed not a flicker of emotion or surprise.

"Okay, tell your grandfather when you see him that I will be in my quarters." He paused. "I have some preparation to do for our journey tomorrow. Meet me at six in the morning in the main courtyard. Don't be late!" He wagged a mocking finger and winked.

Chu mastered his emotions, bowed with a fierce satisfaction, and then wiped his eyes, watching his uncle as he climbed the emerald steps.

Deng paused momentarily on the top step, looking up into the intricately carved and elaborately painted gable. There, in the exact mathematical apex-axis of the Imperial Hall, was the sky disc. Of all the temple's remarkable artefacts, the sky disc was the greatest, probably four thousand years old and discovered in the ruins of Xining and Lhasa in the early seventies by British archaeologist Sir Robin Coningham, an even more accredited discoverer than Lino Crowley.

It was ostensibly a bronze disc, about the size of a small shield, containing a gold sun set in a field of glimmering opaque stars dominated by a small lilac moon. Research had identified one constellation as being Pleiades. Whether perceived or real, the ability to undertake ancient astronomy would have wielded enormous power and influence to its owner, just as pharaohs rose to power in part because it was believed they could forecast the Nile's annual floods.

There were countless theories regarding how the sky disc may have actually been used. One of these suggested that the ends of the two gold bands, one of which had been lost to antiquity, along its outer edges could identify the points on the horizon where the sun rises and sets on the summer and winter solstices, respectively the longest and shortest days of the year. The early astronomer could have followed the sun's path along the gold bands to establish a rudimentary calendar, providing farmers with information critical for planting and harvesting. The disc could also have been used to predict eclipses. Overlaid on the bronze base there was a curved golden object laced with feather-like oars set between the horizontal bands, representing a night ship, a celestial craft which early people believed carried the sun god on his journey from darkness to dawn. But one thing was certain: the sky disc continued to fire the imaginations of archaeologists, astronomers, and ethnologists alike.

Deng remained still on the top step, his eyes narrowing like those of a cat as he allowed them to roam across the banquet and seek out the beautiful dancer one last time. Her hair, now released from its tresses, swung in a glossy curtain across her shoulders. Her skin seemed more vivid than ever, the colours richer and more imbued with life than before. So delicate were her features that they seemed chiselled from Himalayan ice.

Deng remembered his father saying, "Ask for anything you desire," but his natural discipline and his fear of getting too close to anyone assisted him in circumventing that particular avenue of desire, however tempting it was to think that the dancer might be flattered to be singled out for his favours.

She met his eyes again briefly with simple inquisitive smile. In a way, her beauty served only to deepen his disquiet. He clutched at virtue to cover his ardour and, without further hesitation – lest his virtue slumbered – he disappeared into the darkness beyond the high curved doors in a semi-muse, reflecting for a moment on the unfathomable complexity of women.

* * *

Deng's quarters were beautiful. The air was perfumed, but there was a dampness in the temple that did not belong to the air outside. Radiance glittered from jewels and soft flames. The four-poster bed wore hangings of the deepest red. It was a place of pure opulence, bedecked with striking objects made of silver and gold, thick rugs, and a deep armchair in velvet the colour of chilled plums.

There was also a massive table with many chairs and an imposingly large business desk which had a leather top covered in glass. The exquisite carving of the desk was like a live growing plant. The tapestries that covered the walls between the windows and doors were old, rich, and wonderfully worked, and once would have had glorious colours that still showed here and there in the protected folds that the summer sun could not reach. Even the cushions on the chairs were of the finest embroidery.

Deng sat at the desk, a single lamp shedding a bright circle of light as the quiet of the night closed in drowsily. A tarnished bronze brazier, with a steady scarlet glow like the burnish of sunset, battled to keep out the cold. The brazier was itself handsome, standing high on three braced legs like saplings, the fire basket a trellis of cypress and vine leaves discreetly massed with charcoal to provide comforting heat without smoke.

The curtains were drawn back at both ends with scarlet ties. Deng saw that the sky was sheened an eerie metallic blue. The moon was full and fat, and the air was filled with the scent of mountain flowers. As he sat there at his desk, the semi-open window revealing the very tops of the peaks, their faces bathed in the ivory light, he felt chilled with a sense of the vastness of the world.

He heard a noise suddenly, rose from his chair, and walked to the window, where he saw a scattering of earth descending in a rivulet of dislodged stones. But on further inspection he saw nothing, nor heard anything save for the high whistle of the wind.

On a night such as this, one might almost believe in the spirits of the dead, that they were fluttering their limbs like moths and gliding along the lonely track, or through the curved hallways of the temple in sheeted silent crowds, towards the fields where the soil was barren beyond the moisture's reach and which led to the maze of lowland woods and then up to the icy table. It was possible to imagine that the living were outnumbered by the ghosts who dominated the haunted temple and surrounding lands.

Deng realised he needed to get a hold on himself. He had no deep belief in the afterlife, and gave no credence to the ancient Himalayan belief that life may be restored to the dimension of the living, that life may be breathed into that which has gone. The implausibility made it too preposterous an idea to contemplate.

Turning away from the spectral gleam, Deng returned to the desk. His dark head bent again over the books and the map as he tried to work out the safest route to the plateau, refreshing his memory about Tibet's mysterious past. He put the map down momentarily and turned the pages of a dusty book that retold the Tibetan fables.

From the fourth century, Chinese historians referred to Tibet as "Tubo", meaning "the roof of the world". But some archaeological data suggests humans may have passed through Tibet at the time when India was first inhabited, half a million years before. Tibet's first king, who flourished in 213 BC, was supposedly found exposed in a copper box after swimming in the Ganges, the box covered in strange claw-like marks. And at around the commencement of the Christian era, Sakay, the last great scholar of the Buddhists, told many strange and wonderful tales about Tibet's invisible mountain men.

The German zoologist Hans Schröder, who had resided at the temple in the late 1930s, rightly surmised that yeti legends were tightly interwoven with ancient Chinese legends of the Mighty Ape King. Schröder also described Tibet as a Shangri-La, a place that, being sequestered from the world by high mountain ranges, preserved the purity of the species, also reporting that it was almost a hermetically sealed area of retreat for forms of life long extinct elsewhere. He referred to it as *Shambhala*. And he also perceived the Tibetan cult of the dead – "vultures lifting the dead back into the skies" – in Indo-Germanic ritual solemnity. Schröder strove to codify the Tibetan visions and racial ideology into a form of Aryan mathematics, joining ancestral legacy and glacial cosmogony in a combination of racial and temperature studies. He would discover the "secret Tibet", and he would subsequently take it to the grave with him.

Before leaving Berlin in 1937, Schröder visited Dachau in his capacity as a Tibetan expert to observe medical experiments conducted on prisoners by SS doctors to measure human reactions to freezing temperatures and altitude. He also visited Auschwitz and did something similar with Dr Mengele, who was obsessed with a pair of identical twins from Tibet. These twins were of the rarest kind: monochronionic. This means that not only were the children identical, being formed from a single egg, but also that they had shared the same placenta and amniotic sac. It was even rarer that in such cases both twins survived as, sharing the same indefinite space, there would normally be a fight for that space and the stronger twin – as yet unborn – would win. If both twins survived, this indicated nuclein strength and, according to Mengele, could be linked back to their Himalayan origins and be an important clue in the Nazi quest to form the master race.

At the Nuremberg trials after the war, Schröder gave the following evidence:

> 'Himmler had some very strange ideas. He wanted to prove that the Nordic race had come down directly from the skies. Needless to say the whole thing was quite unscientific and so far-fetched that it is hard to believe now. Himmler and the others all dabbled in the occult. They

perceived the Himalayan snowman as a "cold-resistant proto-Aryan", and this is why the Nazis cancelled a Tibetan exhibition that was to be held in Strasburg in 1941, one that included two stuffed Tibetan bears. If the Aryans, as Himmler imagined, were of glacial provenance, and if proto-Aryans were still to be found in Tibet in the form of the yeti, then stuffed bears did not meet the Nazi concept of the abominable long-haired snowman. The Nazi theory of glacial cosmogony was based on the fact that all cosmic energy springs from the clash between fire and ice, thus proving the divine origin of the Aryan race.'

Schröder concluded his evidence with the following statement, delivered clearly and concisely, with the confidence and assurance of someone who had accepted that his role in the world, not just the war, was over:

'Before experiencing it first hand, I had received considerable evidence that the yeti did exist, and one meeting in particular, with an elderly woman in a hut in Salween, convinced me further. In fact she told me exactly where they existed so as to not waste time, like other explorers had done in their search of the remotest mountain forests year after year. It was never my goal to shoot or capture a yeti and drag it into our world. It would quickly have turned into a mere object of curiosity, pitilessly studied under the microscope of science in Western laboratories. There the myth would have died, victim to the same species that

had originally created it. As long as we sought
an early form of human species and dreamt of
a lost world that predated human history, we
felt compelled to prove that the yeti existed, and
that we certainly did. My own wounds provide
statement to that fact.'

Deng sighed. The history of Tibet was like Everest itself, an
immortal object, so why should not traditional horror stories
linger on as well, in the way that European parents scare their
children with "Little Red Riding Hood" and "Hansel and Gretel",
where the tales fulfil longings and dreams, and the fear indicating
the awe in the face of something with superior power?

And what about the long history of wild snow-covered forest
people in Russian folklore? Deng flicked through the pages
further and then read a resonating fable:

'Once upon a time, when Indian mystic Padma
was bringing Buddhism to Tibet, a demoness fled
from him. She offered a turquoise to the people
of Shambhala in exchange for their promise not
to reveal where she had gone. But the powerful
guru transformed the gem to yak dung, and the
villagers, thinking they had been cheated by the
demoness, betrayed her. In vengeance she melted
the mountain snow and flooded their valleys,
which vanished beneath turquoise, and the crystal
blue Phksundo Lake was formed. To ensure that
terror would survive and that no ancient rite could
exorcise her vengeful spirit, she brought back to
life the long extinct human, flesh-eating monsters
that would haunt the mountains forever.'

Whether he liked it or not, Deng had to accept, as did all academics in the end, that there was much he did not know and that some things may not be easily explained by science – and perhaps there was something greater than any human being could understand. He touched his brow briefly in consternation and doubt.

Tibet was certainly a strange alien wilderness, seeming to transcend all human life. It was sometimes referred to as the third pole. To its north rested Mongolia; to the east, China. It was the loftiest inhabited tableland in the world, one vast flattened mountaintop equal in size to three European states. At its lowest point, four thousand metres above sea level, it was possible to scan northern Kashmir and the rugged cactus playground of the Gobi Desert. Here, in ancient mythology, Tibet had laid the boundary between the worlds of the living and the dead, just as the sun each evening would disappear beneath the western horizon, so it was conceived that the spirits of the departed would embark on their journey to the afterlife.

For many years, the only reports of Tibet came from the travel journals of Marco Polo and the Jesuit missionaries. Even Polo reported sighting a monstrous creature, and once wrote a passage that told how he had lost six men in a savage attack from giant snowmen.

And from Deng's own childhood memories of Lhasa, there was the story of the girl who lived in a village high in the Himalayan Mountains. Each day she climbed partway up Mount Everest to graze and safeguard a heard of yaks. One day as she grazed the herd, she thought that a Xiong or a snow leopard might be nearby. She led the yaks to a clear stream, drinking some water and watching expressionlessly as the yaks drank and fed on the tough mountain grasses. But later, when the girl was found by a monk from one of the higher monasteries, her body had been ripped and eaten in a way that did not indicate a bear or a big cat. In addition, two yaks lay dead beside her, seemingly beaten with nailed clubs, and left uneaten.

Then there were the footprints.

Crowley's recent conference had, of course, refuelled the speculative furnace. Perhaps this was a rare occasion when science and legend could coexist? Deng pondered this paradox, closing the book with a strange mix of trepidation and excitement, returning to the map. The mountain roads by which Tibet is reached pass through ravines that are traversed by icy streams to produce the wildest and grandest scenery ever witnessed by travellers. With a patient eye, following a twisting grey line with his finger into the miles of forest, which separated the tracks and the plateau, Deng marked a point fastidiously with a pen.

At that moment, there came the soft noise of his door opening behind him.

Tenzin came into the room and placed two fragile porcelain cups, beautifully glazed and painted, on the table beside his son, speaking no word as he filled them with a hot fragrant sea-green tea.

"Thank you," Deng said uneasily, sensing something which demanded gravity of him. He leaned forward and lifted one of the cups, allowing the sweet smell to penetrate his senses. In spite of the unchanged deathly hue of his father's face, which never seemed to gain a warmer tint, either from blush or passion, there was still the unmistakable beauty to his aristocratic features, which Deng recalled from childhood.

Words were beginning to form on the cracked lips, but then Tenzin faltered, his eyes cast downwards, closing them off from his son's searching gaze.

"It is a very difficult thing," Tenzin began, looking at Deng oddly, although there was no trace of austere intention in his voice as his words fell into a vein of musing.

"I can tell," Deng said, puzzled as he began searching his father's face for a clue. A quiet interlude ensued.

Tenzin met his eyes directly then. "People here are frightened; they do not wish to go anywhere near the plateau anymore."

"Why?" Deng said unblinkingly, nodding for him to speak further, realising how he felt less afraid of his father and less in awe of the secrets he might possess than he otherwise thought he would be.

But for now he kept his defences well-oiled and remained silent.

With a diffident movement of his bony finger and a grey look of pain around his eyes, Tenzin's words seemed filled with dismay. "Can you not read the reasons in these books? Or the evidence of Dr Schröder, who stayed here and whom I knew when I was a young boy? ... I would have thought that it was self-evident." He swished contemptuously with his hand and stood up tall and straight, making the chill of his voice icier and his eyes seem more serious.

Deng stretched his muscles casually and, after a thoughtful moment of silence, said, "Mountain men?" He yawned a little and shook his head in a miniature act of provocation. There was a glint in his eye. Fever in his blood seemed to sing, evidence that much was still subdued.

Despite hearing Crowley's recent tale, following which his mind was sunk for a while in reconsideration, he said in a peremptory voice, "It's all conjecture, a hapless superstition based on fanciful stories that exist only in old people's imaginations, mainly those of the mountain people, who once thought that Everest held up the heavens." He paused briefly. "When science offers no immediate proof, then people turn to myths. That footprint could have been made by anything, probably a combination of things, impressions of regular animals enlarged by melting, leaving a small pool of water in the print, which can enlarge at its lowest point, usually the heel, exaggerating those features." Deng was being deliberately scientific, but deep down he knew that there was more to it.

"Do you think that every broken branch in the forest has been snapped or twisted by a yeti? Are there ghosts entombed within the stone walls of this temple?" He threw a hand up, incredulous. "I cannot believe that you could let Kwei-Lan's disappearance pass so easily because of a damned footprint and an ancient myth, a superstition of the utmost folly. It would not be so terrifying if the truth and facts were to be wholly understood. The only yeti is the one in your head," he concluded harshly. "Nobody has the time to embellish old legends, not even tourists."

Silence fell between them, ominous as thunder, before Tenzin stepped forward to the desk and refilled the cups, a look of calculation on his face.

"One man may observe what another man overlooks." A faint shadow seemed to cross his face. "Sometimes the mountains look up at the sky as if we aren't here." Then there was a sudden rapidity in his speech, which was out of character. "The sightings have started again. From the temple barricades you can see the edge of the great forest, and sometimes, just sometimes ..."

He caught his breath, straightened his shoulders, and frowned in concentration into the shadows of the room, far away into nothing, like a jeweller with a precious stone. "What are myths if not the expression of some hidden or forgotten hints of secret dark truths? Deep truth is imageless." As he spoke, his voice seemed bled to monotone. "As fear, it is buried in the nightmares of our sleep, so secrets lie buried in the past of our land." He paused. "There are forces in the world," he said calmly, "full of power, strangeness, and the sublime ... so much more than an ancient superstition." He concluded darkly.

Deng steepled his fingers and gazed suspiciously into the old man's unblinking stare, deep into that strange reptilian glitter. There was a tension now at the corners of Tenzin's mouth, and deep lines in his brow.

Despite everything, Deng felt the embers of resentment suddenly fading away. He wanted to comfort his father but did not know how, feeling inadequate as Tenzin shuffled over to the window and stared out, unseeing, into the velvet night. Deng was, without question, his mother's son, soft and vulnerable.

Tenzin hesitated a moment, his sharply calculating eyes visibly dilating. "If you deem it wise, then I am persuaded that you should go," he said quietly, sounding slightly dazed. After an ensuing pause, he bowed. "I think I will paint for a while tonight now."

He turned to walk from the room, but as he reached the door, he waited and turned back meaningfully.

"Take good care of my grandson when you travel to the plateau tomorrow." His voice was languishing now, resigned. "And pay your respects to your mother's shrine in the chapel before you leave." He closed his eyes briefly as memory surged like a wave inside him.

Deng met his father's eyes for a moment and inclined his head in silent suspicion, wondering why the old man had become so easily acquiescent. In the end he put it down to old age and lassitude, which seemed at that point terrible, but nevertheless he watched cautiously as the door clicked shut behind Tenzin, feeling a strange sense of something lost.

"I will," Deng whispered to himself with a softening heart.

He returned to the window and was suddenly haunted by the mythical beauty of the land. He gazed at the stars and felt his dreams take wing, until they seemed to fill the sky. A red fox barked somewhere in the rice fields and a forest peacock disappeared below Deng with a dark purple flash into the trees. The breeze carried both the noise of geese above the distant river and the growl of a snow tiger miles away in the hills, faint but distinctive, its night call borne out across the ice by the wind.

He made sure the window was fastened and then walked over to the bed. Profundity could be tiring.

Deng lit as many candles as he could find and placed them around the bed, so that they formed a wall of light. For a long moment he stared into the candle flames, hooded and flickering like ghosts, pondering his father's words. Then he felt a terrible weariness. Before he knew it, he had fallen asleep.

During the night a cold wind screamed through the room and all the candles were blown out, but Deng did not stir. He slept dreamlessly until the morning.

Chapter 6

Deng's Story, Part II

They entered the courtyard together as the sun was drinking the early morning mist, the pre-dawn air fresh and clear. Beyond the trees which fringed the darkling glass of the lake, the eastern sky was brightening. Deng heard wings against the thin dawn as a flock of mallards alighted on the waters.

All the flamboyance and colourful scenes of the previous night were gone. There was just a quiet crowd sitting in the open and a few golden monkeys playing in the shade of the trees. Flowers grew in curved borders at the foot of the cypress trees, which bowed their long fringed heads down. Jasmine scented the air. The crumbling walls of the courtyard almost disappeared under its burden of wisteria, which sprawled over the stones like a crowd of lazy cats.

Tenzin was seated here on a woven mat, sitting tranquilly, cross-legged, palms placed one against each other. His wizened body looked as dry as firewood. He was held by some inner peace.

Deng observed him closely. The tiny wisps of white hair framed the moonlike face. He could see that the eyes were closed.

The edges of the lips were turned upwards like horns. It was a marble face he saw, serene and perfectly motionless in prayer.

Deng and Chu passed quietly without disturbing the discipline of the day's devotions, although Deng remained slightly haunted by his father's persistent hinting at dark mystery.

A little forlorn, he, with Chu following, made for the wide gates, where the northerly facing battlement walls took them down towards the stone-littered cemetery and along the path which led back to where Deng had left the jeep the previous day. He had packed the supplies methodically – body warmers, snow chains, food, torches, jerry cans, a fearsome hunting knife, a pick axe, and waterproof firelighters. From there onwards it was impossible to predict what kind of adventure lay before them.

* * *

From a tangle of mountains in the west, the smaller range of the Hindu Kush spreads east. From the same point, but tumbling southwards, it forms the still greater chain of the Himalayas. Just below this, surrounded by snow and ice on its surface, and miles of thick forest on its slopes, lay the tableland itself. Tibetan history and custom called this region *Sbas-Yul*, "the hidden country", or in peasantry parlance, "a place where crows die".

Deng and Chu travelled in virtual silence, the sky's luminous opacity holding the early sunlight with a smudge of clouds stretching across the moonstone-yellow horizon. Most of the time Chu slept; when he did rouse, he seemed grave and eager.

They crossed the empty expanse in a rambling line, chasing the horizon towards the forest foothills where Kwei-Lan had been on the morning he disappeared. The tilled meadows, peppered here and there with the occasional copse and strategically planted sunflowers, soya beans, and clover, were veiled in a thin ground mist, so thin in some places that the air seemed white.

On the slopes were the remains of prehistoric Stone Age hill forts, enclosed by dry pebble walls, scattered between the patchworks of fallow terrain. And every now and then they passed roadside shrines, some elaborate, dedicated to the Dalai Lama. Others were simpler, containing a figurine of an olive-skinned young woman with long black hair and a red peasant's skirt lying on her back while nursing a baby.

In the distance the sloping grey hills looked alive and in motion, like water. There was an immense feeling of space and silence.

For the people in the lowland habitats, such as Salween, lower than the temple but vastly removed from the plateau, the most important thing was a high rainfall in the spring season; lack of rain and the poverty of the soil would mean the farmer's crops could suffer, a continuous worry that changed with the seasons and could be erased to its bare outlines by winter's cold white hand. So these shrines were a beacon of hope and symbols of survival in a hostile land, where travellers were expected to leave simple offerings, a few cigarettes, a bottle of water, some sweets. If showers came in the spring, then all the fine hair of the fields would grow green again and the bald clay soil would become invisible beneath it.

The forest covering the distant horizon seemed from afar to be tiny patches of moss. The disc of the sun was dull silver, creating a luminous glare. Deng's dark glasses protected his eyes like a mask.

It would take many hours to travel across the fields and then upwards on the forest road to a point where they would have to abandon the vehicle and continue on foot, as they assumed Kwei-Lan had done on the day he went missing, although the subsequent search party had not even recovered his vehicle.

They made good progress towards their destination, travelling over sometimes gruelling terrain. Deng saw a flight of eagles soaring high above him towards the snow-clad peaks. He stared at the mountain scape and thought again about the dark mysteries of the peaks. He also considered the awful snowmen that the Tibetans and Nepalese all swore exists, and whose legend was like a ghost, high on haunted Everest.

In the boundaries between reality and fable, Deng had learned to research reality and dismiss fable. One chronicle of the yeti fable even suggested that the Abominable Snowmen had built the gateways to the next plane via an underground complex in the ice caverns of Tibet, below Everest.

This increased Deng's belief that he was correct to be sceptical, but he also wondered whether his father might be right that myth owed something to truth. Might superstition sometimes veil the germs of fact? He was suddenly not so sure that all the wisdom lay with the sceptics. It was, after all, possible to be sceptical about the sceptics ... and the horrible possibility of this shadowed his imaginings. Uncertainty stuck momentarily like barbs in his mind.

But after a while, Deng smiled ruefully to himself. And as he did so, he realised that he could easily have wallowed in the depths of superstition, which could infect even the most rational of minds, including his own.

He looked at Everest's great summit which disappeared into the sheltering sky, close to heaven; the Tibetans called it the "father of the snows". Every minute that passed, Everest sent towards them its cruel light cavalry, wind wailing like a flute, shape-changing mist, and endless unmelting snow, keeping them ever aware of its deadly forces held in reserve.

* * *

The engine died away and was silent. The day trembled on the edge of extinction now.

Deng and Chu got out of the jeep and stood side by side in the gloom, looking up into the brooding forest on the borderline between the known and the unknown, feeling the cool night air against their faces.

The trees stood and leaned against the fading light. Their dark green fringes, a hundred feet up in the air, were suddenly animated as though by a mystery seeping outwards from unseen forces. Faint noises could be heard in the darkness: buzzing, chirping, scuttling, and twittering – and the rustling wings of small owls, like the unknown tongue of angels.

Where they stopped was a flat area sprinkled with coarse grass, but it was torn and shaped at its perimeter by the upheavals of fallen trees from previous storms, which were scattered everywhere, holding decaying fruit and berries. Beyond this was the darkness of the forest proper and, above the darkness and the treeline, the ice wilderness that they would need to reach on foot.

The sheer size of the incline and the roughness of the terrain made their task seem, at first, to be an insurmountable one. "This is as far as we can go in the jeep," Deng said, looking out into the forest as the woods creaked secretively around them. "The road ends here." The trees were dark bulking presences everywhere, moving slowly in the breeze, rubbing their joints together.

"I understand," Chu replied, frightened at the thought of having to walk through the wilderness area, even in daylight. A cold wind passed through the forest, bringing the sigh and whisper of leafy branches. Chu stood close to his uncle. A dim after light hung in the mountain tops like a sunset mirage. But soon even the shadows were swallowed by the encroaching darkness.

"We will start afresh in the morning." Deng breathed, realising that to be stranded on foot in the alien forest at night was unthinkable. Presently, they returned to the safety and warmth of the vehicle, eating bread, honey, and fruit, before planning to settle in for the remainder of the night.

The night was like a dark tiger.

Deng ensured that the canvas roof was fixed and secured from the outside. After topping up the tank from a jerry can, he removed the body warmers and torches, plus the large hunting knife, which he put on the front seat.

In the forest somewhere, a branch snapped behind him, almost stealthily. He stared towards the sound but saw only blackness. His blood seemed like lava in his veins, thudding in his temples, his hands icy with fear, his mouth dry.

He waited. Nothing.

Then he stared at the black cloud blotting out the stars, listening to hear any further interruption in the brooding forest. As the light drained away, there was barely enough illumination even for shadows. Everything in the forest was hidden. Even the stars and the moon were covered behind a dense layer of cloud, giving the air that tincture associated with the world before a storm. Deng's ears became sharper and his mind paranoid, every snap of a twig a potential predator.

He secured the doors but continued to stare out into the fathomless darkness. Chu was already settled on the back seat. Deng unfolded two body warmers and several blankets and placed them over Chu. He left a flask of water on the floor behind the passenger seat.

Deng remained half awake, listening for the next hour. Shadows, urged by the wind, twisted languorously. He blinked at the growing night, watching the brilliant moon skulking between the clouds.

During the night, Chu awoke screaming, thrashing at the blankets, as though his mind was beset by a throng of phantoms. Deng comforted him, but at times the boy's breathing was so quick and shallow, it was as if some unseen plague were upon him.

"I'm scared," Chu said.

"Me too," Deng said equably, "but we will be safe together. I will make sure of that."

These were the last words they said to each other that night. The light from the moon was suddenly befogged and blotted out, and all that remained was the world unilluminated. A light rain fell, pattering.

* * *

The forest clearing was bound by tall trees. The wind rustled through the leaves, sounding like old men gasping. It was pre-dawn, the lack of bird song making the woods eerie as Deng imagined every leaf flutter or twig snap to announce the arrival of a dangerous beast. He shivered in the inky darkness until the dawn chorus broke the malignant spell. The birds' voices had never sounded so sweet. Streaking through gaps in the branches, the shafts of bronze sunlight tracing down to the ground like light sabres had never been so welcome. The whole area was suddenly teeming with wildlife. Sharp-winged birds soared high above the forest canopy, lazy spiders clambered on flimsy webs, tame squirrels scurried around on the lower tree trunks, and the butterflies danced their unending dance by a shock of bright blue flowers.

Somewhere in the distance, far up in the forest, Deng could hear the sound of a waterfall. Conjured from the jousting between light and dark, he thought he had glimpsed a silhouette move through the trees. He stared for a while.

But perhaps it was only a glimpse and nothing more.

Chu roused a little at a time; at last he gazed out of the misty window. It was still semi-dark. The trees were vague blurs, but the sky was filling quickly with light pouring in from the east.

"I've been out to look around," Deng whispered easily, peering into the semi-darkness of the creepers. "There's a place on the other side of this clearing where we can climb through the trees more easily," he said, somewhat daunted by the thought of doing it.

Chu nodded and pulled himself into a warm ball, hoping the nothingness of sleep would come back, nice nothingness with no nasty pictures in it. An early bee buzzed at his nose, drugged by cold and hunger. The engine noise was soothing, sounding far away. Shades of grey swallowed him again for a few minutes more.

The wind moved through the trees. The sharp points of the horizon blurred and the forest lightened. A bird squawked and blundered heavily away into the air. The slope led uphill into the undergrowth and the mountains rose before the travellers, with little more than a faint mist over the highest points.

The bushes were dark evergreen, and the many buds were waxen green and folded up against the light. Here and there little breezes crept beneath the bright early sunlight, making the larger bush leaves whisper so that spots of blurred sunlight slid over Deng's and Chu's bodies or moved like bright-winged things in the shade.

Deng led the way along the trail. The further he and Chu went, the more daunting were the walls of mingled forest and rock. Above them, crags of ice towered amidst vast ravines.

Presently there was more space between the trees, and many bushes in the spaces. The earth was a reddish brown; the giant trees were covered with spurts of green fire. Deng and Chu went through a small clearing, passing through this until they could see verdant undergrowth again, where at first only the scant patches of fledgling grass and a few bushes leaned away from the wind. The grass was wet. Spider's webs, which broke and clung to Deng's and Chu's ankles as they re-entered the denseness of the plateau's lower forest areas, hitched across the undergrowth.

A cloud moved away from the face of the sun and the trees sifted chilly sunlight over them.

Soon they came upon another clearing which a great tree had made before it died, high up in the undergrowth, a clearing still dominated by the standing corpse of the tree. Ivy had taken over, the embedded stems making a varicose entanglement on the old trunk and ending where the tree had hunched in a huge nest of dark green leaves.

Here, following a sudden glinting of the sun's rays, Chu saw something odd in the earth. He picked it up and inspected it in puzzlement, and then showed it to his uncle. It was a badge or a pendant of some kind, the pin clasp at the back twisted but still intact.

Deng poured some water over it and used both thumbs vigorously to remove the majority of the caked mud from the surface. Although rusted with time with a few tack marks on the rim, the badge's colour was blood red with a bright white circle, in the middle of which was the infamous eagle atop the swastika insignia.

Tibet was one of the few countries not to be involved in the Second World War. Even if it had been, the rising forest terrain culminating many thousands of feet up in an icy wasteland would not have been of any military interest to either side.

"What does it mean, Uncle Deng?" Chu asked breathlessly.

Deng considered the question for a moment and then gave a half shrug with the barest angling of his head.

"I'm not really sure," he said, remembering the fag ends of distant conservations from a time when his memory was not old enough for retention or retrieval. Then he caught sight of something else that was strange, a square metal box attached to a tree, crudely nailed into the thick bark. On closer inspection it appeared to have a rudimentary lens. It was clearly a camera of some sort, although rusted, caked in dirt, and misshapen. This object would normally have fashioned great interest in Deng, but this was not the time to ponder it further.

"We mustn't get distracted now," he said to Chu, who nodded in agreement. He put the pendant in his pocket and they continued their climb, clambering wearily through the intricacies of the forest, clinging onto and tugging at the trees as they moved ever upwards.

A small cloud of birds rose from the tree tops. Something squealed and ran in the undergrowth. Chu's feet swerved and leapt when a puddle of melted ice lay in front of him across the trail as a green snake wriggled past him. The bushes were fuller here, healthier, and seemed to grow upwards from a trench of mud. But thin ice was forming about the reeds and stones, alerting them to the altitude change. The air was becoming noticeably thinner.

On the left, the slope broke away and fell down a sudden cliff to water. Beyond and above there was a gully in the side of the mountain loaded with old snow that the sun had not yet reached. The pelting rain of late winter, combined with intense cold, had compacted the snow and ice that hung perilously.

Water ran out between the melting edge and the warmer rock. It then fell on both sides of the plateau, sparsely where Deng and

Chu were, but more widely and tremendously elsewhere. And where it fell, it was impossible to see through the drifting spray. The sheets of falling water created a milky mist, up-spun into a creamy substance that was hard to distinguish from the spray and mist that rose to meet it.

Deng and Chu looked on in wonder. Thick bushes amongst the trees grew in unvisited profusion, filled with drifts of buds like bright green smoke. The birds fought for airspace with vibrant notes of music and settled randomly on the trees opposite, where the forestland expanded to a small platform, like a tiny amphitheatre.

A rough estimate put them about half an hour away from the edge of the plateau where Kwei-Lan had travelled to on the day he went missing.

* * *

It was still early and cold, but hovering over the plateau there was a dull orange light that expanded to reveal the dark luxuriance of the forest. The arms of the clouds turned to gold, and the rim of the sun pushed in amongst them for the first time. The sill of the great fall glittered vaguely, lights running to and fro along the edge or leaping in a sudden sparkle. The trees of the forest acquired a clearer definition. Dense woodland in the low tablelands became golden and white. Across the spray of water, on the other side of the gap, the distant forest still harboured the darkness, but everywhere else the mountains exhibited their high snow and ice.

Chu looked down at the fall and realised that he was hungry. He breathed in deeply through his nose and half turned away, experiencing a whole mixture of aromas, as the mist from the water seemed to magnify any smell incredibly, as rain will deepen and distinguish the colours of a field of flowers. A light breeze coiled about him and his uncle.

The two made good progress. As the ground levelled off, they took the opportunity to rest. They had food with them, but they also found fresh goji wolfberry fruit via a tiny haunt of bright birds that hovered like insects. Deng carried a small bag on his shoulder. From it he took out two pieces of bread, giving one to his nephew. Chu devoured both bread and the hand-picked olive-grey jelly-like fruit ravenously, looking deeply into Deng's eyes, nodding and smiling for the first time that day. A little colour was finally ebbing into his face.

"Do you believe that my father is still alive?" he asked Deng directly, with a touch of sullenness.

"Yes, I do," Deng said reassuringly. "I have a feeling deep inside me about Kwei-Lan, that he is still very much alive. But he must need our help, so we have to be strong and resolute."

Chu smiled. "I think he is alive too. We will find him and get him back to safety." At that point, the boy's smile was unfaltering. Another spark of sunshine warmed his spirits.

"And we will not allow a million-year-old superstition to stop us!" Deng emphasised, at which point Chu's face opened up and brightened further.

Steeled by such resolute philosophy, Deng went to move, but he noticed that Chu was looking past him now, transfixed, his eyes as nervous as a fawn's, as he stared at a point in space. There was something crouching down amongst the tangled foliage.

The previous open smile had twisted strangely, Chu's eyes wide with anxiety, an ashen expression dominating his face.

Chu pointed weakly and whispered a number of intelligible words. Deng turned his head to follow the boy's gaze.

Something large was moving in the forest by the fall.

* * *

The tall creature with pale green eyes and a fiery-ochre furred back stood at the edge of the forest, unmoving. A little wind pushed through the gap and the tops of the trees swayed. The breeze was cool and calm. There was no noise at all except for the sound of the fall.

The creature turned to the right and loped into the trees. This thing, this marmalade coloured creature, had something of a human movement to it. Water from the fall was cascading down onto the rocks from the melting ice in the mountains. There was a long deep scar in the earth where the branches of a tree had been dragged past by the water. The creature came back. Then it turned the other way and sidled along a shoulder of rock on a virtually imperceptible path.

It was a gigantic thing, more than nine feet tall, but as agile and fast as a squirrel. It began to sway along the path, and then it stood for a moment staring down at the thunderous waters, where there was nothing to be seen but the light blue columns of glimmering haze as the power of the water scooped a vast bowl out of the earth.

The beast began to move faster then, breaking into a queer loping run that made the forearms alternate like the legs of a horse. Deng was lying with one side of his face against the cold earth. Chu huddled close to him, frost twinkling in his hair, but sweat had begun to burst through his skin, making his forehead hot and greasy.

The creature was about fifty yards away. They watched in silence as it stopped at the edge of the path and looked down at the long streamers of weed that were moving backwards and forwards under the water. It lifted a huge clawed hand and scratched almost absent-mindedly at its chin and mouth. Then, with a sudden unpredictable spurt of energy, it ran powerfully and leapt onto the higher ground, pulling itself through the great rocks and trees, moving through the undergrowth as if it didn't exist. Finally, almost out of view, it lifted itself onto the rim of the plateau and disappeared from sight.

For a moment, Deng and Chu stared in raw-eyed disbelief, looking at the place where the creature had been as though it had been a ghost, barely noticed or perceived. Then Deng jumped to his feet, indecision being replaced with a spurt of conviction. "Come, Chu, we must follow."

It took them fifteen minutes to reach the plateau, whereas it had taken the creature barely a minute. They had tried the same route, but the undergrowth was thick and woven like a bird's nest, tangled thickets, and the criss-cross pattern of trunks, making progress almost impossible. How could anything run through the thickets and the underbrush as fast as that creature had? It had disappeared over the slopes without stumbling once, as if driven by some unseen power.

Directly below a sill there came a sudden drop in temperature. Flurries of snow and ice were blown in opaque whirlpools onto the dark canopy of the forest. The ground here was so steep that Deng and Chu might not have actually made it over the rim had it not been for the spine of a great tree which curved like a man stretching after a heavy sleep, its powerful branches coming to rest on the flat ice, the dark green arms flicking snow loose in a fastidious gesture of contempt. They climbed through the bones of the ladder-like tree and jumped onto the hard surface of ice.

For several seconds they could do nothing but just stare out across the vast sweep of nothingness, unsure what to do next. They were astonished by the transformation: one moment there had been verdant trees and forest, and the next there was nothing but an enormous expanse of ice and snow dominated by mountains where veins of salmon pink ran through gleaming white. There was the strangest sense that the world had ended. All was silent and empty.

The ice glowed and the air had an atmosphere of putrefaction. Everest was now standing directly ahead of them, remote and inaccessible, and they were surrounded everywhere by terrain that had seen dinosaurs and mountaintops which had been home to pterodactyls. But there was no sign of the white-ochre beast. Deng spread his arms expansively to indicate the frustration and completeness of that absence.

With less haste, and beginning to be crippled with cold, they started to move slowly across the frozen desert. Beneath the ice were the relics of undergrowth, weed tails frozen as if to preserve an instant of time. But otherwise there was nothing. Everything was chaste white.

Then they noticed something strange. At first not trusting the accuracy of their eyes, they merely continued to tread stealthily across the shiny surface of ice. Pausing then to look more closely, they noticed a series of dark spots. It was unclear what they were, even how big they were. Still some way away, they edged closer. A gust of wind brought against their skin a thousand pinpricks which grew like a frosted dagger to knife points, and then the knives twisted.

They glanced at each other briefly, a depth of feeling between them. The dark spots were holes, entrances to somewhere. Deng peered down into one of them, a vast hollow of relentless white. He turned to Chu, who looked frightened and concerned, and shouted something inaudible against the might of the wind.

"We must go down." These last words spoken on the surface were lost upon the ice as Deng tried to clear his mind of all imaginings.

* * *

Deng felt an odd trembling alacrity as he searched the bottom of the entrance again. Then he lowered himself feet first into the tunnel. When he was safely down, he turned his head nervously from side to side and then looked up, clapping his hands and beckoning Chu to follow.

Both safely down, they followed the short passageway as it sloped sideways. The frozen walls caught the daylight from above, glittering and twinkling like a thousand miniature starbursts and, further afield, casting a pale opalescent glow so that it was just possible to see as they moved forward into the unknown.

At the end of this first tunnel, they came out wonderingly onto a square platform below a massive dome which looked down a hundred feet or more into the centre of a vast hall of translucent ice, seemingly empty and derelict, its far end so distant from them that, despite the whiteness of the ice, it was shrouded in the shadowy mist which seeped in from the plateau. Colossal ice pillars obtruding from the walls loomed like shadowed titans above a complex series of tunnels, like a frozen spider's web. For a moment, complete incomprehension and awe gripped them both.

The platform itself did not lead directly into the ice cavern. In fact, the only way to continue seemed to be by crossing a small bridge, which looked worn and dangerously thin in places.

Deng considered this unusual problem. What was the sensible thing to do?

There was a faint noise. He glanced around, just in time to see, or so he thought, a flitting silhouette, but even as he moved towards the image, it was gone, melted so totally that he wondered if he had seen anything at all and whether it was, in fact, an image half formed in the shadows of his mind. His blood thumped in his ears like a drum.

But all else was soundless and bare.

He decided they had to move across the bridge, so he placed a foot with theatrical caution and felt an imperceptible movement beneath him. Gingerly he moved his other foot forward, taking three small steps, feeling like an acrobat walking the tightrope in a circus – only this was no trick and there was no safety net.

Chu followed. Lighter and more agile, he would be safe unless the bridge became exceptionally brittle. It looked unused. They continued to edge across stealthily. It was a nightmare walk, endless and slow. The ice was caked, and broken in places.

Chu suddenly cried out. He was lurching to the left, arms pin wheeling in slow, wide revolutions. He seemed to totter on the brink for a long time, before standing back safely on the flat surface of the bridge.

"I nearly went," Chu whispered, managing to sound desperate and calm at the same time. Deng reached back and held the boy's arm as they edged along again carefully, inch by inch, his mind contemplating the lunatic space between the bridge and the cavern below. His brain viewed it in spectacular detail, how it would be: the lurch of the body, the diminishing scream, the grabbing for non-existent hand holds in hopeless space, the rush of wind against the face, gathering momentum, pulling the eyelids back, and then … contact!

The ice made a loud cracking sound. Deng leapt desperately for the other side.

"Are you over?" Chu called out in a high, piping voice, several feet away from safety.

"Chu, for God's sake, move! It's going to go."

Chu nudged forward five paces and plunged, one hand flying up like a gull in the darkness. Deng made a tigerish spring to grasp at the hand, and then Chu hung there, gripping his uncle's arm, youthful dark eyes glittering with blind faith. The boy clung with all his might to the quivering arm, pleading in agitating tones.

Then he was up, heaving himself shakily to his knees. He gripped his head between steadying hands as though it might come loose if he were to shake it. Pallid as a ghost, eyes blinking feverishly like the shutters of a haunted house, Chu stood in front of Deng, drawing deep breaths of thankfulness, his ruffled clothes torn in recognition of his final crawling lunge. He uttered an involuntary moan, so abject had his terror been.

They took time to gather themselves and re-establish composure, and then continued in frightened silence along the wide tunnel ahead of them. The air was stale. It penetrated their senses to leave a musty smell in their nostrils. Deng paused momentarily to peer at something on the ground. He picked it up and inspected it closely.

It was a bone of some description, like a human finger.

Several minutes later they peered nervously into one of the chambers below from which they heard movement. Their faces froze as the masks of the dead. There were four of them – huge, hulking creatures, thick with fur tinged red in places, and massive human-shaped ears, mostly hidden.

Their horror grew, intermingling with astonishment and dread, as they tried taking in the scene before them, just as the apes must have once stared at the emerging *Homo sapiens*.

A tiny fire was burning below within a bowl of alabaster rock, making the ice walls look smooth and silky. The crackling flames of the fire produced a thin coil of smoke that reached the chamber's ceiling and disappeared. The fire crackled and shot coloured sparks into the air, making the creatures seem more ferocious and dangerous than before.

One of the creatures, the one that held a tiny fur-clad form in the corner of the chamber, screeched a high-pitched howl. From somewhere unseen, a scrap of meat was torn free from a carcass and given to it. It bit and chewed, trying to feed the baby, and whistled the high wail again.

Lips curled back from great teeth as the creatures all began to feed. The limbs of the carcass were smashed and tinged with dead blood, most of it clotted. The carcass was wrecked and scattered. The air in the chamber was heavy with the smoke of the fire and the rich smell of meat.

Deng could not take his eyes from the massive beast in the centre of the chamber. Larger and more menacing than the others, its feet were broad and flat, the clawed square hands hanging down beneath the waist, its head squarish. The mouth was wide and soft looking and above the fur of the upper lip. The great nostrils flared like wings. There was no bridge to the nose. The moon shadow of the wrinkled brow lay just above the tip. Bigger shadows lay in black caverns above the cheeks, and the pale eyes in those caverns were emerald slits.

Another anguished whistle echoed as the female creature cradled the small one, a high-pitched cry like the highest note of a flute, loud and endless, spinning through the tunnels of ice. Then there was silence and stillness as the beast crouched forward and placed the tiny motionless form onto the fire, which crackled and grew a wide fence of amethyst around the disintegrating fur. The mother stood close by as the flames engulfed the body and then died away. Then she shuffled back to the corner of the cavern, where she sat motionless and silent.

A deep silence filled the chamber, a timeless silence in which at first there seemed to be many minds present, and then perhaps no mind at all. Light sprinkled in from the surface above as one of the creatures disappeared from view, evidently to the place where the meat was, and then came back again. But as it did so, it kicked something forward into the centre of the chamber. Something rolled awkwardly and unevenly, but rolled nevertheless. Deng watched it, trying to catch his breath and calm his accelerating pulse.

It was a human head.

* * *

Deng could feel a great terror now, softly and sickly rising from his stomach and mottling his throat. He stifled a gasp and waited for a moment in braced silence, motioning silently to Chu with finger pressed to his lip. Chu nodded wordlessly at first, but then it was over. A sharp intake of breath and a terror-sick murmur from the boy was all it took.

The shadowed eyes turned upwards with a kind of dream like slowness, meeting the human orbs that stared terrified back at them. Then large clawed hands were raised and the high whistling began.

Deng grabbed Chu by his upper arm and dragged him along one of the tunnels that led in the opposite direction from the crumbled bridge. An empty chamber greeted them.

"Which way?" Chu was near hysteria, his head shaking wildly, the sound of his own voice reverberating through the vastness of the tunnels like an eternal echo. Deng stared at him wide-eyed, furious about being so helpless. "This way," he said desperately. They ran awkwardly across the chamber and into another tunnel, not knowing where in the ice maze it would take them. As they ran, Chu suddenly let out a desperate chilling scream behind him, floating on the air.

Deng swung around in haste and dismay.

"Chu!" As Deng bellowed his name, his voice rose insanely. A look of unutterable terror riveted his face like a vice. Deng was walking backwards, horrified and agonised by indecision, staring ahead of himself, defeated. Fear raced through him like a drug, his eyes frantically scanning the various entrances and exits.

Like a bolt of lightning, a monstrous arm had shot out from a hidden space like a snake. Chu was in the air by the time Deng had turned around. The full size and terror of the creature was emerging from the half-lit gloom. One of the sharp claws hooked into the boy's right ear, the other battering mercilessly at the left cheek, making it a ruin. A piercing shriek filled the air.

Warm blood splattered Chu's face, spreading impossibly fast onto the ice like liquid copper, pitting the ice with gleaming rubies.

Deng noticed the partial opening of one glazed eye and heard a wordless mumble from Chu that subsided as soon as the boy was dropped, like a discarded rag doll. The All Seeing Eye appeared to regain focus for a second, swept across his face, looked directly at Deng and then through him, rolled away, and was gone. The boy's chest was ripped open. The heart twitched like a stranded starfish on the shore at the return of the tide, and then Chu was motionless.

The creature then emerged fully out of the passageway, further mutilating Chu's dead body. The boy's face was curtained with gore, both cheeks hanging in flaps.

The thing moved forward. Every step it took rattled Deng's bones and struck his heart. Deng stared hopelessly for a moment, fighting back fresh waves of revulsion and fear. Then, after a moment's painful hesitation, he ran frantically away through the ice warren, flailing while running, which made one leg rub against the other as though he were sharpening a knife.

Pale penetrative sunlight splashed the ground over an area of perhaps ten yards as Deng stopped, semi-blinded. He watched the sunlight in every patch blinking at him. This was so like the curtain that flapped in his brain that for a moment he thought the blinking was inside him.

Blindly and a little madly, he ran again, neither thinking nor caring. Walls of solid ice reached out to stun and slow him, and glints from discarded bone fragments blinded him, but nothing was going to stop his crazed flight.

* * *

For some reason the creature that had killed Chu did not follow. Deng presently found himself in silence, crouching in a narrow tube of glistening white, shivering and frightened, conscious of the cold cloud of his breath. He hesitated, fear probing just below his heart.

Then he heard a sound, a soft gasping sound which was familiar yet maddeningly distant. He focused his mind. *Human,* he decided – the sound of human weeping. He called out cautiously, but only a listless echo answered him.

He followed the sound anxiously, his mind once again invaded by fear.

Small interlocking rooms revealed nothing, except more human remains. There was a foot and a section of a human arm, the flesh on the arm black and shrivelled to the bone so as to look like a pile of shredded fabric, but in fact it was flesh picked clean in strips from the bones. There were fragments of a torso, covered in a butter-like substance and caked with tainted blood and segments of uneaten flesh. In the furthermost corner, a corpse had been riven in two and hung amidst the other corpses on sharp ice hooks, nothing now but a pulp of blood and bone.

Deng continued to move from chamber to chamber, searching, looking, and listening for the location of the sound. Just ahead of him, a makeshift block of steps disappeared into the ceiling, crudely carved out of a pillar, soaring out around the edge of the dome.

Suddenly in front of Deng, an encrusted wall appeared. Its mounds and bulges of ice, dug into the surface by non-human hands, the same hands which had constructed the mesh-like labyrinth, had transformed the Plateau of Tibet into an underground kingdom of everlasting ice.

And what Deng saw made him, for that moment, forget everything. He shuddered violently and felt madly repulsed.

Inside the mounds were human beings, trapped and held without regard or pity. Arms and legs had been grotesquely twisted, broken at times to enable the individual to fit tightly into the ice prison. Many of the bodies had been reduced to mere lumps of bone, from which the flesh and skin had either decayed or been eaten. Others had been deliberately stripped to the naked bone. These were the fortunate ones who had been granted the gift of death.

Slowly, Deng approached the still intact figure of a woman, narrowing his eyes as he studied her. Her body was ghostly white as if drained of blood. There was something utterly blank about her expression, something dehumanised and strange. Suddenly her cat-like eyelids fluttered and opened. She moaned but could not speak. He jumped backwards, staring at her. He wanted to touch her face, wishing he could help, but instead he averted his gaze as he heard another sound and continued his nightmare walk along the row of frozen prisoners.

Then a face appeared before him, a face he knew – a face wild and lost, the cheeks streaked with tears. There was the faint hiss of breathing and a soft anguished whimpering. The face twitched and the eyelids snapped open in a desperate lunge at survival. Deng stumbled backwards.

It was Kwei-Lan, or at least a remembered form of him, as his muscles seemed to have atrophied.

Tears welled in Deng's eyes. His heart seemed to squeeze up into his chest. Memories and thoughts of eternal sadness saturated his mind in that instant as he glimpsed a memory of his and his brother's terrible childhood together, recalling the loss of their mother and reeling at the fact that it had been so long since he had seen his brother's face.

He touched the amber-coloured skin like stroking silk and then, clenching his fists as though grinding something small, beat hammer-like to try to break the ice surrounding the incarcerating belt which held his brother, but he found it to be as strong as steel.

Kwei-Lan's lips were tightly compressed, and his eyes bulged and yearned.

Searching the chamber, Deng came back with a huge bone, fumbling slightly before using it like a prehistoric club to strike at the ice cocoon with all the strength he could muster. Splinters and fragments of bright azure broke off as he hit at it more and more frantically. But it was no use. He dropped the club, a wild rage dominating his face as he continued to stare through wet eyes at his entombed brother. For a moment he was blinded. When he could see again, he saw that the head had lifted and his brother's mouth was moving slowly. Deng leaned closer. The voice was a hollow spectre's voice, a mere whisper conjured up out of biblical pain and despair.

"Above you, a way out. Go, please ..." Kwei-Lan's voice trailed away like delirium. Simultaneously, there was a sound of a yeti whistling and moving through the tunnel. Deng gazed upwards. There were steps everywhere, but Kwei-Lan was correct: a narrow staircase in the far corner arched a winding journey through one of the titanic pillars into the rim of the dome. At the top Deng could glimpse daylight making coloured shapes as the ice reflected back the surface images, where he could see drunken eddies of snow swirling madly.

He touched his brother's face tenderly. "Do you think I will leave you here in agony?" he asked, incredulous, through tear stained eyes.

His brother replied through half-closed eyes, "You have no choice. Please safe yourself ..." The words trailed away again.

Deng, knowing his brother was right, started to back away. He turned and stood for a moment, pausing on the first step. "Please forgive me, Kwei-Lan. I will come back and I will bring men and guns." A wild hope made his heart turn over.

Kwei-Lan's last feeble words were haunting in the extreme. "Hurry then. I cannot endure it much longer!" He managed a bleak smile.

The yeti had reached the door to the chamber. Deng had no more time. He dashed up the broken ice stairs despairingly, dragging himself into the icy surface winds.

He hardly knew how long he had been beneath the surface, but daylight did not last long on the plateau. There was now merely an image of light above the mountains, a new moon rising.

The wind blew snow off the mountain ridges. The dry flakes were opalescent against the blackening sky as Deng forced his feet across the unsteady surface. The wind was inflating his shirt, and his face was pinched with the pain of the icy gusts.

Soon he could see the backdrop of trees where he and Chu had climbed earlier. He stopped for a moment to search the gloomy blizzard behind him. Something was there. Through the gloom came the glow of green eyes, like sallow lamplight ten feet off the ground, from a myriad of giant ghostly shapes. A dense group of shadows were moving slowly against the haunted backdrop of Everest, and a sharp wailing sound stung Deng's ears like acid.

* * *

Ever thickening darkness made the descent difficult. Deng fell halfway through the ladder tree. He was screaming without knowing it, fighting with thorns. The screaming tore inside him, his face deliriously pale.

There was a diamond glitter in the mist of the fall that was the result of the brightness of the moon. It made the water look like a metal mirror. Once Deng was off the plateau, the wind dropped. The only things that moved now were the fleeing human and the hanging ferns that were being tugged by the water. The tree trunks made great bars of darkness, but when Deng moved between them, the moon dropped a net of light over him. He hurried away, circling into the forest, where the ground was mercifully more firm.

The roar of the cascading water was dulled but still audible. However, the columns of spray were no longer visible. Deng battled on through the undergrowth. Trunks were twisted and roots seemed to struggle with the earth in a tortured hunt for space. Glancing over his shoulder, Deng saw no evidence of movement beyond the trees, which remained saturated with darkness. Above the darkness the trees were black-green and surly, dropping their branches forward like the rigging of a floundered ship.

Faster and more desperately than ever, he fled through the holes in the forest's fabric, vanishing into the purpling night. Urgency tore away at him. He could not shake the image of Kwei-Lan or the echo of Chu's screaming from his mind, nor the vision of the unbearable stream of bronze blood, which bred like maggots in his mind. It was as though the horror of what he had seen could be ripped out from his heart, but even then his heart could not be stilled.

It took him about twenty minutes to reach the jeep. Exhausted, he leant against the vehicle and breathed deeply for several moments, forcing air and calmness into his lungs and sucking his bruised fist to ease the pain, which before he hadn't noticed.

He stared into the depths of the night, visibly shaking. The clearing was empty and silent, save for the distant growl of a snow leopard and a solitary hooting owl. He felt his mind clouded with sickness.

In the madness of all-engulfing terror, which rose like the mighty waves of the sea, he could not halt his torrid thoughts, and wondered whether perhaps only his own madness lay carefully in wait for him beyond the slow pictures which were waxing and waning in his head.

He looked back into the forest, trying to decipher the darkness, the ineffable cold dragging down on his heart. For a moment he wished he could disappear back into the forest and lie as safe as a fox in its lair.

An oblong swatch of navy sky relieved with the incredible lamps of stars hung above Deng. There was still the faint hollow sound of the thunderous waterfall. The moon illuminated the clearing and sharply defined Deng's tired and panicked silhouette in all its gaunt misery.

* * *

In blind panic, Deng spluttered the engine to life. The vehicle uttered a deep guttural roar as it swung around in a semi-circle, stopping sharply then.

Deng's eyelids fell and then bounced open. In that one dreamy moment he imagined he was already back at the temple, telling his father what had happened and gathering help for Kwei-Lan. He was shivering with the inner cold that follows danger, his tired eyes staring up at the plateau. Out of the range of his headlights everything was black and silver. The black forest with trees and rocks was carved cleanly out of the sky, and a white spray with a silver light rippled back and forth along the lip of the fall. All at once, the night was desperately lonely.

The pictures of Chu and Kwei-Lan threatened to overwhelm Deng once again.

In an abrupt movement, his knuckles whitening as he gripped the steering wheel, he skidded the jeep forward, wheels screaming down the dirt track of the foothills back towards the temple.

Chapter 7

Deng's Story, Part III

As Deng reached the arrow-straight road that led back through the lowlands and fallow fields to Lhasa, the needle touched ninety.

The dim light from the dashboard made his skin greenish. His pallor would have shamed a corpse, sitting as he was, hunched like a vulture, his cold eyes flicking only occasionally to note the falling position of the needle of the petrol gauge.

The last traces of fuel evaporated on the road by the cemetery, where he abandoned the vehicle and ran the short distance through the burial grounds. Everything was empty and silent, but then he heard a rustling sound and froze. But he breathed a sigh of relief when only two goats scampered through the bushes ahead of him.

The battlement stones were as washed out as the sky, one grey leaching into the other, all of the shades just as frigid without the sun. Deng descended the worn steps three at a time into the main courtyard, where he tripped on the lower step, falling heavily on the gravel lane. His face was blistered and dirty anyway, but now was there was new blood on his grazed cheeks.

His eyes seemed rimmed as red as the blood on his face. He noticed the rise and fall of his diaphragm with sharp shallow bursts and was shocked to notice how quickly he was breathing, his heart beat almost visible.

A fire had burned that night in the courtyard, but now there was merely a red eye that lit nothing but itself within the piles of rock-coloured ash and a soft cindery sound as the wood fell inwards. He knocked the ember with his foot. A shower of orange sparks flared up in the night, disintegrating into powdery dust and floating on the air in slow dissolution. Above him loomed the temple's gigantic towers.

In the moonlight, the stone was cast maggot white. The temple's windows were pools of darkness, sockets in a skull. The impression given by the whole structure was that it was something quite abandoned by time, de-peopled, a shiver of the past conjured up by the night.

Deng spotted a woman walking on the pathway. He ran arrow-straight towards her.

She was walking hastily with her head bent, almost hunched over, and was richly dressed in sapphire-coloured silk. She was carrying a silver tray which held a wine goblet full of crimson liquid, which strangely bubbled, plus three small daggers of tarnished silver. Looking up anxiously as she saw Deng running in her direction, she curbed her pace.

"I'm looking for my father," Deng said urgently in Tibetan, his eyes wide and his face dusky red. But the woman didn't respond immediately. Her faint smile was dark and bitter.

"Where is he?" he demanded. He was uncaring of his own unkempt and soiled appearance, his clothing in tatters. So lively was his impatience that he laid his hand upon the woman's arm and sought to shake her, the bubbling goblet nearly toppling from the tray.

She stepped backwards and stared at him, clearly not knowing what to do or say. He shook her arm more lightly this time, more as a plea than as an attempt to be aggressive.

"My father, Tenzin. Anyone. Where are they?" He spoke punctiliously from the heart, his eyes wild. He was so grim of face that there was no doubting the urgency of what he demanded.

At the mention of Deng's father's name, the woman gave a sound of positive recognition; said, "*Jiaohui*," meaning "chapel"; and beckoned him to follow her through an adjoining passageway. Deng moved clumsily, knocking over a stack of small barrels and sending them rolling and spinning thunderously in all directions through the empty network of lanes. Birds rose, startled, wheeling and squawking in the air above their heads.

He gathered himself for a moment. The birds resettled nervously. He followed more carefully then, through the old monks' quarters and into the level light of the ancient mausoleum, which represented something much more than a repository of historical details, as it was where Shaolin masters and profound religious figureheads of bygone eras were entombed within the walls of the temple, absorbed into the very stone.

For a dismayed moment, Deng stammered incandescently, but then he followed the lady to the chapel, lively with impatience.

The emptiness and silence were oppressive things. As he trailed her through the gloom, their shapes wove a parallel curtain of shadow so that a raised arm seemed to lift a long weight of darkness with it. His own form, shivered and distorted by the half-light, followed him like some spectre trapped beneath glass.

Still he hurried her along. At one point he glanced nervously over his shoulder as he thought he heard movement in the shadows behind him, catching a flicker of something ... a ghoulish creature, blank eyed, bearing its teeth, cracked and black and as jagged as a mountain range. He waited – nothing. He hurried forward again. There was so much to be said, so much work to be done, in order to save Kwei-Lan.

The chapel was hidden deep within the recesses of the temple. At the end of a long darkened hall, Deng stopped briefly and gazed into the shadows. It was an eerie place. Protruding thistles, amphibious weed, and wallflowers grew matted together over the stones. Above him rose a domed ceiling held up by alabaster pillars and unadorned grey stone walls which, different from the way in which he and the woman had just entered, contained a single door, on either side of which stood tall carved religious effigies. The woman pointed urgently at the door and said, "Jiaohui."

Deng had not known of this underground entrance before. He wondered then about the deeper and darker mysteries of the temple. Only once did it cross his mind to flee, but he knew he'd be swapping the immediate nightmare for hundreds more later on.

There was the soft sound of a religious chant as he approached. Then, as his hand reached out for the tarnished door knob, he heard a single cry from inside. He shivered and his blood seemed turned to quicksilver, as brilliant as the moon, his heartbeat quickening even more and every muscle of his body seeming knotted in discomfort.

The chanting halted abruptly as he burst through the door, its last eerie note diminishing like a banished spectre. A growl of interrupted order and derision hardly needed words of explanation as many eyes turned towards him. He froze, fearful as he scanned the rows of people whose faces shut like doors.

Deng looked ahead, spotted his father, and started moving animatedly along the central aisle, waiting for his father to turn and face him – to chide, to reproach, to blame. But Tenzin did none of those things. He just continued to kneel in what looked like a silent, incalculably strange prayer.

Three women were walking solemnly down the central aisle behind Tenzin, each carrying something, a phial of some description, containing a liquid which glowed with red light, which lit their faces with a rose-coloured transparency.

Next to the colossal bronze altar, in the smoke-wreathed furthermost corner, there was a secondary makeshift altar, created for what seemed to be non-Buddhist worship. The air was heavy with incense, but also with a foetid sweet smell which Deng could feel laying thick upon his lungs. Gazing pensively, he saw wisps of honey-brown smoke curling through the gap created by two high doors, and beyond that a flickering glow of something unseen.

Deng called out, his eyes becoming wild, the tendons standing out on his neck, his face quivering like crystal on the edge of the ultimate destructive high note. His eyes fastened upon the improvised altar. Through the plumes of smoke, he could make out the silhouette of a man now – shaven-headed and dressed in the flowing robes and finery of a high priest, and around whose neck hung the symbols of Ekajati. The shaven head was darkened to bronze, and the face, stooping solicitously, was almost the same fine metal burnishing.

The high priest stood by the brazier that was filled with soft flames. A large pot of boiling water bubbled intensely. Patches of torn fabric were thrown into the pot, thereafter to be shredded and mixed into a dark paste. Deng noticed that a flicker of amusement had touched the high priest's lips as a cloud of incense obscured his view: "How infinite are the beauties and wonders of creation." The voice was calm and unaffected.

Puffs of incense jetted constantly from the brass bellies of the burner like ejaculations of rage.

Deng spotted the lady whom he had seen at the banquet, his mother's ward, and pulled her from her seat into the aisle. She stumbled and fell at his feet and started laughing wildly as if at a cruel joke. It was a shrill sneering laughter, as if someone might have mocked a village idiot. She rose to her feet, shook out her crumbled robe, humbly bowed her head, and lowered her black-laced eyes in feverish mockery, returning silently to her position in the congregation.

There was a strange clouding of Deng's senses. His brow creased with bemusement and fear. Lassitude and a falling heart were crushing him. His courage compressed to fragility, as if infected by a kind of invisible sorcery.

Startled suddenly out of deep preoccupation, Tenzin rose to his feet and swung in a sudden fury to face his son, the familiar wrinkled features cupped by a claret-hooded robe with a gold dragon snaking down the back. There was an object by Tenzin's feet. Deng braced himself to endure whatever might follow, straining his head to see what the object was. He saw something in his father's eyes that made him recoil. The eyes were emerald ice. The shadow of something unearthly flickered across the pallor of Tenzin's haggard face as he snarled, "I have harboured secrets to which your worst comparison would be like sunshine."

Deng stared at the eyes and trembled, acknowledging the situation with a scalding, bitter realism.

The external doors were being unbolted behind the copper censer by the priest, letting the wind billow the brown smoke upwards and to waft twisting swirls of powdery snow into the chapel which melted and became misty raindrops.

A human body was being lifted and carried towards the open doorway.

Deng went to say something, but he was cut short by his father's growling voice. Like a cloud across the sun, he felt a shadow of defeat and irresolution darken his mind.

"You fool, you stupid fool. Do you still not realise?" Tenzin asked with bare menace and contempt, turning on his son a dreadful smile, with a note of something like triumph in his voice. "There are no mysteries anymore – no need for the God Ekajati's All Seeing Eye." The curl of his smile was mocking and cruel, as though revealing secrets too monstrous to pronounce and depravities too terrible for mortal contemplation. Deng could see that he was wrestling against the approaches of hysteria.

"What need do we have for the sorcery of the ancient priests, with their mutterings of secrets and death-haunted mysteries, their promises of an eternity which they refused to explain?"

Deng stepped violently backwards, glancing over his shoulder to note that the entrance to the jiaohui had been closed and was now manned by sentries, cutlasses drawn. For a moment his body shuddered with the great imponderable of 'what might be' searing through his father's mind. He glanced nervously into hell and could feel nothing in his heart but a terrible sickness and horror at the thought of that which awaited him.

Deng dragged his eyes towards his father again, who hissed like a snake. "You see what you have achieved." His eyes glittered with warning and mystery, gesticulating as he did in theatrical wonderment. When he spoke, his voice was like the splintering of ice.

"Is the truth and virtue now wholly understood?" Deng could not break free from the spell of his father's face. A jerk of his head indicated his meaning as well as a jabbed finger in the direction of the outside door, in case there was still any doubt.

Something had entered the church through the doorway behind the censer. Something tall and immensely powerful loomed above the smoke of the copper funnel and wrapped long arms around the sacrificial body. Sharp claws were visible just before they vanished into the flesh of the body, pulling it out into the frosty courtyard.

The outer doors were closed and bolted, extinguishing the thin rays of ashy moon.

Deng searched his mind furiously for a solution, but he saw nothing within the horrified comprehension and the tumult of terror. As his mind faltered, he relaxed his fighting muscles, pushing damp tendrils of hair weakly out of his eyes.

He suddenly felt a languid weariness and a strange detachment from his own fear, a heaviness sinking through his limbs as his spirit melted into black despair. He looked at his father with a mixture of scorn and resignation, his darkest fears realised. His confused eyes continued to stare, as wide and clear as the sky, but a degree more innocent than if they had but newly opened on the world.

Much which had been dim stood illuminated, and much which had been secret now stood revealed. His face was white, full of infinite sadness, full of weeping and revulsion. The dismal truth filtered through to emerge in his mind, the meaning as clear as the sunlight of the day, his elucidation complete. He was witness to a foretaste of his own agony and the knowledge that everything had been in vain. Human flesh was the chemo elixir, and the temple provided it.

People were waiting in the central passageway behind him, the goblet bubbling with a sinister red sticky liquid. The copper daggers were being shown as an old woman unravelled swathes of cloth to the right of the burner, basting the material with yak butter and tea, fragments of boiled garments being added as she awaited the goblet's contents.

All at once a sort of bleak certainty came over Deng like the bursting of storm cloud in his head. He was not going to make it back to Hong Kong. The numbers against him were too great, too numerous, and too determined to defy.

He lost himself in a maze of thoughts that were rendered vague by a lack of words to express them. Mumbling a line from a Tibetan prayer, his voice choked and stricken, he thought of his mother, glancing towards her many-coloured marble shrine fretted with delightful patterns of gold and Tibetan letters inscribed upon the stonework, as though she were still part of a brighter childhood, one filled with ambition and hope, that never became reality. Mi-Sun would never have believed that her youngest son would become nothing more than a morsel of prey for the mountain monsters.

Fresh sandalwood was being thrown onto the burner, which welcomed it with a spray of ginger sparks and a cloud of odorous smoke. The chant beginning once again, the doors were unbolted and heaved open from the outside without the aid of human hands.

Deng looked at his father and felt a ghastly coldness, seeing upon that face an expression of mingled pity, and, perhaps a little sadness. His loneliness was as cold as the depths of space as if he were the heir to the wisdom which had counted the stars and measured the earth. He glanced at the high priest again and then past him to stand by the portraits of the gods painted on the chapel walls.

"Chay-mo!" Tenzin exclaimed. The word might have been a knife going in, the slender kind that is hardly felt for a moment, and then hales after it the pain and the injury. Deng, trying to speak, swallowed half-formed words.

The question he wanted to ask died on his lips.

One of his last conscious memories was of a hefty blow to the back of his head, delivered by an unseen hand, after which the world seemed to spin as he tumbled forward like a sack of coal pushed from a mule's back, the Nazi pendant tumbling from his pocket. All at once, like a sweet and wondrous sleep, he felt encroaching darkness.

A tall figure flashing a scarlet cloak that dropped down his back to his heels emerged from nowhere and strode towards Deng. He could feel tightening hands holding him in place and then a very fine and slender dagger cutting across his chest, which he was allowed to clasp. Berry-red blood in soft bubbles seeped through his fingers and rose in a gentle spring. A rotten stench was thick about him. He choked violently.

He was suddenly aware of being surrounded by a circle of hateful firelit people, like those of the damned in hell, moon-whitened with sparkling eyes. A number of scenarios spanned through his head as his father stood over him, white teeth bared beneath a mass of floating thin hair.

"I will pass my secret onto you now, my son, and your eyes will be as deep and as green and as dangerous as mine."

Tenzin cackled as Deng was made to drink from the goblet, with the remaining bright red droplets being sprinkled into his chest wound. The hands that were holding him released their grip, but he continued to lay motionless. "The reward for following me is to learn the joy of inflicting pain, the love of power, and the ability to remain indifferent as others suffer."

Deng lay there, trying to breathe imperceptibly and not to blink, whilst an inner gloom wavered and tears of effort formed in his eyes. After a moment, apart from a delicate thread of clean air, he was not aware of anything. His eyes were open but quite without sense, and his head lolled as though his neck had been broken. His body was wracked with pain, and his mind seemed empty as the world began to swirl away, but at the same time his soul seemed flooded with light. And then everything went black.

Chapter 8

Thien Hau Festival

Hong Kong, November 2007

Tenzin smiled bleakly as he stared out from the balcony of
the Harbour Vista, taking in the views of water and the bustling
streets in the distance. It was six o'clock. The impending sunset
was evident by the rapidly expanding charcoal line drawn along
the base of the sky, which was melting into indigo. The day
was being swallowed by the night, slowly eaten, and digested
slower still.

The night city had come to life unusually early as it was the
time of the Thien Hau celebrations, with the naturally bright and
vibrant lights of the city being further enhanced by fireworks
and street parties in every district. In Chinese mythology, Thien
Hau is the goddess of the sea. Every year in Hong Kong, carnival
celebrations are held to ensure that the sea is kind to the people
the following year.

Tenzin was glad it was the time of Thien Hau, as it added
a natural flamboyance to the normal colour and noise which
formed an endless backdrop to the daily routine of Hong Kong.
But this was not the point of his journey from Lhasa, which

required a personal guide and three drivers, all of whom would wait for him at their allotted spots for his long journey home. He hoped this would be the last time he would ever have to leave the temple. Indeed, it might actually be the last time he would be physically able to, as his strength and health continued to decline.

Tenzin was seventy-four. Time had slipped through his fingers like water. He sometimes gaped in astonishment when calculating how little time was left.

Longevity could be a form of spite. He knew it and recognised it as his mood control worsened following that night in the laboratory when he'd deliberately ingested chemo poison. After that he was driven intermittently into a black icy fury, to the point where he was literally no longer himself but rather an alien thing of strange and violent rages, so that his mind seemed ever more frantic and unhinged, killing savagely whenever he wanted to.

No one inside the temple was safe.

But then maybe it was only age that gave him this perspective, as when he had noticed, in the orchards all those years ago, his son Kwei-Lan watching as he had struck Mi-Sun mercilessly, time after time, and then took a whip to her arms, he had felt no shame or remorse, either at the time or since. Restraint was a thing of the past; his soul black with vice.

Tenzin was straight forwardly content that his eldest son was dead and that his youngest, Deng, was trapped inside the curse. He was also glad that he had killed his wife on that fateful night after she had announced that she was pregnant for the third time. Scarcely feeling a pang of remorse over the years, he noted that this action had caused him some regret, as the loss of the boys' mother, and the need for him to lie forever about what had happened to her, had broken Kwei-Lan immediately and forced Deng away from the temple, away from Tenzin's control and into the care of his uncle, right here in the very heart of Hong Kong.

Everything was firmly in the past. Tenzin compartmentalised it in a way that only he could, locking all things into a Pandora's Box like container to which he alone held the key. Yes, of course he would sometimes think of Mi-Sun, but he would simply direct his mind towards her briefly, like the shutter of a camera, recalling for a moment her early slender childlike form, and then put her from his memory until the next time he chose to take out the picture.

Penitence existed in the heart, not in words spoken or in sentiment or dreams. It was nothing to him now but a reverie of what once had been. He felt the measureless nature of things. In such a vast universe, what was human love anyway? A bubble, nothing more, on the breaking verge of eternity, a spark, brief and flickering, against the dark of a universal night. Once it was gone, then the void would come.

Tenzin pondered on how much he hated modern life with its lack of reality: artificial silk, synthetic food resembling the make-believe dishes with which mummies are stuffed, and the women, who had become immune to unhappiness and old age but were no longer truly alive.

It was only in the semi-barbaric countries that you still found people who had children one could be proud of. Current times lacked a sense of poetry and magic, and there were no new lyrics to the ancient tunes. Tenzin had searched through the sources of happiness and had found there nothing to fill one's heart with wonderment.

The new generation's pious protectors were evident everywhere, and the ancient gods, like Ekajati, were certainly dead. Museums held nothing but their imaginary marble corpses. No longer was there a need to believe that human beings were fashioned out of mud lit with life by the minds of the gods. With this thought, a crooked grin deformed Tenzin's lips.

He mused a while longer, and then he inspected a street map of Hong Kong, barely able to focus his eyes for a moment. He would have liked to have walked the distance from Harbour Vista to the Yau Ma Tei Theatre, but it would be too much for him, so he would need to take a *sanlunche* rickshaw.

He stayed for a few minutes longer on the balcony, gazing out into the growing night, feeling slightly unwell. His straining moist eyes sparkled, but it seemed as if the pupils had devoured the irises. On top of this, a month of malaria would not have given his skin a yellower hue.

* * *

As the young Chinese man cycled furiously, Tenzin took in the various scenes, noting first the Peak Tram, which headed into the mountains from Robinson road. How he disliked all the British names in this place, thinking of Hong Kong as being a colony returned purely in recognition of its imperialistic legacy. He despised the Anglo-Saxon buildings and attitudes that had survived all these years. Ahead of him, an old zinc-sided building was being handsomely restored and painted, the bamboo scaffolding was following it upwards. The intricate network of bamboo web, however, barely hid the Empire Hotel in the background, by name alone a colonial outpost reminder if ever there was one.

It was a windless and humid Kowloon evening. The rickshaw reached the theatre in plenty of time. Tenzin paid the driver, taking out the pass from his inside pocket, looking at it and smiling disdainfully. In the furore which had followed his last conference, Crowley had decided to hold a second conference, dedicated solely to his yeti sighting. Tenzin was certainly looking forward to hearing what the renowned explorer had to say on the matter.

The conference lasted three hours; afterwards, Tenzin, using fluent English, introduced himself to Crowley as Deng's father.

"Is something wrong with your son?" Crowley asked, distractedly at first. "He was supposed to arrange an appointment with me a few weeks ago, but I never did hear back from him." He looked genuinely concerned.

"It would be easier if we could meet separately so that I could explain," Tenzin said. "The hour is late and I must go back and rest. And you," he gestured to indicate the horde of reporters still milling at the edge of the stage, "are pre-occupied!" Tenzin smiled and bowed humbly. "Do you have any time tomorrow?" he asked.

Crowley's thoughts were vague. He didn't really want to commit to this, but Deng had achieved sufficient reputation and trust in the city and had also become a friend. He looked at Tenzin. To describe the man's facial expression would be like describing a blank sheet of paper.

"Yes, of course," he said assuredly. "We can meet at my hotel for brunch, if that suits?"

* * *

The new dawn came, not with calm beauty, but with a wild sea wind and pelting rain, creating a turbulent harbour. A chaos of boiling surf could be seen as a mini gale swept across the bay, where even the largest junks tossed like model boats in nature's childlike hands. Thunder rumbled in the hills, and the lightning, in a silver sheet, illuminated the sky. A larger boat rose and plunged. The roar of the harbour was rising again. There was a mass of fog in a ghostly white wall rolling in through the harbour's mouth.

Tenzin stared out as he heard a sudden sound of blown water dashed over the window panes like gravel. The sea was wailing like a mother in agony, battering its waves against the distant shoreline. It would seem that last night's celebrations had not made an immediate impression on Thien Hau!

But by ten o'clock the winds had diminished. And although the air remained damp, the sky was painted with the sandy yellow light that normally colours the Hong Kong skyline for an hour or so after a storm.

The hotel where Crowley was staying was, ironically, the Empire, which was located right in the middle of Victoria Town on Hong Kong Island proper.

It was an elegant, cool colonial building with bronze ceiling fans, palms in the lobby, and a famous French chef. In a different time, a more heroic period of the British Empire, today's owner, Sir Thomas Chisholm-Ellis, would have ended up running something very big. The original owner had achieved this exact feat, having been the proprietor of several establishments and also playing an important part in the "one country, two cultures" negotiations. Back in England, he was described by *Punch Magazine* as "an umpire between the empires".

As Tenzin wandered through the opulent lobby, dominated by a black granite and ivory statue of Queen Victoria, he squinted at the framed wall hangings, finding it difficult to focus at first. One of the hangings was the first part of a scroll printed in London from sketches on the spot, showing the first imperialistic expedition in August 1842. Tenzin thought that the artist may have had some guidance as to the hills above Hong Kong, now called Victoria, but the buildings and the quay were purely imaginary.

Then there was a painting of Chief Justice Hulme, who had saved the hotel from closure after a series of murders took place in and around the hotel in the mid-nineteenth century. Looking anything but grave, he was depicted as a cartoon with long skinny legs encased in breaches and black stockings, having nothing like a judge-like appearance, and dancing a hornpipe with a Manchu Tartar, the oriental equivalent of an Indian punkah-wallah.

Finally there was a charcoal sketch of the Sepoy barracks from 1857. This drawing showed the method of constructing mat sheds, the temporary buildings that served many purposes – goddowns, churches, and mini theatres.

The reception room of the Empire had high ceilings and ornately framed mirrors. The wall colours were deep cream touched here and there with faded pink. The overhead chandeliers glittered, and the oblong picture lights had yellow and green shades. The long curtains were wine red, peppered here and there with blue butterfly motifs.

Tenzin had just ordered some tea as he saw Crowley coming down the curved staircase from his first-floor suite into the lobby. Crowley was a wiry and fit man, but he was walking awkwardly, as he had lost a toe during his recent epic exploration into the Tibetan wilderness. He entered the grand reception room, glancing around for Tenzin. He waved a hand and smiled briefly once he spotted him.

The two men shook hands and also bowed in the still respected "one country, two cultures" manner.

Tenzin ordered more tea. An artificial benevolence lay about his mouth. There might have been a worried smile beneath it.

"As you know, I am Deng's father," he reconfirmed pleasantly. "When he came to visit me just after your first conference, he became unwell at the temple in Lhasa, and has not been able to travel back to Hong Kong since."

Crowley looked concerned. "I hope it is nothing serious?" he enquired quietly.

Tenzin thanked him with a genuine sounding tone to his voice. "He has all the medical treatment he needs," he said reassuringly. "We think it might be a type of blood poisoning caused by an insect or a snake bite, as he had travelled into the forests below the plateau the day before."

Crowley pursed his lips. "Some very dangerous creatures in there for sure," he said absently, wincing from genuine experience and thinking about his lost toe.

Tenzin nodded in agreement and painted on another smile. "But my son was very interested in your recent exploration experiences, and also the chemo sighting, and wanted to follow up with you on both, as I think you discussed briefly with him?" He paused to see if Crowley would interject. When he didn't, he continued more thoughtfully.

"Deng asked me to attend your talk last night in his absence and also to enquire if you might like to visit him at the temple and spend some time there as our guest."

Crowley's eyebrows bristled as he absorbed this unexpected invitation. He studied Tenzin carefully, searching for the slightest suggestion of deception in his face and finding none. The man was clearly old but not unhandsome, and his bone structure still perfectly symmetrical, but his smile was one of vague pretext.

Slowly, Crowley's frown became a stare of surprise. A strange tumult seemed to flash across his face. He regarded the older man with concentration, uncertain at first how to respond and trying again to see if there was any small print behind those wizened eyes. A slight shadow of unease passed across his thoughts suddenly.

He gazed at Tenzin, whose skin was like crepe paper, as though you could push something sharp straight through it and draw no blood. This, combined with the old man's sallow tinge and spindly body, made Crowley wonder whether Tenzin himself might also be unwell.

Tenzin's eyelids drooped, so that it seemed he was drifting off to sleep, palely beads of sweat gleaming on his brow. Then his eyelids lifted a fraction. When Crowley couldn't read the small print in his eyes, the shadow of unease passed. He grew visibly excited at the prospect.

"That's a very tempting offer," he said, his mind thinking ahead to any commitments he might have already made in the forthcoming weeks and wondering whether or not they could be postponed or cancelled.

A slightly wolfish look began to curl on Tenzin's lips. He bent his bony face into a salacious grin. His eyes were green, but not the kind of shade that would be easy to describe. It was almost that they were green and black at the same time, with light blue creeping in around the edges as if it were trying to take over.

"My son tells me that, in the past, you have admired our temple from the outside and that you are an avid lover of Tibetan crafts, so," he said, his voice became deliberately enticing, "as well as catching up with Deng, who will be most glad of the known face of a friend, you can spend as much time as you wish looking around the temple, marvelling at," – here Tenzin clasped his hands excitedly and explained that he was not about to embellish or gloat – "the endless multitude of artefacts, the very miracles of ornate delicacy – a thousand wall paintings, vases, sculptures, and general historic memorabilia that the ancient temple contains, being as it had been both a religious epicentre for the Tibetan hill people and a military fortress during the ancient civil war, where battlements were built and manned and the deadly martial arts taught to everyone." At this last, he made a rueful sign to acknowledge the fact that he knew Crowley already knew this information. Then he paused briefly, before adding with some energy, "and remember we also have the sky disc."

Crowley beamed a boyish grin, knowing that Tenzin had not exaggerated at all. He felt a thrill of excitement and seemed to melt with anticipation. "How could I refuse?" he said genuinely. The temple would make Deshi's shop in Xian look like a meagrely stocked market stall!

Crowley was not a scholar like Deng, but he possessed an insatiable thirst for adventure and he had read extensively about the marvels of China, Egypt, and the empires of Greece and Rome. But he wondered, at that moment, whether in fact Tibet represented the most impressive ancient kingdom of them all. And he also speculated about the mighty temple itself, what might have been and what great secrets it might still preserve. Like most adventurers, Crowley clung to the fantasy that he could get into the heart of a place and discover its hidden secrets.

Crowley continued hurriedly, saying, "And I am also keen to learn more about the chemo legend from you. Mine is a recent story, but there must be other, earlier ones that you know about from having lived where you have for so long in deepest Tibet." His eyes blazed with the possibilities.

Tenzin frowned, pretending not to understand, and then laughed hollowly, which Crowley misinterpreted as friendliness. "I have virtually never heard mention of it," he said, "but I shall certainly look into it, as yours is an extraordinary tale."

Tenzin rose to leave. "We look forward to greeting you." He shook the offered hand and nodded at length. "And may our Lord Ekajati watch over you and guide you in everything you do."

As Crowley observed the old man walking from the reception room and then out into the brighter lights of the lobby, he noticed something nightmarish about the his languid movement, something indefinable. There was a grace to him, yes, even a beauty, if slightly spectral, but a wavering doubt still lingered. There was something rather predatory and cold about the old man, as though he were one of those monocle cobras which you occasionally discovered coiled within the shade of the plant pots. He had a composed but unrelenting face, impossible to read unless you knew the language.

Crowley remained for a while, in two minds or more, and for a time appeared completely lost in thought.

* * *

Tenzin's boat sailed back groggily across the sea to Macao and then to Hong Kong. The humidity seemed to grow thicker by the minute. The sun appeared bigger and closer, and the sunset was abrupt, orange turning to ochre. The dark purple strip on the horizon enlarged and glimmered across the sea to engulf the day. The jagged peaks were half-robed in mist. An eagle soared past in a yellow flash in the direction of the higher crags.

The archipelago of small islands which made up the territory of Hong Kong were at that point mere dark spots which came and went from view as natural light intervened. At the end of dusk, a beauteous star-encrusted night emerged, the breezes died, and Tenzin could hear laughter emerging from the boat parties, but those junks now looked closer than they had before because they were strewn with man-made light. And beyond the boats, the open sea was still an irregular arc, like a giant lagoon, blue of all shades and shadowy green and purple.

Tenzin knew in his heart that he had voluntarily transformed himself into part human, part savage beast, an act that history would never vindicate or praise. There would be no redemption, no atonement, and no enduring legacy, merely the memories of that other time before the transformation and the ever-present foreboding of something terrible.

Chapter 9

The Nature of the Beast

Tenzin's Story

Thirty-Eight Years Earlier

The temple, an amalgam of opulence and darkness, harboured a sinister history, but its tradition was vast and it represented the combined influence of ancient Tibet and India, and their subsequent wars with China and the Arab states, which were but the harbingers of bitter schism that eventually tore ancient Tibet to pieces.

Tenzin was well aware of his position within the temple's hierarchy. At the age of thirty, he was the natural heir to the title of lord of the great temple of Lhasa, which was still owned and funded by the Tibetan government, one of the few countries not in financial recovery following the end of World War II twenty years earlier. Tenzin had also already secured the future blood line by fathering two male heirs – Kwei-Lan, who was five, and a one-year-old boy whom he named Deng, after his great-grandfather.

Outside the Imperial Hall, there was a curious monument, a stone pillar about ten feet tall with an ornamental cap. It was built to represent the passing of the last emperors, which his grandfather had told him was an era of rulers referred to as "keepers of the flame".

As Tenzin moved past the ancient obelisk into the hall proper, he saw his much loved father, Kano, sitting on a platform ornamented with gold dragons, lizards, tigers, and leopards. His father was dressed in plain cloth, with his head bound in a scarf of bright red silk.

Tenzin bowed to his father and then sat with him on the platform, sensing an impending conversation of grave importance. Kano was now in his seventies, a tall slim man with a refined angular face.

"Time is flowing, my son. I alone know the true secret of the hills and the terror that dwells there," he spoke with sombre countenance. "I need you to meet me in the great study later so I may show you something and explain everything to you. I must pass my knowledge onto you before it is too late, so that you may protect the temple for generations to come. Meet me at seven," he instructed softly. "The main door will be unlocked, as will be the interlocking door." Kano smiled, knowing that as a child Tenzin had always been intrigued as to what lay behind the bright blue door.

* * *

That night, before meeting his father, Tenzin stood on the old battlements and stared up at the emerging constellations with a clouded brow. He'd come to crave the experiences of night-time, when the stars kissed the sky, decorating the heavens like exquisite jewels.

The evening was cool and damp and full of premature twilight, although the sky, high overhead in the distance, was still bright as if it was adorned with red feathers plucked from the sun. It was beyond human creation, all for simply raising one's eyes.

He caught a fleeting glimpse from his childhood – how he would run through the orchards and the narrow chambers of the temple, towards the distant gold of the light of the day, the glow of the sun above the everlasting mountain tops. He remembered the brightness he had witnessed then and his innocent emotions of joy, which had seemed to presage some great wonder. He would play in the gardens, experiencing the perfume of an infinite number of sweet flowers borne upon the breeze, noticing how lotuses would bloom on the lake and fragrant-leaved trees would bend low as if to transmit the songs of the many coloured birds which inhabited their branches.

Then he would stand on the high walls and stare into the very heart of the sun, imagining that in the mirage created, he was starting to see, almost imperceptibly through the wheeling golden rays, the outline of something else, something other than the sun.

But always this mirage would melt into the haze. Out of curiosity and the nascent urge to explore, he returned like a shiver of light, time and time again, to the battlements in the summer darkness of fine nights, which is never quite so dark as winter, to glimpse the vision beyond the vanishing sun. And then he started to have nightmares, which grew stronger with each succeeding night.

* * *

His father was absent from the great study when Tenzin entered, although he had arrived deliberately early and wanted to look around, as he was normally disallowed access to his father's private chambers. And the study was where, more and more frequently, Kano locked himself away for long periods of time. Kano loved to paint, a talent and pastime he had imbued in his son, but unless his canvases were kept elsewhere in the temple, he did not produce enough work to explain his long spells of solitude in the study. No one knew about the secret laboratory.

So there Tenzin stood, motionless for a moment as if anticipating an act of dire catastrophe. The room was as silent as a church apart from a good fire that was flickering and chattering, the flames sparkling in a hundred repetitions, and the faint sound of a large clock on the mantelpiece which chimed at regular intervals.

Tenzin then weaved his way through a cluster of what appeared to be randomly placed furniture to that tall blue inner door, the paint now flaking, slightly faded in colour but still noticeable against the dark wood that surrounded it.

A wide lacquered table partially blocked the entrance. He nudged the table slightly, preventing the glass of untasted wine from toppling over, but this at least created enough space for him to enter through the door where, inside, a remarkable sight faced him.

It was something that appeared to be a small hospital or surgery. There were two long wooden benches amassed with glazed presses of chemicals, phials, and tubes. Bright coloured liquids bubbled inside them, or flowed through the glass pipes like blood through wonderfully transparent veins. At one table various measured heaps of a white salt-like substance lay on glass saucers.

Jars full of multi-coloured powders were arranged nearby on shelves, and several tables were laden with surgical apparatus, the corners of the room strewn with crates and packing straw. Tenzin looked closely then at some of the crates, which contained imported medical materials, mostly from Germany and England.

There was a profusion of papers piled up on one of the benches. At random, he picked up the top sheaf of one pile and held it up into the light. It was covered in scientific scribblings. The ink was faded and he couldn't decipher the writing easily, but there was one phrase, written more simply, that he could make out. It simply read: "unknown blood."

Three grimy windows were barred with lattice iron and partially covered with a red curtain. An early moon pitched shards of white light through the unshuttered sections of the window, creating a spectral gleam in the laboratory, part sun and part moon.

Tenzin continued to explore the small room with rapacious curiosity.

He looked silently into one of the microscopes' eyepiece. There was something looking like plant material, roots of some kind, with clearly branching fibres. But another sample looked very odd indeed – a sliver of skin about an inch long by a quarter inch wide, the fibres dead straight, very thin with a dark satin sheen and no visible external structure, but still with plenty of ochre hairs, about eight inches long, attached tenaciously to it and largely matted together.

At the far end of the laboratory, ten transparent cylinders glowed with violet light. On one table there were traces of recent chemical work, various measured heaps of the white salt substance laid on glass saucers, he knew not what for.

And then Tenzin noticed, suspended from the high ceiling, a black-and-white picture of a well-known mythological creature. He inspected it for a moment, his stare measured and pale. The image of this beast dated back several million years. The creature was thought to be the first coexistent prehistoric Neanderthal or human mammal to emerge following the extinction of the giant reptiles forty million years earlier, although fusion between the two had often been implied.

The creature, legend or otherwise, was famous in Tibetan mythology, but many thought that it was much more than a fable grounded in the milieu and that these monstrous creatures still inhabited the plateau region of Tibet, below the Himalayan peaks. Stories and sightings still flourished to spellbind villagers on cold wintry nights.

On a recessed shelf there was a neat procession of box files, each meticulously labelled, some overflowing and barely able to contain the burgeoning paper held within. Tenzin read some of the labels: "Zoology Unknown to Science", "Neanderthal Origins", "The Sasquatch Investigation", "The Odessa Iceman Commission", and "Zambia's Voodoo Mothman Casket". Then his dark eyes flickered with heightened interest at one file in particular, the label reading, "Secret Tibet: The Third Reich Expedition".

He was about to inspect this file when suddenly there was a familiar voice from the doorway.

"Legend meets science!" The tone of Kano's voice was soft and calming. "Do you remember Dr Schröder?" he asked. "You were quite young."

Tenzin nodded in the affirmative. "I do remember him, of course. He came to look at wildlife and crops. But I never knew why he had those soldiers with him. ...They scared me."

"But wildlife and crops was not his real mission," Kano said candidly. "We were not involved in the war, but the temple was forcefully occupied by Nazi troops in 1938 who were on an expedition headed by the German doctor of zoology Hans Schröder. I got on well with him, and I helped in his quest." He paused thoughtfully. "And, as it turned out, I helped to carry on his research ever since." He waved a sweeping hand across the laboratory.

Tenzin blew out his breath in confused frustration and did not know what to say. His father continued with measured fluidity.

"The German expedition carried out a lot of what is now considered outdated anthropological work, including measuring the skull shapes and sizes of unrelated local people in Salween, as well as taking saliva samples. Schröder's storm troopers – led by the brute Gerber – shot at virtually everything they saw, mainly bears and yaks, and mocked the Tibetans for being afraid of a long-buried legend which should be uncovered only in stories ...but later they wished they hadn't been so cynical."

Kano moved with graceful old age from the doorway. "The real expedition began when Schröder led his heavily armed party into the foothills of the mountains, aiming to climb through the forest onto the actual plateau itself, where there were rumours of these ancient creatures living in underground caverns of ice beneath Everest, the reason they are seldom spotted."

Kano's expression became one of profound regret and disappointment. "But then everything changed. From the temple walls we heard the sound of far off gun shots, and this was followed by many blood curdling screams.

"The mist was stained with a watery green colour that day, so that I may have been staring out at the dead waters of hell when Schröder returned minus two storm troopers. But Gerber and Alexandru had survived. All were injured and disturbed, particularly Schröder, who had a badly lacerated leg. But they *had* captured one of the creatures, a huge giant, albeit dead. Schröder was also carrying one of the tiny cameras he had used to film a small hotspot area near the plateau where they were attacked. There were disturbing microphone recordings and pictures, including ..." He pointed up at the one hanging up in the laboratory.

"That is an actual photograph?" Tenzin asked incredulously.

His father nodded in the affirmative.

"We nursed Schröder until he was strong enough to travel, and he told us how afraid his men had been, even the hardiest experienced soldier, of what they had seen in the woods and that they had never seen such a gigantic and ferocious creature before. Even their trained hunting dogs, bred to be fearless and aggressive, ran from it. Legend had it that these beasts wanted to eat humans because it is their favourite meat and that they could kill any creature quite easily.

He then told of how he had watched one of the mighty monsters eat one of his storm troopers alive, literally tearing him to pieces and stuffing bits of him into its mouth, with a horrible crunching of bone and crimson saliva dripping over its lips."

Tenzin suddenly felt dizzy, a fluttering of awful possibilities floating through his mind.

"When Schröder was well enough, he returned to Berlin. We made sure that he got safely to Hong Kong. And from there, over several months, he somehow found his way back to Germany. It was 1943 and the world was in turmoil. But at that point, for us, the story goes cold. We never saw or heard of him again." Kano paused reflectively. "I must say that I missed him in a way."

"You missed the Nazi occupation of the temple?" Tenzin asked, his voice expressing astonishment.

Kano laughed with an uncertain pitch. "No, just Dr Schröder. Not your typical Nazi, he possessed an easy magnetic charm. He was merely a qualified man interested in the origin of species who somehow got caught up in a whirlwind he could not control. You liked him too, I seem to remember." He became reflective and reminiscent. "When you had gone to bed, he would sit with me at night under the stars and tell me of his conversations with Hitler, Himmler, and Mengele. It was only many years after the war that I understood the true significance of these people and what they had done."

Kano looked anxious suddenly. "Schröder knew that he had discovered our 'secret Tibet'. He was instructed to understand the DNA – hence the establishment of this laboratory and his carbon dating of hair and skin samples – but he was also under instruction to capture and tame one of the creatures for further research in Germany and potentially to use in ground offensives against their enemies in the East. This proved impossible." Kano stared absently out of the window, the smear of sunset still vaguely visible on the distant rim of the world, the moon beginning to take dominance.

"Since those days I have also been searching for a way to understand this ancient enemy." Kano's tone was raw. He suddenly seemed a little heart-sunken and low. "Trying, if you will, to shine a torchlight, however irregular and faint, into the murky depths of millions of years of evolution and find a remedy that would work today."

He sighed and looked even more deflated. "I don't know whether to attempt to befriend them or just try to destroy them," he said wearily.

Then Tenzin's father gestured towards a heavy-looking metallic door, like a strongroom, virtually undetectable towards the rear of the laboratory. Kano beckoned for his son to follow. Once he turned the key, the door swung open, instantly discharging a gust of the icy temperature held within.

There were more racks of shelving inside, containing fifty or so more box files, crammed into cabinets behind ornate black metal grilles, their spines illustrated with photographs and drawings. The only other object visible was a large wooden structure in the corner of this windowless enclave – a substantial box, like a fallen wardrobe, semi-hidden in a block of dark grey shadow.

"Take a look inside," he said matter-of-factly, his breath a grey cloud on the freezing air.

Tenzin ruminated for a second and then wandered over to the wooden structure. There was a slat missing. He bent down and peered cautiously inside at the shape of something that appeared to be a large bone, partially covered in flesh. He managed to move the lid a fraction. The strange dark shape of the bone became clearer but was still mostly hidden by the lid. He looked up and shrugged.

Kano was standing close to him, a picture of disquietude.

"Allow me," he said, flicking a small switch on the wall, which started a slow mechanical winch. The winch sounded like the clattering of rusty chains, but slowly it lifted the thick slab of wood that represented the lid of the fallen casket, revealing the contents of the box in full. Kano watched his son close the door, thus disallowing further ambient air from entering the room.

Tenzin caught his breath and stared in awe, his eyes widening. Inside the box was a monstrous specimen preserved in clear ice in an insulated coffin with a quadruple-paned glass top and four ultraviolet strip lights shining inwards and downwards, all hidden if you just looked at the box from the outside.

"The captured yeti died of its wounds," Kano said. Then he explained that Mengele had devised the insulation process in 1936, some form of foam for Artic conditions and, specifically, in preparation for the pending war against Russia in the Eastern Offensive. The Germans originally took the idea from Egyptian mummification, but Schröder had brought it here from Dachau.

The block of ice containing the specimen was nine feet long, five feet wide, and over four feet deep. The specimen, whatever it was, was fairly well preserved, having been permanently frozen since shortly after death, the domes of clear ice going up and over the feet, knees, torso, and head. Alive, fully muscled, and moving, it would have weighed over twelve hundred pounds.

The ice above the body was partially clear but for a large number of patches of what were obviously hair-fine tubules, through which, Tenzin could see, gases were forcing their way out of the corpse and causing pencils of white opaque crystals. These were particularly noticeable exuding from the nostrils, the mouth, a break in the left forearm, a gun shot hole in the head, and the groin, with the fur badly burnt in the midriff. The gigantic head was almost entirely camouflaged under opaque crystalline ice.

The hands and feet appeared of strikingly abnormal size and thickness. Tenzin thought that the ice, acting as a lens, might be exaggerating the size slightly. There were short, heavy nails on both the fingers and toes, dyed a deep shade of yellow.

The left arm was twisted behind the head with the palm of the hand upwards. The arm made a strange curve as if it were that of a children's doll, but the curvature was due to an open fracture midway between the wrist and the elbow, where you could detect the shreds of marrow in a gaping wound. The right arm was twisted and held tightly against the flank, with the clawed hand spread palm down over the right side of the abdomen.

The nipples, swollen and pinkish, were positioned as those of a modern human female. Despite the total lack of clarity on account of the clouded ice, Tenzin could see that the head was tipped back so that the mouth and the bottom of the flared nose were the highest points. Despite the position, which in a modern human would free the neck, the neck was not visible, leading to the conclusion that this creature had a short, virtually non-existent neck, or at least carried its head low on the shoulders – unless it had been beheaded?

Besides the fracture of the forearm, the creature had several other visible wounds, the head being the most seriously damaged. The entire occipital part of the cranium was broken and some brain matter was hanging out. In the depths of the ice, large smears of blood were trapped like frozen red clouds, the right eye empty. The left eyeball, containing a ghostly green tint, was fully out of the socket and resting on the cheekbone by a thin thread of fibre.

"What is it and how did it die?" Tenzin asked, a shocked look on his face as though he had been jerked out of deep sleep.

"It is a yeti, and it was shot by the German storm troopers," Kano replied. "It took three of them many rounds of ammunition to kill it. Plus, they burnt it with a flamethrower, before which it had killed two of them. Plus, it crushed the dogs as if tearing paper. The Germans had wanted to keep it alive, to tame it, to breed it for use in their war effort, but it could not be tamed, so a dead specimen had to suffice."

Kano led his son to a tiny enclave where a strange semi-frozen creature was positioned upright in a clear oval jar. The female yeti's stomach had been ripped wide open. The contents of womb, twin foetuses, had been sliced out and placed in frozen water. Wires were attached to the tiny heads, which burned and sparkled. The identical shapes moved. They opened their furless mouths in unison and wailed with nascent life.

Tenzin stared in awestruck immobility now, wearing a mask of incomprehension. There followed a long silence between him and his father.

"Father," he said calmly, "might I be left alone here to read through the files and give this whole matter more careful thought?" He drew out the words as though they were limbs to be stretched after long disuse. "I must confess to being a little shocked and confused. I need time to understand what you have exposed to me here." He tapped the bench in front of him in a nervous and subconscious gesture, but then he bowed politely.

Kano had a smile of acknowledgement on his face, but colour had drained from his face, with only the faintest pink left in his cheeks, like two bruises.

"Of course, my son. Remember that science is at heart a branch of philosophy, based not on opinion or subjective orders from a higher authority like Buddha, but on evidence. Science, as Dr Schröder once told me, aims to make sense of it all."

Kano handed Tenzin a set of keys so that he could come and go as he pleased, and then left him alone in the laboratory.

* * *

In the days to come, Tenzin toiled for hours in that tiny laboratory. He read the entire "Nazi Research Expedition" file, including Schröder's journal, thick with blocks of words and heavily edited handwritten notes, full of crossings-out. But he was able to decipher one pertinent fact. His recommendation to Mengele was that the blood of the yeti, so close to that of our own human nuclein that the two were compatible, might be able to be fused with human blood, with this genetic fusion creating a territorial being capable of human intelligence, huge strength, and uncompassionate violence – devoid of emotion. As a weapon, if you were able to direct it, it would be formidable.

Schröder had colour-coded various chromosome research, each colour representing the ancient origin: blue for Europe, green for Asia, and red for Africa. He noted in a different pattern of blue-green that no red chromosomes could be found in his Tibetan research.

Despite his original scepticism, Schröder concluded that the yeti was a prehistoric unclassified backdrop to *Homo sapiens* origins, living in areas uninhabitable by modern-day humans, principally in deep ice caverns below the plateau, where the yetis preserved human food in a freezer-type environment.

Was this the master race in itself or one that at least could be forged? There was logical reasoning to believe that the cause of humankind's evil lay much deeper in its nature and would turn on some nobler hinge than the principles of hatred and incipient rage.

Tenzin looked again into the wardrobe-shaped casket. Schröder had labelled it "Neanderthaloid". The skull and the brow ridges were remarkably prominent. But other parts of the face were less like a Neanderthal's. The cheeks were not pushed forward, and there was a fairly prominent chin. There were numerous bony lesions on the surface indicative of pathology. Schröder's monograph, containing a very detailed description of the skull, did not come to any conclusion of significance of the brow ridges or the surface irregularities. He simply noted, "Nothing definite yet. Too many provisos and complexities, and no precise taxonomic definition. I wish that Dr Mengele were here!"

One night, Tenzin was lost suddenly in a plenitude of conflicting thoughts as though infected by a darkness seeping from within his own mind. He laughed to himself so despairingly that it sounded like a sob. He muttered something and momentarily lost control as he scanned the laboratory benches, turning in consternation at the strangeness of his thoughts, which he had no desire to explore further.

There was a test tube holding some substance next to a paper record of a series of experiments that had led, as far as Tenzin could tell, to inconclusive results. He walked to the other side of the room to the phial, and then turned his attention to it. It rested next to a tray of powders and another book, this one with more detailed notes. The test tube was half full of a bubbling blood-red liquid with crystals still melting, lightening the colour, and effervescing audibly whilst throwing off tiny fumes of vapour. Suddenly at that moment, as he picked it up, the ebullition ceased and the compound changed to dark purple, which faded again and then turned back to its original crimson.

It was highly pungent to the point where Tenzin flinched and twisted his face with disgust, but then the smell became sweet and intoxicating, infusing his nostrils and senses all at once, clouding his thoughts, and creating a burgeoning sense of fear and endangerment. Then a sudden thought came to him, so sharply and so urgently that it cramped his chest and he panicked like a lone deer cornered by predators. Inadvertently he crushed the phial in his hand. This caused his blood from the ensuing cuts and the strange liquid to amalgamate. No sooner had this happened than he felt unsteady, his mind whirling.

A cry followed. He reeled and staggered, clutching at the wall, staring with injected eyes. For a moment, the familiarities of his human face were lost, the crushed phial cutting his hand with the strong smell of kernels in the air. Devastation fell on him as if out of the sky. He tried to stem the flow of blood but inadvertently put his hand to his mouth, at which point some of the merged liquid dripped onto his lips.

He lost consciousness and collapsed onto the floor, remaining that way for over an hour, his eye lids flickering with vague signs of life. But then his eyes snapped suddenly open, like white balls of quartz, and he stared up with unfocused sight at the ceiling. The eyes were changing colour by the second, alternating between lime green and black. The pain increased, but his thoughts were no longer clouded. That was a dubious blessing, as he was now able to focus on his self-inflicted plight with unsparing clarity.

Twilight was almost at an end, with the last rays of sun battling in vain for dominance against an intensifying moon. The weak golden hands of the sun stroked Tenzin. He was suddenly conscious of the light like a wave, as if someone was stirring it towards him with a paddle. Agonising pains racked his body, grinding in his bones with a terrible nausea. Then the pain began to subside and seemed to be replaced by the first breath of something like a new life.

He pulled himself to his feet groggily and staggered out of the laboratory into the great study, thereafter stumbling through a matrix of semi-lit corridors to his own private chambers.

* * *

That first night Tenzin lay on the dark bed, turning to and fro until the small hours of the morning began to grow large. It was a night of little ease. In his dreams his toiling mind was engaged, or rather enslaved, as he lay in the curtained room of many lamps, unshaken by the wind, drawing a regular pattern of light and shadow upon the walls. His mind, conscious or dreaming, was besieged by questions and regret.

Instinctively he knew then he was a self-destroyer, whether physiologically or by accident he did not know. But time would demonstrate soon enough his new found desire and ability to destroy others.

* * *

Tenzin's mind quickly became a crushing anticipation of calamity. His personality transformed itself from passive, sympathetic, and tolerant to brutal, cruel, and inhuman. His acts of rage became legend in the temple, and the rumours of his viciousness spread beyond the temple into the folklore of the surrounding villages.

When his father passed away, he barely seemed to notice. He developed an open hatred towards his wife, Mi-Sun, and both his sons – but for no conscious reason, for Deng in particular. And as Tenzin was now lord of the great temple of Lhasa, there was little the boys could do except wait until they were old enough to leave of their own accord, if indeed they would ever be allowed to physically do so.

Tenzin no longer had a fixed or stable individual identity. He was not one being but truly two, and this threw insightful consideration on the strength – or weakness – of human nature. Since that day in the temple's laboratory, he had cast an increasingly rugged and impervious countenance that was seldom lightened by a smile. And his brow was like that of a man in permanent mental perplexity.

On the evening of his father's death, Tenzin was walking through the narrow lanes of the lamp lit temple, masterful and distant from human emotion. Outside, it was a wild cold night with the pale moon lying on her back as though the wind had tilted her. The thin trees in the cemetery were lashing themselves along the pathways.

Tenzin increased his speed of step along a westward corridor, feeling as weightless as a storm-swept leaf. In an adjoining eastward walkway, a hurrying servant, carrying a tray of crockery, entered Tenzin's pathway just at the moment he was crossing. A few seconds earlier or later and they would have avoided contact. But they didn't. The two men ran into each other at the crossroads. The servant and the trays went crashing, and Tenzin fell over with a hissing intake of breath.

He twisted to his feet, his expression bleak and brutal. Seeing who it was, the servant stayed on his knees and at once exhibited exorbitant alarm, his eyes widening terribly. "Lord, forgive me," he lamented, stricken-faced, bowing multiple times with his hands clasped in front of him like a praying mantis, rushing out apologies in a voice at once hoarse and clumsy.

Tenzin felt the rich pulse of life flood his body. The very mountains seemed to stir and breathe. He could imagine the blood in their stony veins, so vividly that he longed to tear the rocks apart. He thought this passion would overwhelm him – perhaps a passion of immortality or darkened rage – and yet it did not. His mind had grown colossal, expanded by the beauty of the mountains and his inner thoughts. Nothing could shake the signature of Satan from his face.

His lips were moving inaudibly as the colour came and went from his face.

There was a shudder in Tenzin's blood. The face of prehistoric savagery heavy in all the corners of his mind, which subsequently broke out in a great flame of anger as with a hungry animal's fury, he hailed down a storm of blows and stamps from which bones were audibly shattered and the servant's body jumped upon the stone floor. Then it lay there, mangled and blood stained.

Tenzin kicked away the pieces of broken crockery obstructing his progress and calmly continued his meander through the lower labyrinths of the temple. Later, through the iron framed windows of his bed chamber, darkness moved in ragged blots upon the ever-shifting storm.

Then Tenzin's mind switched, suddenly diluted and uncontaminated. He was able to contemplate his plight in a purely human sense. He thought of it as being a thing caged in his flesh, where he heard it whistle and felt it struggle to be born. It shook the very fortress of his identity and added a desperate curiosity as to the origin of life, his nature, and his status within the world.

Tenzin, and his forbears, had been raised in the old-fashioned Tibetan culture that sought to fix and pin down events, facts, and meanings in order to feel that the rapidly changing world around them remained a knowledgeable and attainable place. That a *Homo sapiens* could be merged genetically with a creature as prehistorically old and deadly as the yeti was a profoundly troubling and terrifying juxtaposition.

The window in his room was open. The stars looked down upon his miserable features. He sipped the chill of the cold night air with a certain sense of release. He awoke to sunshine, bright against his face, and experienced a further development, this one of a different nature.

* * *

Until the end of his life, Tenzin continued his father's experiments, focusing on finding a scientific means by which he might understand, control, and possibly eliminate the chemo in the hope that it might somehow alleviate his curse. Although he did not peruse for long his hopes of finding a cure for his own self-inflicted curse, he knew that he was heavily in debt with humanity.

There was a kind of exquisite unreality to his predicament. These polar beasts would be continuously struggling, shaking the very fortress of his identity, two base patterns raging within him like a tempest. There would be times when he would wrestle against the approaches of hysteria, but there was no way to defeat the fused virus. In the same divided ecstasy of mind, a qualm came over him, a horrid nausea and a deadly shuddering which, even when it passed away, left him exhausted and faint. He would often wake in the middle of the night, trying to remember the person he had been in that lost precious hour before he contaminated himself with chemo blood.

But there was no cure. And as he would live longer than most humans, he would be lonely in the oceans of time ahead. In the end, he would go to the Devil his own way.

Chapter 10

Lhasa Temple

Eastern Tibet, December 2007

A landscape painter could not have put together a more perfect composition: snow-streaked granite peaks, and the battling sun and moon at opposite ends of the sky, hanging full and hazy beneath a cap of dark rose clouds.

Despite its size, the Lhasa Temple looked hunched up like a toy fort amidst the immeasurable openness of the wild topography behind it, a mere pin prick against the backdrop of the thirty-thousand foot Himalayan peaks. Lost beneath the dull violence of the colours in the naked sky, the temple looked like a seabird which had landed briefly on the back of an enormous whale.

Tenzin was in the great study, located in the high eastern part of the temple. The room was lit by an enormous roaring and crackling fire barely able to be contained by the marble fireplace. The cavernous room was filled with an enormous array of quite remarkable paintings, all of which were crafted by his own creative hand. He had taken Kano's inherited gift to another level.

This evening, he had selected a brush which a servant already held ready for him, and began spreading wide strokes of dark silver onto the unfinished silken scroll. His most trusted servant, Rinchen, the name meaning "gem of great value", crouched down beside his feet with ample patience, mixing alfalfa, sunflowers, soya beans, and other plant extracts into a moist paste to create a multitude of colours, which he then poured into variously shaped pots.

Although these days Tenzin had to squint intensely, the mountains grew ever more real under his delicate strokes, rising sheer and inhospitable. The image soon occupied the entire foreground of the canvas. He began adding a touch of pink onto the tip of a cloud perched on the highest mountain. The Tsangpo estuary and the river itself, lit blue by the rays of the sun, mirrored each other with a clarity that surpassed real images, like objects reflected on the wall of a silver sphere. Tenzin painted onto the surface of the water a few small lines that deepened the perfect feeling of sweet flowing waters, plus a swoop of brightly coloured birds.

As Tenzin continued, Rinchen noted the reduction of wax in the candle on the mantelpiece and also the fact that, although the day had not quite gone, he could no longer feel the sun against his cheeks. The new moon was high enough in the farthest part of the sky to peer meekly through the open window and elucidate the study with pale ivory light. Darkness, like some stealthy predator, was rising through the great peaks and would swallow the sun within the hour. The far horizon had already bruised to purple. With the threat of a gathering mountain storm, the peaks flickered with gleams of electricity.

The brushes were laid down. Rinchen stood up with grim resolve. His rust-coloured trousers barely reached his ankles, and his faded cotton shirt matched the tones of the sky in Tenzin's current frieze. A gust of moist wind swept against the window. Rinchen locked the catches, as though barring the night, and then, still silent, he rested his forehead against the window pane for a moment before turning to address his master.

"I am My Excellency's servant." Rinchen breathed and made a soft and gentle bow, sloping his shoulders with the meekness of a sick lamb, fearing to disturb as he looked at Tenzin, who was still painting.

"To hear is to obey. You asked me to remind you at this time that there is something you have to do." His timid voice trailed away wetly and he sat down again placidly, continuing to mix the pots of colours. He had served his master with devotion since childhood.

Tenzin raised an eyebrow, swept a wavy grey tendril of hair across his otherwise bald head, and sighed audibly for a moment due to the weight of thinking. His fingers were getting stiff, and he supposed that he would have had to stop painting soon anyway.

"Thank you, Rinchen," he murmured in a silken tone. "You alone of all my servants are the one that I trust and depend upon." Tenzin knew that Rinchen had not one scruple of complexity, possessing a mind that looked no further ahead or behind than the length of his own eyelashes. He was as loyal as a dog permanently on guard, simply waiting for his next task or his next meal. For that reason, Tenzin was never condescending about his servant's epic simplicity, nor did he ever get angry with him.

The current canvas would have to remain unfinished for the time being. Tenzin stooped to rinse his hands at the iron sink, but as he prepared to do so, a drop of blood splashed onto the porcelain of the lemon-hued basin. This was a frequent and continuous problem, as if his body was trying to rid itself of a venomous substance.

Tenzin blotted his nose, turning on the tap and the water. As he swirled the water, it became stained a pinkish red, before it emptied and drained away. He turned as he dried his hands.

A large telescope jutted out of the far window, pointing inquisitively into the twilight sky. World by world, star by star, universe by universe, he had searched for a God but had found nothing.

"We are alone," he concluded darkly. "God speaks in stones and rocks as much as in religious verses. There is nothing new under the sun. Everything has been invented and everything has been written. Time has stopped."

At that moment, lightning stabbed across the Himalayas. The whole room was lit silver by its glow.

Before leaving, Tenzin paused to look at his most treasured work, the painting of which he was most proud. It rested on top of the cedar chest which he had retrieved from Deng's Kowloon apartment in Hong Kong. It was a depiction of the Lhasa Xining civil war, known as the era of fragmentation, which took place in the fifth century. Xining once formed the ancient trade link between the kingdoms of Ladakh with both China and Tibet.

And Tenzin knew the history well. It was a terrible war, excelling in all the grim arts of medieval conflict.

* * *

For a time, after the centralised Tibetan empire collapsed, the land was dominated by the remnants of Imperial Tibet and the rise of regional warlords, such as the much feared Cetan Kalsang and his trusted Red Guard. Kalsang realised that a land at odds with itself offered great opportunity as well as great threat.

This resulted in an attack on the capital city's temple and an uprising, at a time when, for whatever reason, a vague tale about sorcery and the unnatural terror of long-buried evil was not enough to bedevil foolish peasant minds or justify belief in their worst suspicions. The villagers gained much support from some of the disgruntled workers inside the temple. A mutiny ensued, with the temple being attacked both internally and externally.

The usurping village elders, led by the Xining infidel Kalsang, were backed by the tribes who lived in the foothills and fallow villages like Salween.

A great determination and zeal had settled upon the hearts of Kalsang's followers as they raised the cry of battle and gathered in purposeful numbers, the din of strife rising high into the heavens, the raven horses neighing wildly with a clatter of hooves on rock – and with the thunder of a million footsteps, crowds of villagers, their torches flickering in a line along the western plain, as they marched on the temple, which was lit a blazing red that evening by the setting of the sun, as though formed by living fire, the tip of each flame a vaunting, jagged tower, whilst around the temple stretched walls of colossal stone. And then the flame was lost, as the sun was slowly swallowed by the west.

"They are coming," was the holler from the temple battlements, followed by the grave command, "Kill them all." Swords were drawn so that steel flushed yellow in the dying light of the sky.

Pandemonium ensued for the next ten days, but the common people's tortured hopes of great change were, in the end, crushed.

Lhasa, led by the then emperor Tubo, the last true leader of a unified Tibet, assisted by the Mongol and Ghurkha mercenaries, and whose savagery was respected and feared by the most bloodthirsty of races, bore down hard on the uprising, defending the city and temple walls successfully, allowing only minimal breach. As the strength of the enemy began to ebb, the defenders crushed the twin uprisings and impaled the disloyal elders upon hideously sharpened spikes, many already lifeless, but others twisting and shrieking out violent curses and screaming prayers, writhing, their cries of lamentation and grief ignored.

The impalements decorated the ramparts for days afterwards, until the stench of death under the pitiless summer sun got the better of victorious gloating.

In the courtyard, the many lesser sword-gashed and arrow-disfigured men were impaled on stakes. Multiple bodies lay on top of one another, mangled and piled high near the tall lacquered gates that led out into the sprawling cemetery, their dead, dismaying eyes protruding with a look of inexpressible terror, with their throats cut so wide that their heads had been virtually lopped from their necks, their stomachs slit open and their guts spilling out in the courtyard dust in mystic climax. They would be buried under piles of stones or simply exposed to the hunger of vultures and crows.

Everywhere the close air was spiced with blood and the courtyard ran red. The fly-blown corpses of dogs, also slain in battle, lay amidst scattered arrows and garbage, already being eaten by the vultures and swarming insects, as the cruel Tibetan sun that summer chose not to discriminate between shrivelling the crops and scorching the fleshless bodies of the dead. A rapidly expanding repugnant stench infected the air. You could smell the dead throughout the mountains that summer.

The right order of things had been restored.

The victorious Lhasa Temple, protected from the sun and the gathering flies by the shutters, celebrated the event from the pale rooms that overlooked the central courtyard, looking out and smiling as the sun's lamplight stabbed through the wooden slats.

Kalsang remained alive for entertainment, howling with vexation and terror, before Tubo threw his head back with a shout of scornful laughter, his sword rising and falling. He felt it puncture the soft sac of the heart. Kalsang shrieked, a terrible unearthly wail of pain and hate. The shriek echoed through the temple and across the lowlands. Everything seemed stilled by it.

A fountain of blood spouted up into the sky, bright scarlet against the deeper tones of the horizon, like rain from a crimson cloud. Kalsang fell like a beast in a slaughterhouse. Tubo then slashed him across the throat. There was silence, save for the sweet washing of Kalsang's blood against Tubo's victorious face. The withered corpse seemed to disintegrate into powder as bright-plumed birds rose into the air from the head of a shattered statue. They dismembered Kalsang's body into fourteen parts, scattering the pieces far and wide.

The temple workers who had remained loyal to Tubo spat on the dead, glad that the early autumn moon would soon rise above their silent graves. The head of Kalsang remained impaled on the stockade for five days, open to the elements and all indignities: birds, flies, and insects savaging the head like hornets on a honey-dripping fruit.

Such usurping sacrilege could not be forgiven easily. A heavy hand was used to crush the disorder. The temple set up a war tribunal to try the lesser betrayers – Kalsang's underlings – and no one was dismissed without penalty. Sentences of public flogging, human humiliation of the worst kind, and imprisonment were meted out in line with what the court considered would be necessary for the offenders to reconsider the nature of truth.

But after a summer lost to warfare passed, a winter of uncertainty ensued. The temple walls remained unrepaired, the high bronze gates still broken, and the recrimination seemed never ending; the Lhasa vengeance knew no bounds, covering life and limbs and lands, hurrying through the darkness towards the fires of the villages, bodies continuing to pile up on the undermined banks of the Tsangpo. It was all described in such extravagant detail so as to make it the work of giants rather than that of mortal men. Blood seeped through the fields as though the soil were a bandage laid across an unstaunchable wound.

The victory represented the manifold proof of unsettling power and an eternal curse on the deposed Kalsang's ignoble blood line. It became the stuff of legend and story-telling in the years that followed, a nightmarish proclamation to all who might wish to repeat the attempt of usurping the noble blood line which had flowed since the dawn of Tibetan time. The high priests, who had sided with Kalsang, skulked in their castles for years.

Seven long summers and seven winters passed, until at last, such was Lhasa's triumph that it was no longer considered necessary to kill peasant villagers at random for their previous sacrilege. Fugitives and renegades, previously in hiding as hunted men, to keep village wives unwidowed and children still fathered, could re-emerge and resume some sort of normal life.

The damage to the temple was restored, swords could be sheathed, and the Tibetan lands seemed at peace once again.

With continued peace and good rains, Tibet could rebuild. And King Tenzin Tubo's legend was sealed like that of an ancient pharaoh, many believing that he was still alive today, for even if he were to be sliced into an infinite number of particles, were his blood to be mingled with the waters of the world, were his bones to be crushed and ground into a dust, the essence of his mighty ruling spirit would remain.

Tenzin's painting showed Kalsang in the background pointing his sword towards the blood-red moon, but in the larger foreground was his decapitated head, sliced with a thousand cuts, hanging from a hook, blood dripping like the finest rain with its death-imposed imbecilic grin; sharp black eyes still twinkling out of the thicket of his hair and beard, both matted with gore; and an expression of wondrous horror still preserved upon his frozen face, with no one able to hear his wordless screaming. A hideous wound was painted across his throat.

* * *

Tenzin believed that, even in the modern times in which he ruled, he had the run to rule the temple with the same heartless efficiency to ensure that no such uprising ever happened again.

Peasants were peasants and could be stamped on or ignored, but leader warrior peasants, such as Kalsang, needed to be publically destroyed and humiliated. It was a natural hierarchy – the stronger must feed upon the weaker, the greater upon the lesser, blood upon blood, for the world was nothing more than a demonstrable pattern of such destruction. Tenzin had learned to take his place within life's order, and he understood with a midnight clarity what that order was.

He looked at Rinchen before exiting the study. The servant's face seemed haunted by a sudden dread. Loyalty and gratitude had paid off, but even in his slow, simple mind, Rinchen knew he was nothing more than a salvaged man in the great flow of the world. The flames blazed and crackled in the fireplace. When the shadows flickered, Rinchen stared at them as though afraid that they might shelter some dark demon.

Tenzin passed through the procession of musically hinged doors that led, ultimately, to the chapel. For an old man who normally semi-shuffled, he moved quite swiftly and with purpose, his mind now firmly fixed on the dual tasks that awaited him that evening.

* * *

In the chapel, accompanied by a handful of guards and servants, Tenzin observed the semi-naked man who outwardly shivered as he stood facing him. The door behind the bronze censer let in the violet dusk, along with the ever-changing ghosts of gathering storm mist.

"You have betrayed the secret and dishonoured me, Ling." Tenzin's face seemed contorted by bitterness and loathing, his lips tight and pale. "And in order to lock your blasphemous form up in the only cell from which there is no escape, I have decided to burn your eyes out." He breathed in a ghastly whisper, watching Ling's facial reaction piteously. "Because your eyes are the two magic gates into your own kingdom."

He advanced forward with idle pace until he was barely the length of his own shadow away, touching the man on the shoulder. Ling shuddered at the contact.

"I hate you, Tenzin," Ling shouted in terror and indignation. "You murdered my mother and my daughter." His face was a twitching mask of hate, but his voice sounded distant and frail in his own ears. He grimaced rather than spitting the words, which for him was a gentler way of crying and exhibiting despair. He showed a grin of terrible bitterness, knowing there was no chance of forgiveness or escape anyway.

"Ah yes," Tenzin said haughtily, his eyes glittering and a faint smile curling on his lips, "I remember now how all night their screams and moaning kept me delightfully awake." He laughed, an evil sound of intermingling mockery and triumph, worse for its intermingling.

Two guards seized Ling as Tenzin fixed a stare directly at his face, moving a little closer, speaking in a soft menacing tone. "The only empire which is worth reigning over is that which you alone can enter. And my empire is this temple, made of one thousand curves and ten thousand colours, and the mountains covered in snow that cannot melt. But I have an equal, and these creatures must be fed. Do you understand?" Tenzin amplified the question theatrically.

"I alone can venture in the dead of night along that road which no living creature other than the chemo dare take." Tenzin twinkled for a moment at his own omniscience. "And," he said, pausing and smiling ruefully. "I cannot help my blood. But my inner demon protects me."

Ling babbled something unintelligibly. The two guards struck him fiercely. He fell at their feet onto his knees, tasting blood in his mouth. He staggered to his feet with difficulty, like a pine tree wavering under the forces of the wind. He continued to protest, frail as a reed, childish as milk. And now he did cry, no longer ashamed. When he spoke again, the words came out of some deep well of the past.

"I will not kiss your feet or beg for forgiveness." He was moaning through gritted teeth, desperately attempting to stay true to his resolve. "And I would rather be a slave than rule in hell over all the ghosts of men."

Tenzin's eyebrows raised. He looked at his captive with an unblinking eye, as one might when finding a crab under a rock.

"Dry your tears; this is not the time to weep," he hissed, chuckling at his own cruelty. "Your eyes must be clear so that the little light that is left in them is not clouded by your weeping as you enter a world full of dark and fabulous mystery. And in the afterlife," Tenzin paused in serious thought, "do not underestimate the joys of hatred. I wish you an eternity of disgust at everything you own and an unattainable desire for everything you shall never possess. It is not only the cruelty in my own heart that makes me want to see you suffer, for you are damned. You are accursed."

Tenzin's face took on a hideous ugliness. He seemed more like a demon than like a mortal man. His eyes seemed ablaze with a hell-like fire, and his white teeth grinned with a terrible vile menace. "Or I might cut you open and clean you out. I will pull your brains through your nostrils and fill your skull with liquid fragrances."

Then he bent down and picked something up with an animal-like grace, holding aloft a gleaming cutlass in the half-light, brandishing it in slow motion. He considered his options with a carefully crafted and eloquent smile.

The guards released Ling's arms but forced him to his knees, and at the same time seized him by the chin and strained his head upwards, as if raising it to the sun. Despite his agony and struggling in perpetual vain to shake himself loose, the captive Ling cried out, "I would rather die than obey you."

Tenzin licked his lips, his eyes narrowing like those of a cat. He said nothing for what seemed like a very long time. The seconds lengthened as pity and desire mingled as one. "Rather die?" he queried then, his eyes gleaming like emeralds. All the emotion and life seemed to bleed from his face. He laughed with a fierce contempt and rage, and then fell silent.

His face seemed chilled by the kiss of death.

His decision was made: "I will bestow on you generous justice," he said. "Forget the eyes, oh hated son of Kalsang. Forget the eyes." A horror shrieked in his blood like wind against wire. He was screaming and foaming like a lunatic, swinging the cutlass above his head like a berserker as if about to perform some act of fearful magic.

Ling's head fell from the neck like a cut flower, and the corpse started spreading blood instantly, a very faint movement still flickering on the eyelids.

A young servant girl, who had entered inadvertently, dropped a basket of fruit in an unintended gesture of disapproval, her hands cupping her face as if to contain the horror and fear. She immediately regretted her mistake as the basket's contents despoiled and entered the flow of sticky red slime.

"Clear that up," Tenzin commanded darkly, his eyes bulging. "You do not need to conceal your revulsion, as I can see it in your face and the way that you stare at me. But," he said, his voice now taking on a morose, glowering, warning quality, "I would advise you to do as I say. You know that the grave is better than poverty."

It was both a shrewd and cruel point, but Tenzin had been informed that this particular servant girl may have stolen items from the temple to sell in the local villages. More than anything, it reaffirmed his belief that greed or desperation will, in the end, always conquer fear. She was, to him, nothing more than an insect to be crushed under his foot at any time he chose.

She rang the servant's bell. Her face darkening further in violent disgust, she swallowed before replying in a stammering unctuous tone, obediently setting about the task of cleaning up the gory mess as other servants frantically mustered to help. They scrubbed aggressively, refusing to admire the beautiful light russet colour that the foul discharge of wonderfully smelling fresh blood created across the jade tiles.

The decapitated corpse was wrapped in blackened swathes of linen and transported out into the misty courtyard. The head followed, gathered up in revulsion in the skirt of the servant girl's gown as she rose nimbly from her knees, holding the head away from her like a child holding up a drinking cup. Her hands were wet with blood, and flies already stuck to the tears of blood on Ling's eyelids. The head was tossed out into the courtyard; it made a heavy thud as it hit the ground. Tenzin turned to the guards. "You know where to take the body and the head. I will check presently that you have fulfilled your duties." His tone remained unmistakably threatening.

The guards bowed rigidly in obedience and set about following their orders.

* * *

Barely ten minutes later, Tenzin stood at the bottom of the ice dungeon's spiral staircase in his starched robe, which was splattered here and there with crimson flecks of Ling's blood. He carried a tall candle, trying to resist free admission to the echoing empty corridors of insidious memory that greeted him there.

This was the place where he had murdered Mi-Sun.

* * *

Mi-Sun means "sun spirit".

She had been born at the temple and worked in the kitchens and pantries as a child. When she was the age of twelve, people could glimpse the fear that already resided in her eyes. She became distrusting of Tenzin's intentions towards her even then. She knew she had beauty, but she did not fully understand the broader effect this could have on men. It was true that she had done nothing to deliberately attract his notice.

When several years had passed, her beauty grew and she arrived upon the bloom and loveliness of womanhood, becoming a lady of sense and fortitude. Now he looked at her with genuine intent, his smile more wolfish and hungry, gazing at her black silk-lashed eyes, as though it was the first time he had ever truly seen her. He would cast crazed lustful looks upon her as on some precious stolen object, as if a mist that had made him blind had suddenly cleared. But when he spoke to her, it was always with a hard heart.

He ordered her to be bathed and dressed in lavish unfastened robes, and time and again he would call her to his study, or to the throne room, with the same look of ravishment, heated by the fires of lust on his face, tugging at the sash of her robe so that her upper body was no longer concealed by material, cupping her breasts and pushing aside her slim-fingered hands. Her waist was as fine as silken thread, her breasts like twin fruits of ivory, her face the hue of pale honey. Mi-Sun's looks put the fairest ebony to shame.

Tenzin kissed her as if feeding, like an infant drawing on mother's milk, and so urgently did he seize her, so tightly did he grip her, that she stumbled and half sobbed, seeking to break away.

"I am entitled to command you!" he insisted with a merciless heart. "Your body must obey me even if your mind does not." She still protested but reluctantly allowed herself to be clasped. She cried with displeasure until he silenced her, crushing her lips beneath his own. His physical rights were sacrosanct, and her purity was burned away as he claimed her as his birth right.

Mi-Sun shared Tenzin's bed and his throne for many years and bore him two healthy sons. She became busy and zestful amidst the unexpected ease of life. But it wasn't long before her life in the temple began to worsen and her sense of passionless violation increased. She saw that her husband was lazy and loved only his own pleasures, and so she made herself adroit in providing him with these. But still she hoped that he would be glad and grateful and perhaps, gradually, loving towards her. But it never happened. Despite their marriage, and his random munificence, she knew that she was really no more than a concubine. Often, staring out from the window at the wild beauty of the mountains that stretched for thousands of miles, she thought how true a daughter of the land she was.

As her husband bedded more and more women over the years, Mi-Sun got on with life with a heavy heart and a vexed mind. Resentment and envy never darkened her face. She feared Tenzin as a mouse feared a rattlesnake. She thought of her life as being so much clouded in shadow that there was to be no distinguishing between the shades of darkness.

On the night in question, Tenzin stood by Mi-Sun's side in the dungeon, half resolved not to do it, but the yeti in him – a darkness lurking like a spider in his heart – had been caged too long. It came out roaring with unrestrained delight for its release, but with hatred and dislike for the human form beside it. It was its birth right!

In the same divided ecstasy of mind, a qualm came over Tenzin, a horrid nausea and a deadly shuddering, which presently passed away but left him faint. He thought about the situation from the human perspective for a moment – how his wife's long-lost kisses now irritated him by the very thought of them, how her faded beauty no longer pleased him, and how her sweet smell was now like that of mellow grapes or a scented blossom at the end of its spring zenith. Compared to his first portrait of her, which still hung in the blue-columned gallery, he was shocked to notice how much her beauty had faded. She failed to arouse him, and her nakedness revolted him like the slithery skin of a snake.

He had thought of her as a once beautiful, rare, and expensive fruit which he had reproduced on canvas, before the fruit lost its illustrious skin and freshness. But then he also knew that he could not expect her to be beautiful forever.

Mi-Sun was also too protective of her sons and had tried to limit Tenzin's control over them. He remembered her bellowing once in a fit of suspicious and stupendous anger: "Never again will you rock my children; never again will I fill my lap with delicious fruits for you, sitting beneath the cypress tree that gave us both nourishment and shade. The rivers of milk that flowed from my breasts made my sons from the same stuff as my heart, and you will never understand it or be truly part of it."

Her tone of voice was a surprise. It was soft and musical with just a tinge of melancholy. She managed a fake smile that for a moment buried the pain deep inside her heart. But her eyes remained cold, like nothing in this world could melt them. For Tenzin, her ruby smile had cracked and faded, and his attempts to discover an elixir to restore her previous beauty and preserve it in the face of the passing years had failed. He had thought her to be a beautiful, ageless woman, but that was not the case. And a third child was certainly not required, lest he become a breeder of monsters. She had told him that night that she was pregnant and how she hoped it would be a daughter this time.

Since that time in the laboratory, Tenzin had been constantly aware of an awful darkness coursing through his veins. He was possessed by a creature to whom power was given and who made him rise to do its bidding – bidding without an essence of human mercy. The chemo had long been contained, but that night with Mi-Sun in the dungeon, it came out raging and lusting after violence and the chance to inflict pain with prehistoric severity.

Mi-Sun's head sank as though her whole body were a poppy stem and hardly strong enough for her weight. She shrugged despairingly. "You have a face like murder," she said, her look darkening into a combination of despair and hate as she clutched herself and shuddered.

Tenzin's resolve snapped as he asked her savagely. "Who do you think you are?"

Mi-Sun did not reply. She could see his cruel, detestable smile forming into a permanent sinister snarl, as sunken olive-green eyes stared out of his face with mindless menace into hers. She nodded miserably, understanding her fate, and started to sing lightly in a voice strained with raw fear, looking at the teal tint of his hardened eyes.

Rage in him came out faster than magma. Just as destructive, and without hesitation, he pulled out the nail from his left-hand pocket, grabbed hold of her raven hair, dragged her head backwards, and drove the nail into her neck. Calmly, his face barely changing, he then drove a second nail into her forehead.

Reaching inside his coat, he withdrew a stony thorn-shaped object and began stabbing at her eyes. Satisfied, he prised opened the rusty-hinged door and dragged Mi-Sun's now limp body out into the cold air, her hair stained with brains and blood.

She barely moaned as her languished eyes died out like the reflection of stars in a bright summer's dawn. Lastly, Tenzin decapitated Mi-Sun and threw her head into the courtyard pool with a soft splash. He watched for a moment as it bobbed like a water lily. Her long dark hair, black like the most pitch-black night, rippled around it like floating roots. He watched as the ripples spread and diminished until the pool was as glassy and still as before. Mi-Sun had died without a sigh. The water turned a cloudy crimson with her departed life-blood.

He knew that neither the body nor the head would be there in the morning.

* * *

As Tenzin pushed the memories of the past away, he noticed how the dungeon that night had become more hauntingly cold, with a vapid mist seeping surreptitiously through the multitude of cracks and gaps in the walls and slender lattices of the window frames. There was a rumble of thunder, remote and far away, like a mouse walking across a drum.

Two servants were standing on the plinth, next to the frozen footprint, which Tenzin glanced at with philosophical detachment. They were talking and laughing, but then Tenzin himself laughed. It was such a fearful sound that the servants were instantly hushed, as though offering their souls to an evil spirit.

"This is not a sky burial." Tenzin scowled, his voice flaring with the tone of recrimination. He cackled again. The noise seemed dissonant and strange. For the second time that night, he appeared more of an evil spirit than a man. His fashioned eyes remained large and commanding, and he knew, despite his age, that he could still inspire universal fear in the minds of idiots, although he also understood that his influence was under mortal threat.

He gave the servants an imperious signal. Worried into silence, they began pulling large barrels of dry wood onto the plinth next to the frozen footprint, stacking the containers carefully so as to be easily consumed. They set fire to the wood with flaming brands, lunging forward to scatter flares of light into the gloom.

Tiny wreaths of blue smoke rose like pallid ghosts, here and there at first, and then they thickened. It was much like a forest fire would start, by rising amongst the creepers that festooned the dead or dying trees.

As Tenzin watched, a flash of fire appeared at the root of one wisp. A small flame expanded and scrambled up the firewood like a bright squirrel. Within seconds, the barrels were small pyramids of expanding light. A yellow wash flickered across the room. A thick plume of black smoke engulfed and obscured the plinth momentarily. The tubs were kicked still closer to the footprint. The servants stayed bent over as they tended the flames.

When the melting process of the footprint was past the point of no return and the firewood was curling and becoming as black as dying red roses, Tenzin left the men in the dungeon to finish the job and clear up any evidence.

Drawing on unexpected reserves of energy, he walked with purposeful haste through the Imperial Hall and out into the blue paved courtyard near the gardens. He paused below an archway.

As he did so, the clouds overhead became ragged and frayed, and then scattered altogether on a gusting shriek of wind.

The storm was almost upon them.

Beyond the archway, there stretched more flowered gardens, with lush banks and a bridge from which Tenzin could hear the indistinct conversations of servants as they sat on the stone benches by the green lines of shaped hedges and the crowns of trees. It was a good place for them to exchange news and views without being overtly noticed or overheard. Tenzin crossed to the steps, where the waters of the lake were gently lapping and shimmering against the stone surrounds.

Smaller than the lakes, the courtyard pool, made out of cream and white clay, was circular and full of water lilies and needle-like reeds that grew seemingly of their own accord.

The caged monkeys fidgeted and scratched but were mostly silent, semi-enveloped in the clandestine mist and growing darkness. It was still palely bright in the west, but a cold wind was blowing consistently now, condensing the clear spots of icy rain that started to drop from the heavens in the east, making the earth damp and the battlements shiny.

Tenzin made his way along the path which many of his trusted servants had smoothed for him, clearing even the smallest pebble in fear that he might trip. His face, pale like an immaculate moon, and though betraying no emotion, was tarnished by poor vision and the unstoppable encroachment of old age.

He seemed like a leaden mirror whose beauty reflected only itself.

* * *

Tenzin moved beneath a long under croft of stone buttressed and pierced by two additional archways, wide enough for carts, but for most of its length it was underpinned by thick wood that formed a lacquered awning. As the stone walls struck inwards, he stared at what first looked like a hatch to a cellar, meaning it might simply have been a storehouse containing supplies of firewood or coal. It was like a door to a large wardrobe but was lying flat, about the length of a tall man.

He approached with measured steps and considered the stout door with a sense of challenge. He was wiry and still quite agile for his age but conscious that his bones were too brittle to sustain a fall. He clenched both hands on the handle, set a broad foot against the timber frame, and heaved at the hatchway, his square but fragile shoulders gathering in one great breathless heave. The door, its wood old and unpreserved, lifted slowly and then fell backwards on its hinges with an echoing thud onto the stone pathway, tiny splinters of cedar spanning lazily downwards into the darkness.

Tenzin stared at the opening he had uncovered, brushing away the cobwebs. There were steps leading deep into the earth. He could see the first two steps, and then nothing but yawning black.

He carefully placed his foot on the first step and began his descent into the multi-layered vault, penetrating the ancient underground levels of the temple. The ceiling of each chamber was ever lower and the darkness ever deeper, lit by fewer lights. He then found himself walking through a long, thin room held in place by a series of plump stone pillars adorned with intricate carvings. Set back in the wall there was the mortared outline of yet another doorway.

This miniature door was adorned with emblems, the carvings of strange talismans and aristocratic demons, the symbols of a dark and dangerous magic which no living human being could read. Above the doorway was the face of a whorish and cruel women. A large stone figure of a jackal guarded the doorway, and a replica sky disc was emblazoned into the grey surface of the stone. Like a gaoler, Tenzin took out a key, stained with rust and forced it into the lock.

It scraped grittily but did not turn.

There was a sound from inside the room. A moment of combined fear and sheer delight coursed through Tenzin's veins. He had to steady himself against the cold wall. He tried the key again, this time with added strength. Again it scratched against rust, but this time the mortise of the lock gave a soft click and then snapped open. He unbolted the higher locks with ease and pushed a shoulder against the door.

Directly ahead of him was a small set of steps leading down into the blackness. He took a-pace forward and passed into the gloom of that interior cell, glimpsing it then – a large silhouette, a giant shadow, as if the shape were chiselled out of the darkness itself, and yet it was blacker than all the shadows around it.

He heard a lumbered movement. The darkness was pitch. Tenzin paused, his eyes widened, and he stared into the obsidian as though it were the vanished past, thoughts rising like incense to cloud his nerves. There was a faint rattling of chains as, although he couldn't see clearly, Tenzin felt his way along the wall to a shelf where he knew he had left a supply of fire-lighters.

The door gently swung shut behind him with a gentle click. Through the darkness came the glow of two green spots, like sallow lamplight.

The spurt of candlelight was like an arc of brilliant gold in the blackness; the miniature flame held firmly in a rusty sconce. The brush of the torch burst into flames, flashing an immediate and intense brightness. Within seconds the candle burned like a miniature sun. Tenzin peered through the burning cloud with a feeling of wonder and awe, paralysed and exhilarated by the dense red mist before his eyes.

The colossus was loaded with padlocks and heavy coils of chain, which were buried deep into the stone floor. An iron cage with wide bars running from ceiling to floor provided further metallic restraint. The chain lengths disallowed the monstrous arms and claws from reaching out through the bars.

The chemo snarled defensively and seemed confused by the sudden influx of light, becoming momentarily enfeebled by its brightness, retreating into the dark shadows of the cage, and lapsing into torpor. It stared at Tenzin through the green sparks. Tenzin pressed his face against the bars as if to goad it, picking up a shred of human meat and putting it in his mouth. 'What pleasure,' he thought. All other joys would taste like ash in the mouth. This was the cannibal's dream, the taste of human meat in all its exquisite simplicity.

Despite its wounds and evident exhaustion, borne out of its permanent struggle to escape, the chemo's eyes were still agleam, as if lit by some inner light. It was a magical mix of beauty and power. It half rose to sit on its haunches, perching like a bird of prey and squatting like an incubus in the flicker of the torch. It seemed to yawn very slowly as if considering its options. Then it hissed a loathsome high-pitched sound of warning.

As Tenzin had instructed, the body of Ling, including his deflowered head, lay on the filthy blood-caked floor of the cage. He leaned his forehead against the central bar. The chemo suddenly made a desperate lunge for the bars. Although Tenzin knew it couldn't reach him, he leapt backwards as if snatching burnt fingers from a fire.

The chemo uttered a sound half of pain and half of triumph and then, coldly and methodically, began to tear the head of Ling apart, ripping the flesh to shreds, and then the body, so that the heart was exposed and the limbs and chest were be-slobbered with yet more oozing blood. Satisfied at both the disposal of Ling's remains and the ongoing imprisonment of the chemo, Tenzin turned, his footsteps echoing as he crossed the uneven stone floor towards the door.

Leaving the torches to quench and sag naturally, he slammed the door of the windowless cell behind him with a solemn boom.

* * *

Tenzin made another arduous climb onto the high walls as the consequent darkness seemed kept at bay in the concluding rays of the sun. For a moment, he was unable to see anything. Tiny arrows of light fell on him with yellow and orange tips. He prayed that the sun would rise again tomorrow, for what was the sun if not the source of all life, power, and force in the world? Every bright-petaled flower, every sweet smelling plant, every shade granting tree, every wondrous kind of animal, every living thing of beauty, was granted breath by the sun.

The mist increased and the sky was clouding over in the deep copper of dusk as the giant disc slipped rapidly beneath the sill of the world, having lost its battle to the rolling overcast horizon. The horizon itself became a curtain of thunderous brass that rang out with the storm coming. Tenzin's face contorted slightly; his vulpine smirk flickered and became malevolent. A rack of clouds played tag with the moon, which ducked in and out of them and turned their edges to beaten silver.

Tenzin saw a chemo standing in the cemetery grounds in a cone of darkness, lit intermittently as the moon, deathly pale, stained the monster's pelt in a silvery red streak. The creature fidgeted, its wide nostrils flaring rhythmically, seeming to scent the air. Tenzin could smell it, its hair, its sweat, its savagery. The upper lip, the colour of liver, wrinkled back to show its heavy tusk-like teeth, unbearably foul.

Then it disappeared from view for a moment, fading as if within expanding cloud cover, before reappearing below him. The creature was a terrible representation of grotesque power. It screeched a high pitched howl and the entire world seemed bleached with desolation and pain. There was nothing of God or light in that heartless sound; it was all black winter and dark ice.

A vulture hovered on the overspreading cypress tree, its two blood-shot eyes visible in the satin darkness. Disturbed by the noise the chemo had made, it took off like a flying dragon, wheeling and crying in a startled manner above the tree tops, a clamorous silhouette against the sky. And then it was gone.

Tenzin understood fear; and his own fear was almost palpable in the gloom as he leant through one of the alternating parapets. But then, within him, inexpressible emotions combined again to make his imminent rage elemental and awe-inspiring. With his conflicting inner personalities, he wanted to both love and defeat the chemo, but he was suddenly drained and felt impotent, although he longed for one final confrontation. Hope may dissipate, but surely it cannot be destroyed completely?

It was true that the chemos could not scale his walls, at least not yet. And he had managed to capture and imprison one – something that Schröder had failed to achieve. But despite myriad experiments, involving a mix of kindness, cruelty, and both primitive and sophisticated communication attempts, it had not been possible to tame the chemo one iota. As past laboratory experiments had revealed, the blood was ostensibly human, the make-up of cells, plasma, proteins, glucose, minerals, and irons so closely resembling the genetic human structure that it was virtually impossible to tell them apart.

But there was a great freedom in despair. Once reached, even despair could be a type of paradise.

Tenzin shuddered and clenched his fists, as though fighting to control some desperate monstrous urge, whilst staring into a profound future, face-to-face with it.

He also thought that the chemo probably feared him too, as Tenzin was a hybrid, hungry for prey – two linked species in which the parallels were genetically exact, merely separated by millions of years of evolution.

The high whistling fell away. Tenzin remained motionless, a gaunt silhouette barely visible, like a phantom turned to stone, save for the faintest tremor which passed across his face. All was perfectly but unnaturally still around him, as though frozen in a moment outside the flow of time and space.

His limbs were horribly thin, like those of a water-skimming insect. The florid flesh appeared to whither upon the bones, paled into waxen austerity. He looked nothing like a mortal man any longer, seeming more ancient than the mountains but holding a power far beyond his mortal origins.

Tenzin stared at the terrible whiteness of the face in the cemetery, and for a moment a dark shadow flickered. He thought he saw an image of self-loathing there, plus horror and regret, but he did not really know. So rapidly had the shadow passed that he could not be certain it had been there at all?

He had hoped to see in the prehistoric features some infallible sign of pity, but in the glaring and terrible sparks of green-gold, the blackness remained. Then the creature vanished for good with a shrill whistle, running on two legs with terrible muscular ease, painted with moon-fire as it disappeared. There was a wild, terrifying smell in the air.

Tenzin stared beyond the tree-lined cemetery. Darkness was sweeping in from the margins, flooding everything. The only indication of any form of human civilization was the great open space to the west. The village of Salween, deep in the foothills, was already half asleep or half preparing for the violent weather. Old lanes rutted by ox-carts criss-crossed the flatlands and were winked with occasional dispersed torches and twinkling braziers. Carried on the upward flow of wind came the murmuring of studious voices from the local yak herders and the whinnying of a horse.

The Tsangpo River, hidden by a haze of soft blue mist hanging like a floating veil, and unstained by the moon, was just perceptible as a reflected pale gleam between the trees. A barge, glowing with man-made light, with a large prayer flag flapping in the wind, moved slowly down river.

The fringes of the tree tops tossed and fluttered in the teeth of the sudden gale. The golden monkeys made protesting noises as the wind chased them everywhere. They knew and feared the coming of the storm.

* * *

A cluster of dragon fruit, fibrous lumps the size of water melons, were loosed from their stems and, beneath the battlement walls, fell with a series of hard thumps. Deep within him, Tenzin felt a spurt of liquid ice. The storm began in earnest then and intensified with a roar, the wind shrieking as though in violent agony, driving branches, earth, and graveyard stones in all directions, continuing its tirade.

A monstrous orchid and three giant sunflowers swayed to and fro upon their long stems. Birds flew backwards. And Deng's jeep, still unmoved from where he had abandoned it on his way back from the plateau, slithered across the gravel path as though on ice, moving like a toy.

The distant Tibetan sky flashed intermittently with lightning, and the thunder in the mountains sounded like heavy machinery. Then the sky was shattered by a blue-white scar. A moment later an enormous crack of thunder came like the snap of a gigantic whip. The rain fell profusely. The higher leaves and branches were roaring like the sea. The wind became a living thing, violently punching holes in the glass windows of the temple or sending spirals of dust and earth into the air like miniature tornadoes.

Tenzin's face was twisted with agony. Between the livid zebra stripes of lightning, the air was dark and terrible under the increasing threat of the sky. He remained still, unflinching from the heavy strokes of the drops as they pounded down on his face.

Up in the cloud canyons, the thunder boomed again like an angry god.

* * *

Although weary from trials and vicissitudes, Tenzin stayed on the ramparts for another hour. The rain eventually stopped and the wind was silenced like a scolded dog, but the storm remained on the brink of violence. He stayed until it had abated to a muted hush and the golden monkeys slept fitfully once again.

The air was soft and clear as the moonlight lanced the temple and threw great blocks of shadow into the trees. Servants were already repairing the windows. The new moon-decked night gave a pale hue to Tenzin's uplifted face, which seemed carved in white jade against the alabaster walls. He raised his face up to the sky and felt the moon's light replenishing his cruelty.

He tried for a while, in vain, to formulate the future, before concluding that the world had depths of wretchedness too profound and that everything was probably nothing more than a mass of muddled colours thrown into the void by an insane painter, smudged here and there by tears and the bloodied mess of the tortured.

Thoughts beat rampantly about his heart with awful wings.

So Crowley wanted to learn more about the chemo? It would be a delight to educate him, a delight that made all other pleasures, at that moment, seem like dust. And, as an explorer, Crowley would also no doubt appreciate a sky burial, the body left whole for the stray scavenging vultures or, just maybe, to be consumed by a species so ferocious and intelligent that all other animals, without exception, were afraid of it.

* * *

As streaks of tawny light began to jab the sky, the maze of darkness sorted into near and far. At the high point, the cloudlets were warmed with pastel colours. The mist in the distance was lifting from the river, shot through here and there with oblique gold. The blonde monkey gang came to life, and a single bird flapped upwards with a hoarse cry that was echoed by another and then another. Now streaks of cloud near the mountains began to grow rosy. The canopy of the forest was green and friendly once again.

A sunbath under an unbearably blue sky subsequently emerged as the yellow orb gazed down like a scornful eye and soaked up the torrid rain from last night's storm that had scythed vegetation flat and swept the forest clean like a scoured blade.

The silence in the courtyard became oppressive as Crowley came through the high gates. Tenzin's robe that morning was blue, to symbolise winter, and green to remind everyone of the hope of spring. His withered throat was adorned with a pharaoh-like necklace as if he wore the Crown of Egypt.

Tenzin stood with arms outstretched, as if greeting the welcoming rays of the sun, noticing immediately the mulberry-coloured birthmark on Crowley's temple and the fact that Crowley's face disagreed with him as much now as it had done in Hong Kong. Crowley brushed his thin red-brown hair back away from his eyes and beamed a smile of acknowledgement at Tenzin, looking up at the temple walls and imagining the silken delights that lay within.

A smile of almost painful happiness began to draw itself upon Tenzin's lips, which were fluttering as if about to kiss. He thought, '*No more than a skull can tell us what a dead man once dreamed. And who knows what dreams, what wondrous dreams, what uttermost desires or memories, Crowley may have or still possess?*'

Having waited with laboured patience – and on Tenzin's command – the noise of the crowd sharpened, starting with a mumble, and then whistling and howling, which broke into a sort of chant that ebbed and flowed at first and then rose towards the sky like a long-lost lullaby.

Crowley had arrived. Only time would tell what fate awaited him at the temple.

* * *

That freezing night on the fortified walls, just an hour shy of midnight, Tenzin realised, with a convulsion of the mind and a little fall of the heart, that if he ever came face-to-face with the darkness of God, he would prove to be impotent in his attempt to explain humankind's essential illness.

And whatever had happened might be a judgement or a jest of the ancient gods that people worshipped from the safety of stone circles on ivory-strewn nights. But he knew, deep down, that there was no profound meaning to existence, that everyone was equally incomplete – mere pieces, fragments, shadows, and matterless ghosts – and that all humanity's ambitions, in the end, became nothing but dust.

Tenzin glanced up at the stars and realised that the time had come to slowly begin his own death. He looked deeply into the past. As a boy, he would seek to put the terror from his mind; yet he knew, as he grew into a man, that he could no longer afford to do so, for it was that terror alone which served to keep hope alive. He would rise to the ramparts as the evening light cast deep shadows under the northern most parapet and half across the courtyard pool, above which floated a faint, moving cloud of fine dust, glittering in the twilight rays of the brilliant afterglow. There, he would stare for hours until the cold and the need for sleep forced him back inside the warm walls of the temple.

Tenzin knew that, for him, darkness would begin before death. His sight was failing rapidly as if all the tears he had shed in silence for things he had done were slowly burning out his eyes. He could not endure the length of living for much longer.

But for now the moist straining orbs still reflected the enshrined mysteries of the stars and the immutable heavens, beneath which he felt very small, even superficial. He would make no complaints. His life would disappear like ancient herbs on a rooftop, with the night wind and the mountain witches toppling his tower as a different God had once felled the towers of Babel.

He would find the strength to meet death with a bright hope and would not complain of a destiny that he shared with flowers, insects, and the stars. In a universe where everything passes as in a dream, humankind would resent happiness and a contentment that would last forever. Tenzin was not sorry to know that objects, beings, and hearts were perishable, because part of their beauty lay in that very misfortune – and yet he could not accept that Mi-Sun's beauty had not remained in perpetual spring. He was unable to bring himself to feel the slightest regret, and not even the keenest grief could pierce his consciousness now. Indeed, if he could rake up all the dying embers in his heart, they would stir scarcely a fleeting flame.

Other men's hearts would burst beneath the weight of unbearable love, but their tears shall not be his tears. Hands of desire would continue to join under the jewelled cypress tree in bloom, but the same rain of petals would not fall twice on his human bliss.

"Blood of blood, dust of dust," he whispered to himself grimly, feeling like a man carried away by a flood who wished that he might find a single corner of dry land to leave there yellowed letters of his life, flaking with time.

He wished that, as life and death each mirrored the beauty of the other, his brushes, paints, and inks would occupy his last hours, like offering the favours of a harlot to a man condemned to death. But even then his imperious hand would not tremble on the silken cloth. Infinity would enter his work to be ever preserved in colours that the canvas could not show. His counter-fear would be that as he dragged his brushes and pots to the life eternal, they would turn out to be less clear in his memory than in his dreams of travel. Thereafter he would enter peace, the kind of peace which only the dead can truly possess, away from the darkness of the unclean practices of modern life.

Tenzin could still just about admire the beauty of nature. As he looked along the stone barricades painted with a soft mask of lost mountain snow, the century old cypress tree, sixty feet high, flung forward its leaf-weighted entwined branches, creating a thick dark green and mauve thatch. In amongst the wish-fulfilling gems, a corresponding scrawling blue-blond plant hung from a temple roof and spilled lavishly amongst the canopy of the tree.

The solace of the battlement walls comforted him no longer. He found no reassurance in the noises of the remote Tibetan night, the whispering of the cypress tree, the swaying of the tall grasses. When the breezes died, he felt oppressed by an unexpected sense of closeness, as though the stars were crowding in on him.

Tenzin noticed his own shadow, cast in spider-like directions against the temple walls, and thought that a shadow was a dark extension of a man which is perhaps his soul, and that the shadow is imprisoned and dies as if suffering from a broken heart or an eternity of regret. His mind and soul were filled with a great anguish caused by a combination of fear and repentance.

But what had he done earlier that night which now made his shadow flicker like a dark grey flag in the wind? There were now hawks and buzzards, normally indifferent to the temple, hanging over the limit of the battlements, gazing at what was taking place below.

There was moaning and a babble of panicked voices rising. Smoke was seeping through the branches in white and yellow wisps, the sky turning the colour of rotten orange. The shadows blew wildly in the wind.

He had been in Deng's quarters, he remembered now, the brazier moving easily from its serpent-shaped legs with a single unthinking push to hit the floor with a frightful explosion of scarlet flame, sending out a thick yellow tongue like a furious dragon. Crimson anger rose from the burning blaze within seconds.

Tenzin flinched as the glowing coals cascaded over the floor, starting a red furrow, a flurry of smoke. Amidst the stink of burning wood across the nearest rug, the dragon reached the dry tinder skirts of the tapestries on the wall between the two windows, at which point there was a sound similar to a great intake of breath, like the flyby hiss of a monstrous arrow.

A serpent of flame climbed the wall, and after it a tree of fire grew, thickening and creating lightning branches on all sides, enveloping all the space between the windows and coursing both ways like hounds at fault, to reach the dusty hangings on the neighbouring walls, which instantly glowed into quivering life.

The brittle shell of the room was ablaze in seconds, timber at the window beginning to cry out in loud cracks and splitting groans, spurting thin jets of flame. Tenzin, his narrowed eyes agog at the ill-considered thing he had done, stirred from his horrified stillness. He shielded his face and moved as briskly as he could from the terrifying heat and from the smoke clogging his lungs.

He descended the wooden steps like a black gale with a speed he did not recognise, the very threads of the stairs burning under his feet and the framework of thick smoke rolling along the stair roof. The opening of the door as he fled provided a way through for the wind that nourished the flames. Such brightness burned up at the far side of the room that he would only have had a minute or two before the inferno swept over him.

Dogs at the bottom of the stairwell were barking with fright. Several birds flapped hysterically in their cages, unable to escape.

Deng's quarters were next to the great study, where the fireplace burned. Within a matter of minutes, the two species of flame met, merged, and expanded like an alien species, now unstoppable in their crackling intention to engulf all matter, living or otherwise. Above him, Tenzin heard Rinchen shrieking for help against the furious voice of the fire.

Rinchen knotted his hands in tapestries on either side of the door where the flames had not yet reached and tore the rotting fabric down, rolled it up tight to resist sparks, and hurled it into the furnace on the other side of the room to, at least, make the door semi-passable. But somewhere in that abrupt hell, a length of blazing tapestry was blown towards him. He rolled and shrieked in agony.

He lumbered onto his feet, trying to swallow, but his tongue seemed thick with fiery dust.

The doorway was still clean, but the circling flames were licking both ways towards it. Smoke was thickening quickly, stinging and blinding Rinchen's eyes and flashing idioms of fire. Then the heat burnt through the brittle blue door and engulfed the mini laboratory. Within seconds there was the sound of shattering glass and multi-coloured explosions, one after the other, creating sudden forces that scattered books and papers like a plague of insects. These fluttered in the air before falling into the fire, adding more to the fuel of the inferno. The ice-encased specimen in the strong room melted in moments as the heat from the metal door intensified and created an internal vacuum.

Rinchen clutched a wide sleeve over his face, placed his trust in God, and stumbled towards the doorway.

* * *

On the far side of the Imperial Hall, the *Keepers of the Flame* obelisk fell. The musical doors offered no resistance as the fire tore through the wood and then engulfed the interlocking rooms beyond the courtyard, scorching the blue stone pillars and devouring the mini gallery. Mi-Sun's portrait behind the thin curtain gave a frail, forlorn look before being defaced by the licking flames. Her memory and all she had ever known was gone forever.

On the battlement steps, Tenzin was joined suddenly by Deng, their hybrid union of human and chemo blood complete. There was an urgent horn call behind them, but Tenzin continued to look ahead with his back to the temple grounds, refusing to grant personal recognition of the loud cry of the growing firestorm which he had created.

"They say fire purges everything," Deng said to his father. "There should be some solace to be taken from that." Then he was gone, moving swiftly and agilely from the battlement walls.

The dull blue shadow of the mountain maze was like a deep cancer inside Tenzin's body as he drew on all his Tibetan teachings and searched with his inner eye along the long pilgrimage of life. Tibetan piety had not changed for thousands of years, except perhaps for the quality of the souls that are taken at the end. Haunted suddenly by an evil throng of memories, each one individually immeasurable, he found that sickness clouded his thoughts, so much that he half stumbled, shivering and feeble. Daring not trust his legs to stand, he had to support himself against the high wall, his head lolling and his chest labouring as intermittent swirls of smoke eddied around him like ghostly serpents. His eyes smarted, tears swimming down his cheeks as trails of smoke snaked into his eyes.

Gone forever were the megalomaniacal beliefs that he was the mortal heir to Ekajati, who created and taught the arts of life to humankind, or even that he was linked in any way to the earthbound Emperor Tubo, the slayer of Kalsang. There was no echo of a great ancestor within him – that he could alter and shape the world – and he had not achieved his imagined rise to ubiquity that he had sought after so much since childhood, when he stared out into the mountain-clad sunsets with his father.

With a deep gleam of pain, Tenzin now seemed to belong wholly to an alien thing, a thing apart, a spirit amongst clay, a stranger amongst scenes that had once been his own. His mind was filled with sickness, for it seemed that all the stone of the temple was melting and that its massive weight was becoming nothing but an inconsistent mass of fire and smoke.

He rubbed his eyes. When he opened them again, he stared bleary-eyed but intently at the scene that was taking place below him. Deng was in the cemetery standing alongside a giant chemo, which made no move towards him.

Crowley's body, dragged out of the temple, lay now in the cemetery, still vaguely twitching and his arms by his sides like the burnt flags of a defeated country. His head had been snapped around by giant hands as he continued to stare indistinguishably and incomprehensibly into the pitiless green eyes. A claw-like foot ripped at him for a while, almost playfully, tearing one of his cheeks away in a flap, exposing the teeth on the right side. Warm burgundy blood spurted instantly, splattering on the ground. The mess the creature made of Crowley's head was revolting.

Crowley managed a final scream out of his mouth and his ruined cheek as Deng and the chemo fed on his flesh together.

Over the chemo's shoulder, the moon flooded down white light. Moonlight was the last thing Crowley saw. Beneath the gore was a final look of rest. He died covered in a saturated shroud of basted cloth within a maelstrom of powdery snow.

Soon Crowley's corpse was unrecognisable. It could have been the carcass of a sheep or goat for all anyone could tell. The chemo headed for the graveyard fence about a hundred feet away, leaving behind sets of twelve-inch-long, five-inch-wide footprints – the space between its footprints twice the length of any man's.

And the chemo would return tomorrow, as sure as the colour of evil was black.

Tenzin, breathing deeply, averted his gaze from the slaughter with mingled pleasure and disgust. He could feel his sinews giving way as his arms stretched towards the sky. He begged heaven to free him.

He turned abruptly to peer with mute fascination into the heart and heat of the inferno behind him. There was a deep grumbling noise, as though the temple itself was angry with him. The thunder of the fire increased in intensity. Frantic servants screamed and ran in confusion, scurrying and scattering around the courtyard in all directions, dragging out from the dormitories and kitchens whatever belongings they could, salvaging items from the food stores, which were located dangerously close to the original wooden structures of the temple.

A terrified horse shrieked wildly, stamping its hooves but unable to break free from its tether. Guinea hens scattered frantically, wildcats and foxes behind wire netting panicked desperately in their confined spaces, and groups of workers huddled by the courtyard pool for comfort and protection. Birds were squawking madly; smaller creatures shrieked and cowered.

The dancer from the banquet whom Deng had so admired lay ungainly on the moon-white path by the pool, charred and unmoving, her wrist stretching out slim fingers as though her nails were claws, her soft, silver face virtually unrecognisable.

No one paid any heed to an effigy of All-High Ekajati, the highest of the ancient Tibetan gods, as it was violently engulfed in flame; their lord could roast before they would risk a burned hand for him.

The cleverer ones took refuge in the sturdier parts of the temple, where the heat would be less intense, as the stone walls there were thick and the floors laid with flag stones. Here, the only enemy would be the smoke that gnawed acrid and poisonous upon the first intake of breath.

Unexpectedly, Tenzin saw Rinchen in the courtyard, tearing off what was left of his shirt to bind it round his face so as to shield his nose and mouth from the fumes. He began to move like a shambling bear towards the gates of the temple walls, which were now broken open. Kicking aside anything that might obstruct his route, Rinchen was determined to survive as long as his breath and strength lasted.

Elsewhere, columns of steam rose in places where water had been thrown over the encroaching fire. Men still carried buckets in a human chain from the well, dampening down the entrances to the lower quarters, where families of workers remained hemmed in.

Tenzin stared at the tower of smoke that rose into the sky above the spot where he had started the funeral pyre. The fire had already engulfed the central halls of the temple. The gigantic stone structure of the Imperial Hall would stand, though as a gutted shell, but the braced timbered annexes would become a furnace.

Panicked men and screaming maids blundered into the courtyard by the pool. The disaster and danger had overtaken them so suddenly that they did not know what to do. The first tree in the orchard caught ablaze, being devoured noisily and casting a flickering glow over the lake, where ducks, swans, and anything that could float sought natural refuge on the surface of the water. A flame, seemingly detached, swung like an acrobat and licked up the leaves of an adjacent tree, and then another.

The sky overhead was thick with smoke.

Suddenly, and very unexpectedly, the imprisoned chemo ruptured forth from the hatched doorway, the lock and hinges bursting asunder as the wreck of the door fell inwards. It emerged from the underworld like a mythological ogre set free from the ghosts of Hades, its monstrous image seeming to trace slow-motion patterns in the radiance as it entered the here and now.

The surround to the large cellar door was shattered into a multitude of wooden fragments with a single lunging blow. One of the snapped chains still clung to the creature's leg.

The chemo straightened upright, its high whistled scream becoming continuous and foaming. It shot forward into the open courtyard, snarling and blood stained. It paid no heed to the heavy weight of the chain, immediately clawing and savaging two people within reach, but it did not eat their flesh, as it, too, seemed panicked by the jungle of fire that engulfed both its near and far vision, including the area from which it had just come, the buttressed archways now having burst into flame to become a tinderbox.

The entire temple was ablaze and shuddering with flames. All at once, the lights that flickered ahead of the chemo merged together, the roar of the fire rose to thunder, and a tall brush in the creature's path became a great fan-shaped flame that raced forward like a tide, flapping at its face. The chemo forgot its wounds, its hunger, and its thirst and simply became animalistic fear fleeing through the courtyard, tensing against more terrors.

As he watched this from above, Tenzin's teeth were bared like the grin of a dead thing. So wide and bulging were his eyeballs in their sockets that they seemed like baubles placed within a mask. Spots jumped before his eyes and turned into red circles that expanded visibly.

A blazing portion of moraine hit the chemo. Its thick fur burst into flame, which brought the creature crashing to the ground with surprising speed. It screamed a terrible unearthly scream, its flesh shrivelling away from muscles and bones almost immediately and melting into a hideous soup like substance on the stone pathway.

Tenzin's face remained a living skull as he gazed again into the aubergine night, holding aloft the sky disc, hefting it in one hand above his head and looking beyond it to the storm-injured moon. Like a werewolf, he produced a nefarious and desecrated cry, as cold as the moonlight and as silvery as when that light shone upon the glittering plateau or breathed upon the waters of the lake urged by the faintest of breezes. The mountains echoed the sound.

It was a terrible sound of pain and regret.

"Free me forever," he shrieked, his eyes gleaming as though lit by the fire. His face was darkened by confusion and despair.

The cypress tree shimmered with a fierce light as the singing of the fire rose to a chorus, like a rioting crowd, but better harmonised – the triumphant utterance of a single will. The great tree ignited before Tenzin's eyes, three centuries of wisdom disintegrating into glittering dust within minutes and vanishing into the night air like banished spirits.

With the sky disc still held above his head, and the fathom wide grin of the skull inside a great heaviness of smoke, Tenzin allowed the vicious, malevolent scream to discharge. It hissed upon the wind and resounded multiple times, at first downwards through the temple's burning labyrinth, and then outwards across the cemetery grounds where the golden monkeys fought for their homes, moving up then into the forest, and finally drifting like winter mist across the frozen plateau.

It was a call for the second Bardo, the Buddhist belief of being conscious of death whilst still being awake in the physical world.

Chapter 11

The Second Bardo

The image of the moon fell into the river and danced there for a while before breaking up. There was a change in the sky. Just over the dark outline of the horizon, and in the expected place, the clouds lightened. Half the foothills and then the mountains were suddenly drenched in a milky light that moved closer and closer towards the ruined towers of the temple. Minutes later a winter sun entered the open space like an angry red eye and dominated the light blue fabric of the sky.

Tenzin, with Deng's assistance, hobbled with a painful stiffness, making audible sounds of discomfort as he moved slowly through the wreckage. His limbs bore the appearance of being too heavy for him, like he was personally struggling against more gravity than anyone else was.

All around him in the courtyard, and everything within view, seemed utterly destroyed – cracked marble and the pale relics of lost glory. The scene was like the aftermath of a war. A canvas awning above the servants' quarters still etched a chalky line of smoke into the sky, and here and there the wind scattered charred debris over the ground and threw black ash into the air in ghost like shapes.

The only thing untouched and normal was the glimpse through the ruined trees of the lake's crystal water, where a few ducks floated in seeming ambivalence. Tenzin shuffled out through the snow like ash and shattered tombs, where the sight of the many shrivelled limbs and wish-granting jewels of the great cypress tree, no longer claiming immortality, made him weep.

Tenzin pulled a non-wavering curtain across his mind to separate a natural instinct to flee from his conscious decision to manifestly select the method of his own demise. The divergent beasts within him would be continuously struggling and shaking the very fortress of identity, two base passions raging inside him like a cyclone, even after all these years.

There were several chemos in the grounds by the fields beyond the cemetery, gorging on the unusual morning feast of charred human flesh, or just moving around slowly together and occasionally simply standing and looking about themselves, like people admiring the view. It was clear that they had noticed Tenzin and Deng, but they paid them no heed. A flock of goats scattered in fear, heading for the safety of the hills.

Over the mountains in the east, the pinks of dawn were painting the snows. Deng moved to one side. Tenzin's frail form stood motionless, with his arms at his side, his head turned upwards to look at the dawn wounds across the sky. Perhaps a god did exist, but if so, he clearly had no interest in humanity, and humankind would never be able to locate him to ask why he was indifferent to them. Tenzin had passed through horrors and flirted with eternity. He had tried to plumb the interminable realms of space and the infinity of ages. He had spent long nights absorbed in strange sciences, trying to measure the secrets of the ancient spirits of humans and even wondering at one point if death itself might be able to be conquered.

The chemo could no doubt reveal strange wonders too, about the history of the earth back to the dinosaur epochs, and perhaps even the demoness who brought them back from extinction in Tibetan mythology.

The aeons of space passed before Tenzin's eyes. Winters of memory rolled over him in that drop of time; everything was boundless and he seemed to attain a higher state, opening his stagnant mind to the universe, tightening his perceptions like the strings of a lyre, so that his visionary senses were immeasurably increased. And he glimpsed his own eternity, also discerning that he was still close to some great secret, near to unravelling the riddles of life, and maybe those of death as well. Immortality lay in a dimension beyond life where the body is cleared of clay and the mind of mortal thoughts, where whispered voices have the sweetness of angels and where eyes are like the waters of a beautiful lake. Gone would be the earthbound buried wisdoms and long-forgotten truths of the past.

Tenzin became a boy again in his mind, tender, delicate, and thinking of Dr Schröder.

From behind the remnants of a ruined tower, a lone chemo, a colossal beast nearly twice the normal size, stepped out into the open and moved lazily towards Tenzin, huge claws scratching under its chin, seeming to regard the human being before him as a man might regard a complex problem. Tenzin felt his heart rate slow. In the near distance, the lesser chemos paused from their feeding in the gardens and rose on their haunches, silently staring at the giant beast as it towered above its human counterpart, making Tenzin's feeble form look no more than a discarded and neglected toy. Tenzin felt withered, cold, and powerless.

It was normally the time of year when the chemos moved into the higher territories of the Qinghai Plateau to graze in the uppermost hills and to live and breed in the underground caverns, hoping that they had managed to collect and encase enough meat in the ice chambers to survive until the spring. This would be their last foray into the foothills this year.

In the final moment, as the alpha male chemo towered above him, something eminently human beaconed from Tenzin's eyes. He felt crushed inwardly in that second by all he had done and the years of sordid neglect of his birth spirit and human nature as he fought in vain against a more powerful inner force.

Pride, desperation, and shame commingled at that moment and passed across his face like the passage of a storm. He saw his life as a whole. It was as if God had adjusted the colours of the world in the night and everything seemed brighter than it should have been.

He followed the brightness from the days of childhood when he had walked in the gardens holding his father's hand, moving through the self-denying toils of his religious life in the temple, to arrive again and again, with the same sense of unreality, at the demented self-inflicted horrors of that evening in the laboratory.

If Tenzin were the chief of sinners, then he was also the chief of sufferers. But in those final moments he was aware of the primitive duality of his life, the furtherance of knowledge or the relief of sorrow and suffering from both sides of his intelligence, the moral and the intellectual. He had been relentless, like a man of stone, but would now pass away like the stain of breath upon a mirror. And so would the inner dominant savagery that he had ingested sixty years earlier.

"Goodbye, Father," Deng said, bowing and walking slowly backwards inside the crumpled temple walls.

In his enervated state, Tenzin was carried effortlessly by the chemo with extraordinary speed through the tunnels of ice to the chemo citadel beneath the plateau, where he was allowed, that night, to die a natural and respectful death. There would be no feeding on *his* remains His body – persevered by the cold – was laid with some care next to the small Tibetan alter that Deng and Chu had spotted in the domed cavern as they had once peered down from the frozen bridge high above; what they hadn't noticed was the faded Nazi insignia laying behind it on a weather beaten flag. The shine of Tenzin's human eyes, brilliant and as cold as jewels, had faded from green to onyx, like an endless stretch of midnight sky, and then lost their colour forever.

His last swirling memories were that the gleaming snow was freedom, and the longing to run like a wolf, wild and cruel, hunting across the bright new-fallen snow. He longed to kill, a murderous hunger for blood. Bright poisoned blood would look beautiful splashed across the snow.

The frustration of this gave him an air of bewilderment and anger as if some perpetual source of astonishment and outrage hung in the empty air. But his last thought of all was one filled with guilt, rage, pity, and shame, all rising up within him and fighting for supremacy in that last moment.

The lord of the temple died without the faintest moan.

The alpha chemo remained there for a while, staring at Tenzin, seemingly deep in thought. Occasionally it made a gentle move towards the body and prodded it tenderly as if trying to reinstate a microbe of life.

Presently it rose and ambled away, pulling itself mournfully out onto the surface of the plateau, where even the howling wind could not cover its high-pitched scream, which continued unabated for several minutes. Then all sound had fallen away – including the birds, the insects, the wild cats, and even the water's flow. The silence, like the sky, was cold and dead.

Across the white surface of the plateau, no living thing moved other than the chemo.

The chemo was a vast ghostly shape in the gloom, stretching away high amongst the peaks, a dark form of a shadow, as if praying to a higher being, until its mammoth silhouette merged with the blizzard of snow being swept off the mountain ridges by the wind, at which point its image was overpowered and vanquished like everything else.

Chapter 12

Future Legend

Lhasa Temple, September 2020

Thirteen Years Later

Free independent thought had long been suppressed in Tibet. That suppression culminated in the invasion of the Chinese and their relentless assimilationist politics. The people of Tibet suffered terribly under Chinese rule, resistance being met with torture and death. Thirteen years before, there had been a thousand monasteries in Tibet and every fifth Tibetan was a monk. The lamas disappeared with the arrival of the Red Guard, and many of the holy sites were brutally ransacked.

Beijing officials were now the rulers, and Lhasa, rather than being the Holy City, was now merely the autonomous province of Tibet. Tibetan art had been replaced by Chinese kitsch, horses by bicycles, and religious heads by soldiers. Only certain gilded pagodas still glittered high above the confusion of everyday life in the nether regions of the mountain monasteries.

The great edifice which was the Lhasa Temple lost its position at the heart of Tibetan culture shortly after Tenzin's "disappearance" early in 2008, the once home of the Dalai Lama now becoming a tourist attraction, as was the village of Salween.

The temple had crumbled in slow motion, slower than the eye could detect even over a lifetime. Only the sun and the moon themselves witnessed the steady deterioration of the turrets, ramparts, and courtyards. These were walls that have defied aeons, the temple more ancient than any bone left in the soil.

More significantly, civil funding for the temple had subsequently been stopped, but it was provided a multi-million pound joint grant from the Chinese and Indian governments to turn the oldest part of the temple into a museum, housing the impressive array of historical artefacts for members of the public to see for the first time, locals and the nascent tourist trade alike, including the sky disc, which, because of Deng's father, had resisted the action of the great fire. Deng had personally designed the museum displays, overseeing the careful movement and written descriptions of each item, much in the same way that he had at the Yau Ma Tei Theatre in Hong Kong in 2007. Amongst other things, there was a skull set in silver, a flute made of yak bone, and a drum covered in human hide.

The remainder of the temple, mostly destroyed in the fire on account of its historic wooden structure, was being rebuilt and would become a luxury hotel, modern in its making but replicating the traditional temple imagery, amassed with beautiful suites, candle-lit ochre corridors, and hallways sparkling with opulent chandeliers, tier upon tier of intricate crystal decorating the ceilings like frozen fireworks.

Every room would have its treasures, an oriental Aladdin's cave of never-ending wonder, with carpeted indigo material containing elaborate golden designs and draped with tapestries and dark cloths, making everything look regal.

The floors and the walls would be stone, but the fittings would be wonderfully beautiful: glittering ornaments, many-coloured rugs, rich woods, bright flowers, paintings, and rare books.

Deng stood on the battlement walls and at first beheld the complex number of degrees and hues of twilight, for here it would be dark, the back-end of evening. There was a glow of rich lurid brown, like the light of some strange conflagration. Presently he turned his attention to the great scene of restoration that sprawled out behind and below him.

The restoration was nearing completion. Towards the end of the year, both the museum and the luxury accommodation complex, along with intricate ancient looking towered restaurants, would be open and fully operational.

Deng would reserve certain areas for his own private use, including the restored buttressed walkway that held the way through to the worn battlement steps which overlooked the cemetery on one side and the hotel, museum, courtyard, and sprawling slate-coloured brackish lakes and gardens on the other. He looked again towards the gardened cemetery and smiled in appreciation at the young cypress tree, the leaves purplish and sprinkled with black dots, barely standing ten feet high. He knew it would grow tall and strong in the decades to come.

A nightingale spilled a rill of song, assured of enough shade and privacy, and blessed the cypress tree with her natural music.

Deng would conduct tours of the 'Museum in the Clouds' personally, cutting a shape of clean distinction in his traditional

Tibetan dress and talking eloquently and enthusiastically about each item, which included a stuffed brown bear's head, another Schröder trophy, mounted on the stone wall along with its giant protruding teeth.

After you observed that example of taxidermy, as you turned into a cloudy lane, you beheld the sudden view of the yeti, which was a complete specimen enclosed in a nine-foot tall display cabinet, creating an optical trick. To add to the mystery, the creature was only partially visible, as it was on a rotating plinth and bathed in an eerie grey light, seeming to appear and then disappear as though from within a mountain fog, wading through snow and crossing glaciers. It had one arm raised across its enormous chest and two green-glass eyes, made luminescent and glowing out of the mist, staring out from a face of blended savagery and intelligence.

A combination of the moving platform, the deliberately restrictive viewpoint, and of course the glow of the jade light made sure visitors had only a fleeting glimpse at each rotation. The brass plaque simply read: "Fact or Fiction?"

This creature had pronounced nostrils and a long sloping nose that was covered, like the rest of the face, with short amber-white hair. The region around the open mouth and gigantic yellow teeth was heavily reconstructed with plaster or clay, while the mouth itself held a vast array of teeth on both the upper and lower jaws. There were long vampire incisors embedded in both jaws, but at the front of the mouth there was what looked like molar teeth, looking as if they had almost been inserted upside down. The rest of the body was covered in shaggy hair about six inches long, darker on the legs, white on the chest, and marmalade on the back, as if it had been made up from parts of different animals. The hands and feet were huge and splayed, humanlike.

In the museum there were winding curved walls decked with maps of the Himalayas and inlaid panel plates describing Tibetan mythology: the turquoise demoness who brought the chemo back from prehistoric extinction, the history of the sky disc, and of course, the dark legend surrounding the yeti species itself. This was the legend existing in the minds of the local people, so, for the tourists, it would mirror what they heard as they explored the local towns and villages.

The legend still had an influence on the everyday lives of the people in Tibet.

There was a mountaineering section, displaying ice-climbing gear from two centuries. And a Nazi section, stating how the Third Reich viewed Central Asia as a sanctuary for a pro-Aryan race and sought the remnants of a Nordic spiritual aristocracy, whilst later, contemporary adventures used satellites to make thermographic scans of the entire Himalayan territory, to seek undiscovered species and legendary hominids – whose images, once captured, would be sent around the globe on the Internet. This research, of course, only served to push the yeti legend even further into the realm of fantasy. Not even modern day thermographic scanners could reach below Everest into the ice caverns.

Deng smiled to himself.

Other artefacts were speculated, but one in particular was not speculated but proven. Whilst on his SS funded mission in 1938, Hans Schröder had discovered an ancient Buddhist statue buried in the foothills between Lhasa and Salween. It was called the *Iron Man*. Heinrich Himmler's belief was that the Aryan race originated in Tibet. As such, he was eager to recover artefacts from the area, including the much sought after but, at that time, undiscovered sky disc.

Schröder took the *Iron Man* back with him on his return to the Fatherland in 1942 but never told Himmler about the *Keepers of the Flame* obelisk or indeed any of the other genuinely historic and rare objects that resided at the Lhasa Temple.

In Germany, the *Iron Man* statue became part of Hitler's private collection in the Berchtesgaden. Analysis showed that it was made from an extremely rare type of meteorite, millions of years old. The *Iron Man* was returned to Tibet after the Nuremburg trials.

Deng never failed to marvel at the wondrous treasure trove of precious relics, more of which were discovered virtually daily – in the lower layered tiers of the temple, in long forgotten and abandoned rooms, behind hidden doors in the temple, and in randomly locked cupboards that held no key and had to be broken open.

He was going to enjoy his twin role as the mysterious curator of the new Lhasa museum and hotel complex.

Chapter 13

Schröder's Story, Part I

Auschwitz-Birkenau, Upper Silesia, 1944

Seventy-Seven Years Earlier

Hans Schröder sat in the commandant's villa staring at the fire. Amon Goeth had doubtless charm and his face seemed open and pleasant, but underneath he was a lunatic, lost on power and on his perceived untouchable status as the commandant of Auschwitz. He was steeled and knew he could not be touched, the very thought of which gave him the same delicious excitement a long-distance runner might have before an event he felt sure of winning. Goeth was a practical man. By no means a thinker, he nevertheless considered himself somewhat of a philosopher, especially when he drank too much, which was nearly all the time.

Goeth had arrived smiling fraternally and, in his freshly tailored Waffen SS uniform crafted precisely for his enormous frame, seemed to instantly dominate the room. His complexion was inclined to be sallow, as though he had been for some time in the tropics.

On his way through from the high iron gates, Schröder had realised with blood curdling dread how greatly the experimental and extermination camps had expanded since his time in Tibet and his long spell in hospital following the yeti attack. Although night and day were largely irrelevant in Auschwitz, tonight was gruesomely cold.

A small railway line ran from the quarry up past the administration building and the large stone barracks, bringing fresh Jews daily. The aged and the sick were to be shot immediately, and the healthy were to be marched in the direction of the work-houses.

Trolleys of limestone, each weighing several tons, were being hauled by teams of women, twenty or thirty to a team, dragging cables set on either side of the metal truck, doubled up to compensate for the unevenness of the railway track. The women who tripped or stumbled were trampled underfoot or instantaneously executed, as the team had an organic momentum and no individual could be allowed to affect the process. Sometimes the eyes in the domed watchtowers would become visible and a bullet or two fired into the terrified pack.

Schröder shuddered at the tangled pyramid of frozen corpses in one barbed wire passageway beyond the electrified fencing of the rustic railway siding – fifty or sixty deep – shamefully exposed and jumbled in a red-stained mass, their limbs madly contorted in an acreage of mud. The following day the ovens, furnaces, and pyres would work on clearing the backlog.

Many captives, barely alive, stank horribly and were seared black by the cold, mere skeletal figures at the mercy of either bullet or frost as they shambled down another pathway towards the door of the armaments hall, where piles of wire and timber lay to either side. The electrified strands of fencing, spaced at intervals, ran with several hundred volts per section.

And then there were the bloodied wheelbarrows used to transport some of the dead to the woods where already many thousands were buried in mass graves or on the verges of those eastern pinewoods that the Russians would later discover on their march from St. Petersburg and Moscow through to Berlin. Between the wheel-barrows were the gas chambers and incinerators. Nearly two million people were turned to ash or buried on the pine needles of Birkenau. As the years unveiled the particulars, it came to haunt the world and represent the ultimate example of humankind's inhumanity to humankind, unless something could be done to halt the carnage. Centuries of Jewish Poland, literally, was in the process of becoming history, flattened into ruins.

The immense complex at Auschwitz, in its safe ground in Upper Silesia, was designed to complete the great task in the east. Once the job was completed, the crematoria would be ploughed under the earth, because without the evidence, the dead could offer no witness and would become a mere whisper behind the wind, an inconsequential dust on the aspen leaves in the woods.

Outside Goeth's villa, through an opening between the gatepost, there was a way through to the camp proper, where row upon row of low-ceilinged, miserably annexed buildings, looking much like hospital wards, stretched away into the darkness with only tiny stabs of moonlight showing thin boned, hollow-faced people peering out, racked by extraordinary hunger and cold in their four-tiered bunks, some squatting, their knees pushed into their chins. Their breath froze on the walls as they crossed the borderline that separated the cavernous living from the good-as-dead. There existed not even the faintest daydream of rescue.

Schröder had mostly recovered from his ordeals in Tibet, but he appeared pale and a little shrunken. He still had some trouble walking. From time to time he shifted awkwardly as torn muscle sinews came to life with renewed pain. However, the mental anguish of the yeti tearing through his thigh muscles with claws made of something equal to the tensile strength of steel – when he allowed himself to think about it – was far worse than the physical pain had ever been.

Mengele and Himmler, both sitting next to Goeth by the fire, nursed tumblers of cognac, sipping frequently whilst Himmler blew clouds of smoke from his ubiquitous cigarette, waiting with an air of expectancy and avid tolerance as Schröder threw himself into a deep leather arm chair and took a mouthful of brandy himself.

What story did he have to tell?

A Latvian maid possessing a dark radiance, wearing a safely anonymous faded floral dress with no stockings, put down a tray of various meats and cheeses and then brought in an enormous silver pot of coffee and placed it on a sideboard underneath a picture of Jesus with his heart exposed and in flames.

She was at the same time childlike and sophisticated. She stood to attention with a jerky suddenness. Schröder noticed then the injury to her lower face, an alarming purple blotch, not covered by her collar at the junction where her lean neck joined her shoulder. The previous night Goeth had made her run up and down the villa's four flights of stairs twenty times because he had discovered a faint line of dust on a picture in the corridor. She was then beaten by Goeth and had been struck so savagely that she went sprawling. She rose and tottered when Goeth started complimenting her. He was amused to be speaking endearments to a prisoner, or even speaking to any prisoner at all.

The maid did, however, receive extra food that night compared to the other Jewish inmates' ration, but in a way this was simply a further degrading compensation.

The Latvian maid curtsied and, with shooed permission, left the room hurriedly.

* * *

Hans Schröder, like so many people before or since, had fallen in love with the Himalayan part of the world and with the people who lived there. His interest in Tibet lasted until the end of his life. The way his eyes sparkled when he began his story showed this was no invented passion. That said, and considering the audience, he took a very deep breath. He looked at times like he had a death warrant written legibly on his face.

He bit lightly on his lower lip, took a second slug of cognac, and briefly closed his eyes, as though in mourning for its forgotten taste. He had developed a defence mechanism to believe that one could drink with the Devil and adjust the balance of rights and wrongs over a tumbler of cognac. It was impossible otherwise for him to work within the SS schemes. He saw himself as Caligula the Good, more seduced by mercy than by the fear of reprisal.

Then he began talking in a slow, measured fashion, beginning his story with sombre testimony.

* * *

"I did as much research as I could before leaving Berlin. I knew that I could not just understand the yeti story scientifically, understanding purely in the" – he paused and waved an apologetic hand in advance – "the possessed genetic factors." Mengele nodded in a considered, dignified manner – a bare acknowledgement only, but one indicating that he had to accept some credence to Doctor Schröder's pretext.

It was also important to understand the genesis of the legend and its beginnings in Tibetan folklore.

"The quest for the yeti goes back as far as Alexander the Great, who in 326 BC set out with his Macedonian army to conquer the Indus Valley. He progressed almost all the way to Kashmir. The yeti, people told him, could not function properly at low altitudes, and this is why the invictus Alexander could not find one, as he was unable to reach the higher planes and plateaus of the mountains. Pliny the Elder, who in AD 79 fell victim to his own thirst for knowledge in the eruption of Mount Vesuvius, describes a yeti-like creature in the Land of the Satyrs, in the mountains to the east of India, that are 'extremely swift, able to run on two feet, have human like bodies, and because of their speed and strength can only be caught when they are ill or old'.

"The first Western description of a 'giant hairy wild man' roaming the mountains of Asia came from Mongolia, written by a thirteenth-century poet and hermit who said that the yeti, living above the snow line, was a supernatural being and forest deity that only appears to the righteous at the time of the fall moon, and that human sacrifices should be made to it on every full moon.

"And there have been second, third, and fourth testimonies. As recently as 1921, the Englishman Colonel Howard-Bury published his auto biography about leading the first expedition to the north side of Mount Everest, explaining how he saw dark shadows flitting over slopes at ten thousand feet. Later, in the precise spot where he had seen the strange creatures, he found gigantic footprints. What these dark creatures wandering over the glacier slopes were, nobody knew. But since the day of that sighting at such extreme elevation, the stories surrounding a wild man of the snows have grown in number. The yeti has become central Asia's most compelling mystery, and scientists have sometimes attempted to draw conclusions about the yeti from two million year old bones found in the vicinity of the Himalayan range.

"But, I still wondered, did legend have a real base, or were these simply the same as the fairy stories we all still have in our memories which we heard from the grandmother and the grandfather? And was the yeti just 'a different kind of mountain bear', as science and geneticists had tried to categorise it with irksome taxonomy?

"Zoologically, I found that there were three species of bear that lived in the Himalayas. One is the sloth bear, which inhabits the forest foothills up to five thousand feet, feeding mainly on termites and ants. Although the smallest of the native bears, about three hundred pounds in weight, the sloth bear is considered the most dangerous, having killed or injured more than the other two species, although mainly because they populate the low-altitude regions and they attack instantly when surprised, being equipped with long curving claws on their front legs that can disembowel a man with a single slashing blow.

"Higher up the slopes, to an altitude of six thousand feet, is the habitat of the Asiatic black bear, larger than the sloth bear, omnivorous, with exceptionally fleshy build and powerful claws that are covered with thick fur all the way down to the soles of its feet.

"Both types of bear have a crescent-shaped white mark across the chest that distinguishes them from the largest of the Himalayan bears, which is the Tibetan brown bear. This huge animal, with alpha males up to eight feet tall and weighing a thousand pounds, lives at an even greater altitude, seen at over nine thousand feet, well above the tree line. It is able to walk upright on two legs for short distances."

Goeth yawned elaborately. "You are boring us, Herr Doktor," he interjected impatiently. "It is your 'secret Tibet' that we want to hear about, not bears." But then his somewhat arrogant interruption was silenced by Himmler with a dismissive hand. Himmler was one of the few people Goeth could not challenge. This clearly rankled with the junior officer. He walked in the shadow of Himmler whether he liked it or not. With his half-completed technical education, he also felt intellectually inferior to Mengele, who sat to his left. In a way, this was an awkward session for Goeth.

"Let him finish, please," Himmler said, his voice biting and abrupt. He flared a match towards a cigarette and was momentarily lost in a fog of light blue smoke. "He is merely setting the scene." Himmler then requested, "Please continue, Hans."

Mengele said nothing, simply folding his arms and continuing to remain impassive and expressionless throughout, his face guarded and closed. Schröder took a further slurp of cognac and a large gulp of air almost simultaneously, before flashing a cautious smile of acknowledgement and continuing.

"I had decided that the brown bear's size and its high altitude habitat made it by far the most plausible candidate for the confusion with, and creation of, the chemo or the yeti, which I had discovered are merely names created for the same thing by regional dialect differences.

"I had also researched the journals of Marco Polo and his travels through Mongolia in the early thirteenth century. A leading historian suggested that Polo's reported sightings of 'mighty mountain men' might refer to polar bears, or alternatively giant pandas, both animals unknown in the West at that time. That said, *Xiong* – the Tibetan name for bear – have no real methodological significance, perhaps because they can be found from Pakistan and northern India and the Himalayas all the way down to southern China, Vietnam, Korea, and Cambodia."

Schröder explained how, with the initial research undertaken, both zoological fact and fairy tale fiction, he left Berlin as instructed, hoping to discover how closely the legend corresponded to present day reality.

"We reached Transylvania in good time, having passed through ravines of wondrous beauty in the Borgo Pass, where fog hugged the mountain flanks. King Carol greeted us at Bran Castle, as arranged. I must say that I found him a good host but one who was both haughty and strange, and more intent on control than on helping us in our expeditionary venture." Schröder paused thoughtfully. "That said, he made my stay at the castle very pleasant and provided onward supplies for the journey and also one of his highly trusted guards, Alexandru – which means 'defender of humankind' – to complement our already well-armed military contingent. We were well prepared.

"As we were leaving at dawn, an early winter sun touched the spectral hills with a streak of orange. A quilt of bare trees lined the castle courtyard. We continued east along the Silk Road, following the old caravan route which is surrounded by the Tian Shan Mountains, home to the snow leopard and lynx.

"We stopped at a busy bazaar in Kyrgyzstan to refuel and buy fresh water, and then we took over a converted tower in the primordial city of Osh, where we stayed for another two nights before heading through the Qilen Mountains on the Dunhaung-Golmud road, which is the widest and safest pass-through towards Tibet itself.

"On the morning we left, wafts of smoke and shreds of fog floated above the sparsely forested mountain meadows in the hills surrounding Kyrgyzstan. As the multitude of engines started, virtually in unison, a cloud of the most beautiful crown-necked loons rose up, flew wildly into the rain heavy fog, and disappeared into the valley. They made a sound like one I had never heard before, nor even read about. It sounded like a rusty handle being turned. They were a joy to behold."

"Oh please!" Goeth hooded his eyes, waved his hand dismissively now as if to shoo Schröder away, and stared at him with renewed impatience, but Himmler smiled at Schröder in a non-threatening way, which turned into a chortle of laughter.

"Your love of all wildlife is one of your undoubted charms, Hans, so pray continue, but please stick to the main theme as much as you can." Schröder nodded and apologised, taking yet another generous slug of bandy. Schröder despised Goeth in the simplest and most passionate terms. It was strange in a way. And despite also being a callous monster, Mengele was a man whom he respected far more, a man who at least channelled his cruelty into medical research. Goeth was murdering on a daily basis for fun.

Schröder ran his fingers through his hair in a restless, troubled manner. Sweat beads started to form on his brow. Then he blew out his breath lightly. His face seemed more composed, as though he had reached a positive conclusion on some pressing matter.

"The Arun is the largest of the trans-Himalayan Rivers, rising in Tibet and cutting through the main Himalayan chain between the peaks of Makalu and Kanchenjunga. The lower levels of the Arun basin are heavily populated, but the steep-sided valleys leading to the high peaks are virtually unexplored, even today," Schröder explained carefully. "They are thickly wooded with dense vegetation between native hardwood trees. We traversed with some difficulty but made it through. The tree line was about ten thousand feet, giving way to a barren icy landscape that, when the expedition arrived, was partly covered with fresh snow. It was here that I suspected I might have seen my first yeti prints, larger than an elephant's, with the sage brush and grass around it trampled flat."

Himmler learnt forward with his eyes twitching behind his glasses, clasping his hands like a school boy listening to a ghost story.

"*But,*" Schröder emphasised, raising a finger as Himmler deflated slightly, "I could not be sure, being aware that native encounters with the yeti are often tinged by the suspicion that the people are confusing ordinary classified animals with the mythical creature. Plus, these prints were much distorted. I was not prepared to add to the legend at that stage."

But Schröder then explained that as he lay that night in a town manor house midway between Osh and Lhasa, he heard howling high whistles and deadly growling nearby.

"I rose from semi-sleep to peer through the grimy windows of the master bedroom. A metallic sheen lay on the rocks and weeds, the mountains were obscured by a haze of silver mist, and the night seemed rich with mystery. I heard another strange cry echo across the empty sky, and then a whistling call. This could not have been the wind. But had the call come from far away or nearby?

"I stood by the window for at least twenty minutes but saw or heard nothing more, although I had a sense that something was out there, something hidden between shadow and mist.

"When I eventually went back to sleep, my dream was of being lost within a dream. A castle. Towers like slim fingers topped with witches' hats, the cladding bright through a haze of dust, as zombie humans shuffled towards a cave entrance guarded by a gigantic long-lost primate, too dangerous to be permitted to live, something that only God himself could eliminate.

"The next day, we headed due south to where the bulk of snow-capped mountains rose up from amidst steep and broken ridges, arriving at night with a wind blowing tattered storm clouds across the stars, reaching the temple in Lhasa, where we were met at the gates by a man named Kano, the temple's lord and religious leader.

"It was clear that from the fortified towers of the temple they had seen our cavalcade of armed vehicles coming along the mountain road, for behind the main gate there were two rows of temple guards with shields that gleamed like miniature suns, and ordinary temple workers massed behind them on either side. Kano stood at the front. The threatening mob in the courtyard were clearly willing to defend the temple upon his instruction."

Goeth laughed snidely with a sound like that of hailstones bouncing off a roof. "So you shot him through the head and splayed machine gun fire into the courtyard?!" Mengele smiled.

Schröder blinked twice in fast succession and was fidgety and jerky. He pulled a face of awkwardness that flushed a delicate pink, trying to control an anger that he knew would only get him into trouble if he were to let it loose.

"No," he said piously, "there was no need. And besides, going forward, I would obviously require the help of the temple workers. And we would also need further supplies." He paused. Goeth said nothing. He just sat there, grinning horribly and waving a trivialising hand. Like some dismal swamp, he was both dark and deadly.

Schröder continued undeterred. "I explained that our mission was peaceful and that the weapons were only for protection against dangerous wildlife – snow leopards, river monsters, and jackals – not people.

"Kano accepted this on face value, although he remained wary of Gerber and the mini German-Romanian army who were always egotistical and unruly, sometimes firing rifle shots into the air for the sake of it.

"The soldiers were found rooms in the servants' quarters, where I would have also been happy to reside, but at Kano's behest, a maid led me to a private bedchamber. The door was covered with a red baize. The room was large and filled with fabulous luxuries, satins and plushes, embroideries and gilts. All the rugs were Persian, mainly pink and white, the furniture ornately carved from various woods. There were candles set on antique candlesticks, and in the adjoining room there stood a marble bathtub being filled by maids with steaming water, where I presently washed away a thin layer of travel grit.

"That first night I couldn't sleep. I must confess to being filled with an electric excitement of pursuing a myth whilst based in a vast ancient temple in Tibet and so close to the mysterious Himalayas. I took out my binoculars and inspected the stars and the mountains. The air was crystal clear, and the night sounds, both near and far, were full of exquisite unseen wildlife. The night was cloudless and the pathways brilliantly lit by a full moon.

"Presently I fell into a dream of musing. The next morning I passed from my own bed chamber through rooms which in the early sunlight already seemed faded, walking down corridors with cracked flag stones, eventually finding myself in the Great Hall, where a musically hinged door led out to the gardens and lakes.

"I sat at a bronze-iron table and started to plan the early weeks, deciding that we should continue warily at first, concentrating on our secondary mission whilst still planning the ultimate journey through the barren fields, entering the lowland forest and then going on to the frozen flattened desert itself, in real pursuit of the yeti.

"But I needed more information first.

"The brightly lit gardens were deserted. Each square of lawn was like yew-clipped velvet. But presently I was joined in the gardens by Kano's son, Tenzin. I watched him come out of the grey tunnel of the Great Hall into the confusion of green after images.

"Tenzin, only ten, enquired politely if he might sit with me a while. He had a sensitive face and a marked delicacy about the baleful eyes, but because his height was outgrowing his weight, he was rather ungainly.

"I folded away my note book.

"Of course you may,' I said, smiling. He was a tall good looking boy with radiant dark eyes and a mop of black hair. There were thin furrows in his forehead, as deep as youth could make them, and his eyelids were half closed as if they bore an unendurable weight. All around us, the gardens were overwhelmed with the sunrise.

"May I ask what you are doing here?' the boy asked precociously, but also with a combined mature directness.

"I explained about our quest to identify new types of wildlife, crops, and flora, mentioning that we would be here a while, if that was okay with him. The boy smiled excitedly. 'Yes,' he said. 'My father says it is important work, so we must support you.' He paused in a considered fashion. 'May I help you too?' he asked in more child-like fashion then.

"With his father's permission, I enlisted the services of young Tenzin. And through Kano I also met and employed the services of a local naturalist. Between the three of us, we set to work, rambling through dripping woods, or over silver-dewed rice fields, marking the birds and their custom and their songs, and carefully packing up a voluminous natural history collection – animal and bird skins, butterflies, bees, ants, wasps, and other insect specimens; fragile dried plants for the herbarium; packets of seeds containing one thousand and six hundred varieties of barley, several hundred varieties of wheat, and many more of oats and teas; not to mention multiplicities of seeds from other potentially useful plants."

"These seeds collected from my various regional expeditions in Tibet, especially in the lowlands near Salween, were important, as, Heinrich ...?" Here Schröder offered an opportunity for interjection, but then he continued when Himmler signalled his approval. "We also planned to develop hardy new varieties of crops in order to boost the agricultural yields of our new colonies across the Eastern territories of the Ukraine and Crimea. I set to work with vigour, as you have seen from my report. You will also have noted that I have proposed the founding of a teaching and research institute in plant genetics. I would of course need a staff containing several research scientists, but I will call it the Ancestral Legacy Division." Schröder paused and scanned his mini audience. There was no response other than from Goeth, who issued forth a short obsequious snort.

Schröder ignored this and continued unabated.

"I led a small armed expedition into the lower foothills to capture a brown bear, the closest known creature that I could find associated to the yeti legend. After a day or so, all we found of interest was a takin, a rare antelope-goat creature, but then we managed the feat quite easily, although it was against my natural instinct to kill such a beautiful beast.

"The bear was placed in the ice dungeons. Later that night, I tried to persuade Kano that I needed some dedicated space at the temple to set up a small laboratory so as to undertake examinations, experiments, and tests of a varied nature as the need arose. Kano considered me with a profound professional interest, and smiled in the affirmative.

"He suggested I use the annexed chamber inside the great study. I inspected this facility later that night and concluded that it would be perfect – enough space, with hidden inner rooms, and completely shut away from inquisitive eyes.

"Only Kano and I had keys to this hidden laboratory.

"My analysis of the brown bear was quite conclusive in the sense that, despite its size, weight, and predatory disposition, it was a simple unalloyed sub-species of bear and not in keeping with the wild tales of a giant humanoid monster that could slaughter yaks with one blow and live in the coldest terrain for months on end, even underground. Also, whilst the brown bear would eat any type of flesh quite happily, it had no great preference for human flesh, which was one of the key facts associated with the yeti legend.

"But it was midway through my time in Tibet when I realised that I might be on the edge of a great discovery.

"It started when I was taken by a guide and interpreter from the temple through the unpaved winding lamp lit backstreets of Salween early one evening.

"The guide assured me, being from the temple and amongst his own kind, which meant I did not need an armed guard, but Gerber insisted I take Alexandru with me, who mirrored my movements with a loaded rifle and two grenades fixed to his belt. Alexandru was the Transylvanian soldier assigned by King Carol; he was quite an old soldier with a mahogany-coloured face and who seemed indestructible, but in fairness he was doing his job rather than overtly looking for trouble. He said nothing throughout the trip, simply looking out for me as King Carol had instructed him to do.

"The village was adjacent to a tiny tea plantation and surrounded by thorn bushes, termite cities, and stone barriers. As such it appeared eerie and desolate in the red light of the setting sun.

"Piles of firewood stood like sentries in front of the lime-washed mud huts and half-timbered houses, all of which had colourful window banners and bright prayer flags fluttering from the thatched roofs and trees. Bluish spirals of smoke rose over the roofs and were blown into the valley by a cold wind coming down from the mountains.

Men and children stood by the edge of the water, virtually motionless on either side of a beaten track that lay parallel with the river, heavy with melted snow, and only a stone's throw from the bank, whilst women carried stone blocks weighing hundreds of pounds on their backs.

"The river was bearded with plant life, like a pebble entwined with weed. The reeds themselves might have been made of bone. Smoke from braziers dirtied the air and cast a myriad of shadows. The last of the sun glittered from the river water in molten shapelessness.

"Trees lifted busy green crowns heavenward. Bright iridescent winged insects buzzed as they flitted from branch to branch, birds trailing long tail feathers as they dipped and soared in search of insects. Beetles scurried amongst leaves and fallen branches like ambulatory jewels. A deer appeared, saw us, and bolted back into its pen.

"I felt a sense of eyes, thousands of eyes, watching me across the deceptive embroidery of the water like sparks of cold fire. But then I convinced myself that this was the ripples of the water lit in the dying sunlight.

"Then I saw something else – something that startled me. In the middle of a grassy copse of barley stood a dung-smeared scarecrow made of wood, rags, and scraps of stained cloth. My guide explained that it was a traditional belief – a way to protect the village from demons, monsters, and spectres. Another bird came out of the sunblind but did not go near the scarecrow.

"The guide took me into an impoverished yak hair tent, close to where the fishing boats danced by their nets. The tent consisted of a single large space but was tightly packed. To the right of the tent's entrance was a sack of pressed cheese, a container of cooked meat, a trunk filled with other supplies, and a yak-hide bag full of barley. To the left were water containers, two of wood and one of clay, a cask of butter, a pail of milk and a bucket of yogurt. In the corner there was an oven covered with tarnished pots and utensils and a separate special oven for roasting barley.

"The dying sunlight crept down the trees, touched the hide curtains on one side, and then slid down and shone from the surface of a polished bench.

"The light found a face. I met an old woman of some wisdom and character. Her face was craggy, but not in an overly worn way, the way that tells of a life too hard. It was rather one of a lifetime of experience, of a life well lived, with ample degrees of respect, laughter, and kindness.

"She was known locally as the Sky Woman, having been born in the higher ridges of the Himalayas and raised in a mountain monastery. Her face had been ravaged by sun and frost, her lips were cracked, and she knew how fleeting time was, how soon the present becomes the past and the important becomes the irrelevant. In this hallowed and ancient Himalayan village, the trees had seen the centuries blow past in the winds of each season and witnessed the folly of human struggles.

"The dust of the place was on her face and her body. It was also in her hair, which was tangled as a briar, pinned back with a coral pendant. A golden shimmer seeped through the makeshift window. On the walls of the tent, masks hung alongside skulls painted on cloth. Above them were stuffed animal heads, hunting trophies of elk, wild boar, deer, and yak.

"Next to the Sky Woman was a family altar on which sat bowls of holy water, butter lamps, and a treasure chest, the last of which could be added to but not taken from.

"She blinked, put one hand up to her forehead, and initially seemed hesitant. But after that she spoke quietly, like a physician explaining a disease. I heard not only the village stories of spirits and ghosts and of an ancient fear seeping out from the mountain forests, but also something else.

"Real evidence, perhaps?

"She unravelled a piece of cloth, which seemed baked in some dark paste, and handed me a savage fang some eight inches in length, half an inch thick, and slightly curved. It was rotten and stained and looked like yellow ivory.

"I knew from the experiments and research I had already done that this was no bear's tooth. It was the wrong shape and larger than even the tooth of the high mountainous brown bear. I was slightly perplexed and asked if I could take it back to the temple with me. The woman was at first resistant, but then my guide explained that Lord Kano would ensure that it was safely returned to her the next day. She paused for a moment, rewrapped the fang in the cloth, and handed it to me.

"I stayed a while and drank some butter tea with her. Then I asked if she knew where these creatures lived.

"She didn't hesitate before saying, 'Shambhala.'

"Research had told me that Shambhala was part of Tibetan Buddhist and Hindu culture. It is mentioned in various ancient texts, including the Kalachakra Tantra and the Zhang Zhung Scripts of western Tibet. The Bon scriptures also speak of a closely related land called Tagzig Olmo. The name is also to be found in ancient Sanskrit.

'But isn't that a mythical kingdom?' Schröder asked the Sky Woman.

"Her response was both nonchalant and definite: 'No. It has become mythical due to thousands of years of fear. Shambhala is "hollow earth", a land beyond the horizon.' And then, more precisely, she said sharply, 'The yeti lives in the opposition between civilization and wilderness. They dwell in a gigantic ice palace beneath Everest, where nothing else on earth could ever live, and they have flourished there for millions of years.' Then she leaned forward and carefully lowered her voice.

"'They roam at night in search of human flesh through the vast regions between the uppermost villages and the glaciers. They are basically night creatures, wreaking havoc with the native herds, tearing humans to pieces, and then dragging them up into the mountains and down under the plateau into their ice caves.'

"She then told a story of how a woman in her late twenties, having heard her small son screaming, ran to where the child had been tending the herd. The mother was horrified to see a huge unknown creature carrying the boy away, teeth and claws bared, ripping into his face and seemingly eating his feet. The boy looked like a doll in adult hands.

"She didn't have weapons. And by the time she could have rounded up men with clubs and knifes, it would have been too late. So she instinctively grabbed a thick branch and began beating the creature until it dropped the child, but not before damage had been done.

"The Sky Woman looked half-blinded with tears as she waved a summoning hand, whereby a man with a face so pale it was almost paper white appeared in the hut. From a distance it looked as though he was smiling, but as he drew closer, I gasped. The man had two horrendous scars, one on each side of his mouth, twisting all the way up to his ears as if someone had attempted to cut his face in half. I also noticed the stubs of his amputated toes.

"He was a gaunt man of indeterminable age. As he perched on a cushioned footstool, crossed his legs, and leaned back, he put the tips of his fingers together. An emerald ring sparkled on one of them.

"I asked for his story. Although he considered this for a moment, he merely stared at me. It was as if he had lost the capacity for speech. The colour of his face deepened, catching up the sunset and passing on the colour. I indicated a second time that I wanted him to give me the details about the features of the animal that had mauled and scared him. There was a long pause. But then he laughed and simply ambled out of the hut.

"The woman turned to me and asked abruptly, 'Do you believe in them?' She pulled her pelt scarf around her shoulders as if suddenly cold.

"I thought about this and replied, with a short laugh, 'I am not here to believe. I am here to search and discover.'

"However, there was something bothering me, so I decided to ask her something directly. How these creatures had managed to survive was deeply mysterious, but how they could die without leaving a trace was a deeper mystery. The Neanderthals died out many millennia ago, and yet we have found their remains. If yetis or chemos really did exist, there had to be bones, or at least a hide.

"She laughed with a backward shake of the head and said, 'Wherever a chemo dies, the body is taken to the ice caverns and allowed to be preserved. It then slowly disintegrates over time. All the bones are piled up in a vast container inside Shambhala.'

"I felt exhilarated suddenly at the thought that I was looking for a breed of hominids with an incredible capacity for survival. I knew that one of the explanations was that about a million years ago, there were many species of hominid apes in Africa. These apes then spread across the African continent, Europe and Asia, and here in the mountains they turned into yetis, whereas in Europe they evolved into people – but we had been one and the same at some point in evolutionary history.

"As I got ready to depart with my good natured guide and superfluous rifleman, I asked the Sky Woman to draw a chemo for me. She drew a sketch of an animal I did not recognise. She also showed me a yellowed newspaper clipping of a yeti hand, which looked like an oversized hairy human hand but with vast claws. It was clear to me now that I was examining a type of creature of which we had no previous experience in the wild, Schröder in zoos, or in literature.

"Just before I left, the Sky Woman froze as if facing a poisonous snake. There was a faint whistling noise down river at the same time.

"'The water of the river raises not a bubble; it wells,' she said drearily. 'It dances to itself night and day and spews a stream of clearness and life for the grasses and the flowers. The mountains rise about me, the river runs by me, but the water is dark for all the sun.'

"Men outside the hut looked at each other and rubbed sweaty palms on their linen kilts, then held them up, palms outward. The semi-clothed children began to call out and run round, until the women bent down in their threadbare robes of thin linen and shook them into silence and stillness.

"The Sky Woman murmured in a mild voice. 'The river is filled to the brim, and the blue poppy lies open…find the chemo and kill them!' She handed me a cross. It appeared made of gold and was beautifully worked with semi-precious stones.

'Where did you get this from?' I asked in surprise. I was no expert, but its value seemed far in excess of anything that might be owned by a lowly village elder. The Sky Woman didn't answer my question. She just simply said: 'Take it with you to Shambhala. It will help protect you,' at which point she simply shrank back into the shadows.

"Later that night in the laboratory, I undertook a more detailed inspection of the giant tooth and the cloth in which it was wrapped. A rudimentary test revealed that the dark stains on the material were human blood and that the fabric also contained, strangely, traces of calcium and caffeine.

"Turning my attention to the giant fang, I could see that it was probably canine, although it might possibly have been a secondary incisor. It had a helical inner structure. Continuous growth would have been enabled by formative tissues in the apical openings of the root of the tooth.

"It was also denser and much heavier in weight than would be considered normal for modern tusk species, completely different, for example, from elephant and walrus ivory. I could think of no zoologically categorised creature on earth that possessed such canine characteristics, although I did remember an analysis of a mammoth fossil found in Colombia that had similar qualities.

"At this point I therefore concluded that the tooth must be a prehistoric relic of some kind, a type of humanoid ivory. However, I then undertook a basic radiometric dating test, which revealed that the tooth still contained trace matter of residual soft tissue, meaning it could not have been more than two or three years old." Schröder paused dramatically for effect, and suddenly his mini-Auschwitz audience seemed captivated, particularly Himmler. He continued: "Although the yeti myth had spread globally and in many ways did not fit into a rational, tangible world and seemed largely a product of imagination, the creature's actual existence, in which I now believed firmly, could only be established by going to where it lived, so leading an expedition to the plateau to search for the Shambhala ice chambers was the next logical step."

Chapter 14

Schröder's Story, Part II

Travelling to the Plateau

"The night before we left for the plateau, I had a meal with Kano and young Tenzin, and I consciously thought then what I had already come to realise about Kano, what a deep and wise man he was.

"He had said, 'How all of life is but a dream. Although we may think we see it clearly, it is we who are the shadows, for the world is but an image of spirits and our passions are naturally as swift as the winds. How else but by the enlargements of anticipation and memory does our human instant differ from the mindless movement of nature's clock? Life is a personal matter with a single fixed point of reference.'

"In my bedchamber later, I thought about what he had said as I listened to the storm rumble and growl in the mountains. It was dry to the south. The double darkness blew cold on a sudden wind towards the temple.

"Mountains surrounded the temple on all sides. The black storm crept into view. I watched it without expression. Where it passed there were flashes and dazzles lower down, so that the storm cloud left a glittering snail trail behind it. I watched the cloud drag its smears of falling rain out of sight. The wind elected to drift my way so that the giant cypress tree just below my window stirred its leaves, woke, roared, and then was silent again.

"For seemingly no reason, various ill-defined thoughts were suddenly spinning madly in my mind.

"I awoke to moonlight, cheating the nascent sunrise by about an hour, and then started preparing myself for the adventure that lay ahead.

"Presently, the sky on the horizon was breaking into day, crimson enhanced with blue – not the dark blue of midnight, hardly to be distinguished from black, nor the dense, grainless blue of midday, but azure with specks of white in it – seeming to shine from beneath the surface of the sky.

"As we set off, the emptiness of the landscape spread before us like a threat. Everything seemed fierce and barren. A sea of mist enveloped us, with only a scrap of forest visible in the distance.

"Far to the right there stretched a ridge of mountains. In the still semi-darkness to the west, there seemed nothing but rock, gnarled and bossed and blackened like an Egyptian corpse. The grasses in the fields by Salween were abundant and blonde-topped, restless with the fiddling of crickets, and the skies plentiful with the music of the many vesper sparrows. The distant hills seemed to hold no life at all.

"Our heavily armoured vehicles drove forward until they came to a point where the slopes above the cleared area were blocked by tall trees and the forest floor appeared coated in thick green fur. The sky was mostly grey. Just when it began clearing, new clouds rolled in, fast and ominous, making us feel trapped within the tree line. Further penetration through the forest and up to the plateau would be possible now only by foot.

"The engines were silenced. The guards jumped down and started to off-load the critical equipment – weaponry, munitions, ration packs, night-vision equipment, flamethrowers, and flashlights. The flamethrowers were an after-thought. But Heinrich," Schröder said, acknowledging his superior officer with an open hand, "you had made a perceptive comment in Berlin, that being, 'However ferocious, gigantic, intelligent, and strong they are – every species on earth is afraid of fire!'

"There was a basic military unit of four storm troopers, plus Gerber, Alexandru, and me. Gerber, a pair of binoculars in one hand and a sniper's rifle in the other, barked out the orders and assigned duties. The jeeps were refuelled in case there was ever the need for a rapid escape. A large tent was being erected. One of the soldiers collected wood for a fire that would serve a triple purpose: the provision of warmth, a means of cooking food, and a constant flame to ward off unwanted visitors, as bears, tigers, and snakes are all prevalent in the foothills of the Himalayas.

"The storm troopers would take it in turn to tend the fire and stay awake to guard the entrance to the tent.

"The guns were loaded with ammunition, and the three flamethrowers were tested, spewing forth a red ejaculation of fire in the direction of the farthermost trees, where the nesting birds took off in a multi-coloured cloud, startled and wheeling above our heads. Two huge Dobermanns, which Kano had lent us from the temple, trained to kill under order as temple protectors, were unleashed to roam freely in the nascent campsite. They would stand no chance against a tiger, but they were, nonetheless, a dangerous deterrent against smaller predators.

"Gerber, clearly in control, stood in the centre of the campsite, a bandolier of grenades fitted neatly across his chest in a harness.

"Whilst all this activity was going on, I sat on a moss coloured rock, took out a map, and looked at the tangle of red and blue veins which outlined the way up to the land of snows we would need to reach. The Sky Woman had described the route. Although not an easy trek, at least we had a basic target area to head for.

"We didn't have a plan for how we would go about photographing a yeti, nor indeed what we would do if we encountered one, but I had brought with me several motion sensitive cameras, a recent German invention which I'd been privileged to have demonstrated to me in Berlin. I decided that as we had no real strategy for finding a yeti, we would just affix the cameras at various points and I would send temple workers to collect the evidence later in the hope the devices had captured something of interest. I put one of the cameras on a tree in our campsite to watch over the vehicles. Three more would be placed en route to the plateau.

"It was damp and cold, a sunless day. I stared up at the forested slopes. A flock of birds rose above a clearing – vultures! What did this mean? Maybe a yak had died or there was something lying amongst the rock ridges, bluffs, and gnarled weeds? Whatever it was, the flock of vultures kept hovering over the same spot.

"I sincerely hoped it was not an omen of some kind."

Chapter 15

Schröder's Story, Part III

Shambhala

"The following day, ice crystals glittered on the inside of the tarpaulin of our tent. The air was clear.

Objects and sounds could be seen and heard at great distances. With the storm troopers leading the way and covering the rear, we spent the vast majority of the day climbing from our forest campsite, heading upwards towards the frozen desert.

"The mountain winds blew harder, and the birdsongs below us in the trees became softer and more intermittent. I could hear nothing but my breathing, the echo of my steps, and the distant sound of the waterfall as it flowed with an endless supply of semi-melted ice from the plateau to keep the lower forestry verdant.

"The path up through the tree line was arduous. I was worried that at any moment it would peter out. I struggled for a moment to navigate a giant cedar tree in front of me. The armed troops, despite their training and fitness, also struggled, yet we pushed on, eventually coming upon a small clearing, where we rested for a while. It was obvious that we were close to the plateau, as tiny particles of ice were forming on the soil, there was not a single form of life to be seen, and there was no scent of animals in the air.

"However, what I did notice were strands of ochre hair, like threads of fire, caught on twigs, plus snapped branches and heavy rocks, the latter of which appeared to have been moved or thrown in a seemingly effortless manner. As I tilted my head back, pleased for a pull on a flask of schnapps, I noticed oblique movement. Then, all of a sudden, we heard a light whistle as a cloud of snow fell through the trees.

"Something was there.

"Instinctively, Alexandru opened fire, shooting multiple bullets upwards, which shattered the edge of the plateau and caused a tonnage of ice to cascade downwards. Fearing a full avalanche, we moved swiftly to the other side of the clearing and watched as the dislodged sheets of ice hit trees and rocks around us.

"Gerber's eyes locked on him like gun sights: 'We wait until we see an enemy before we shoot,' he said angrily. 'Next time I will shoot you.' Alexandru nodded imperceptibly and adjusted his stance in acquiescence.

"We perched on a rock spur and stared downwards through the forest, in case an attack should come from below. We were shivering with cold and couldn't sit still anymore. I found myself sweating despite the chill in the air. The trees created a canopy of darkness. The soldiers scanned the terrain ahead with flashlights. The cream sunlight which inhabited the sky above the trees made virtually no penetration.

"I fixed the last of the cameras here.

"The slope ahead was extremely steep and arduous. We knew that any creature that lived here, if indeed any did, was stronger than any of us. We rose up onto the plateau with difficulty. You cannot imagine such a sudden drop in temperature and difference in landscape. The winds screamed, and the particles of ice in the air stung like needles. The wind carried every sound up to the mountain ridges and over the edge of the forest's canopy. The air was strikingly thinner, the ever-present cold our nemesis. For every step forward, we slipped backwards as much.

"We continued out across the plateau. The wind made talking impossible, howling sharply. Crossing the icy desert was a soulless endeavour until we saw something that defied belief. It was an entrance to what looked like a white castle, glowing like crystal, sparkling like a cut diamond. It rose out of nothing, disappearing and reappearing in the freezing fog. It was windowless perfection. Shambhala! The underground ice kingdom of the yeti. There was no question that this was an entrance created by design and purpose, and not by nature, the openings being carved too precisely.

"Naturally, we entered with trepidation, my mind a whirl of options. We soon found ourselves in a vast chamber, at least two hundred feet high and several acres wide. Everything was white – everything. Just as the Sky Woman had described, it was an everlasting palace of snow and ice, the gleaming complex extending incredulously before us.

"Intricate chambers ranged in size from half a metre in diameter to several metres across, all seemingly interconnected. Some tunnels arced deeper into the maze, whilst peculiar conical pits dead-ended in the floor, so precisely was the underground complex forged. There were also sub-floor conduits. My mind was spinning like a dynamo, exploring options, considering and disregarding possible solutions. Moving forward didn't take much thought, but choosing which way to go in the rat's nest of connections was recondite in the extreme.

"Then I made my decision.

"Gerber barked an instruction. For the first time I was grateful to be accompanied by the storm troopers, who, sensing danger, made arms ready, preparing for any uncertainty that might lay ahead.

"The multi-coloured reflections that pirouetted around the ice caverns illuminated our way, but also played tricks, our own shadows flat as if cut from cardboard, the silvery patterns deep and clear-edged. The wind that howled above and around us buffeted nerves more than bodies.

"It was becoming increasingly difficult to distinguish between harmless natural phenomena and inimical movement. Through a hole in the ceiling at the end of the passageway, thick mist swirled in from above. And, just then, without hearing movement of any kind, a monstrous black shadow loomed before us like cancer and darkened the passageway ahead. One of the storm troopers opened fire. The ice wall in front of us exploded into a thousand smithereens just as if someone had thrown a diamond hand grenade.

"The shadow vanished. The wind on the surface of the plateau howled above us like a defeated spirit. Then, as the swirling frozen dust settled, everything seemed for a moment silent and still. But beyond the now fragmented wall, we came upon a cavern full of the sounds of agonized moaning, the semi-daylight casting flickering movement against the tortured walls.

"We stepped inside the chamber, a dead smell in the air. Another encrusted wall lay directly in front of us. It was marred by bulges and ripples and had been sculpted by some unknown hand, a teratogenic birth of Rodin's *Gates of Hell*. We walked around this wall which did not entirely block the entrance to the chamber that lay beyond. I must admit that I was trembling with a combination of trepidation, cold, and intrigue. What we saw therein would haunt my dreams forever.

"I found myself staring in a horrified daze. And despite the temperature, I felt sweat pouring down my forehead and under my arms. Anxiety and nausea raced in the pit of my stomach. Dante could not have imagined this in his wildest nightmares, nor Poe in the grasp of one of his uncontrollable delirium moods.

"Like the sound of a stone being dropped into a well, comprehension at first came slowly.

"The walls around us subsumed human shapes, the bodies of the unfortunate who had been brought here to become frozen food for the yeti community. Their entombed figures gleamed like insects frozen in amber. Some dead eyes met ours immediately, whilst other figures writhed and moaned.

"Encased in the first section of wall, like a butterfly on a mounting pin, was a terrified child, barely able to move or speak. The child was emaciated, dirty, and wounded, the skin taut around her small face. She looked more fragile than a toy doll. Her dark hair was tangled and matted, a garland of steel wool framing her face.

"We now had some idea of what we had stumbled across and were all momentarily too numb with horrid fascination to converse with each other as we scanned the chamber and saw the numerous men, women, and children held captive by ice clamps, their skin preserved by the freezer-like conditions, just waiting to be eaten.

"My gaze returned to the child. I have never known such heart felt emotion. I gestured to Alexandru and said, 'Free her.' Alexandru looked to Gerber, waiting for orders.

"You're not hearing me.' My voice rose to a level I had never known before. 'I am head of this expedition!' I shouted. 'Free her immediately.'

'You are the more senior rank,' Gerber acknowledged, an edge creeping into his voice, 'but I am head of security. Do you think you can help any of them anyway?'

"The girl's eyes fluttered open, pleading. At that moment she became briefly aware of her surroundings – cocooned in the pillar-like structure. She was unresponsive but not comatose, silent but not mute, and she let out a soft groan of pain. Her gaze darted right and left, at which point Gerber stepped forward and drew a Luger from his waistband. The cocking of the weapon made the girl's eyes and attention spin into sudden life. A high pitched scream reverberated from her tiny vocal chords, at which point Gerber shot her straight through the head.

"Her head exploded like an over ripe melon. Brain matter hit the wall in a grey and brimstone-red splat, hung there for a while, and then began to drip in thick globules to the floor.

"It was, in my opinion, an unnecessary crime of singular ferocity. I staggered back, appalled, not trying in the least to conceal my disgust, my skin physically crawling, my face contorted by bitterness and loathing.

"But Gerber gave no heed to my anguish, and again did not consult me before instructing Alexandru and the other soldiers to kill all the entombed prisoners, each one caught in a rictus of agony.

"The soldiers carried out their orders with a combination of bullets and flame. The flamethrowers went to work, heat and light filled the chamber, searing the walls. Deafening screeching echoed all around as fire leapt over the entire area of the chamber. The walls melted and puddled around the soldiers boots like liquefied steel. It seemed at one stage as if even the ice itself was on fire. There was a thick organic stench of burning flesh in the air.

"What could I do? I could only stand and watch the horror unfold around me. This action did put the traumatised victims out of their misery. I could predict there and then that if this was the yeti's 'freezer of food', then the yeti community were not going to accept what we had done lightly.

"On the far side of the chamber, blocks of ice had been used to create a makeshift balcony. Turning my back on the carnage behind me, I peered over the edge of the balcony. The scene that faced me was astonishing and, again, was exactly as the Sky Woman in Salween had described. The entire space, descending some fifty feet across and God knows how deep into the earth, was filled with bones, thick structures of tarnished ivory-mandible, the remains of hundreds of dead yetis that were brought here to ensure that their remains were never found. In some cases, with the newer ones atop the pile, hair and skin was still attached. As we stood close, the stench of rotting flesh was putrefying and mordant.

"Regaining my senses, I took back some control of the situation and told Gerber that although I respected that he was responsible for security, if he didn't now adhere to the zoological objectives of the mission, then I would report back directly to Himmler that he had destroyed any chance of our understanding the origins of humanity and the creation of the master race.

"Gerber thought seriously about this. After a moment, he nodded, saluted me, and asked for instructions.

"But just at that moment, we heard a high pitched whistle echoing through the web-like tunnels. Something was upon us. We could sense it even if we couldn't see it, like a wave rushing up a black sand beach at night. Uncertain movements were glimpsed dimly, nightmare shadows moving in ghostly silence beyond the decimated wall, the vast shadow of a creature clearly visible.

'Do we fight our way out?' Gerber asked, almost sardonically, as he swung his machine gun into the ready position on his support arm.

"I looked around the now decimated cocoon chamber. The chamber suddenly had the image of a dome pulsing from within. The effluvium of death was all around us. The chamber had been baptised in blood, and the mordant perfume of burnt corpses emanated from it amongst the flamethrower smoke. The dead lay twisted in fantastic postures. It seemed to me – staring at them through the smoke – like they were the victims of a volcanic ash explosion.

"Alexandru made his flame thrower ready and awaited further orders.

"I pursed my lips, trying to analyse rather than react emotionally. 'Schröder, we just need to get out alive,' I said. 'Now that we know what's here, we can come back better prepared and with more men from the temple, and more ammunition.'

"In the midst of the chaos and confusion, I looked around and saw that on the far side of the chamber there was a route down into the adjacent side of the maze complex via vitreous steps where a corridor forked, a frozen chute.

"But before we could move, a faint hint of movement caught our attention. Suddenly an enormous beast emerged from behind the shattered wall where the shadow had been. For a moment, the beast seemed to simply examine the situation, taking in all the bullet riddled and charred human remains, all melted out of their ice prisons and lying in various crumbled disfigured states.

"The yeti raged into the chamber, front limbs flailing. Two soldiers opened up simultaneously, laying down arcs of fire like welders sealing the skin of a tank. In the confined space, the din from the heavy weaponry was overpowering and a virtual curtain of ice dust flew up like a curtain.

"Alexandru's fingers tensed reflexively on the trigger as a steady blue flame hissed from his flamethrower muzzle like an oversized lighter. A jet of flame engulfed the ice dust, turning it into a multitude of raindrops, which fell splattering.

"Behind the curtain the yeti had vanished.

"We made a dash for the steps, speed more important than visibility or silence. One of the soldiers slid all the way down, landing unsteadily on his feet, clutching his rifle in one hand, ready for action.

"Then we worked our way through the maze. The deeper we went, the more everything took on the appearance of having been grown or secreted rather than built. The frozen labyrinth looked like the interior of a gigantic organ or bone, but not a human organ, nor a human bone. The wall substance was opaque. What little colour it displayed was muted greens and greys, and here and there a touch of some darker green.

"One passageway was so narrow that we had to stop momentarily and turn sideways to slip through it as mist swirled into the corridor from jagged gashes in the ice walls, concealing what lay ahead. I was grateful for the respite, no matter how temporary. Then the mist cleared enough for us to examine the shaft. It definitely led to the surface. The climb was steep climb but not long. Dim light marked the end of the ascent. From above we could hear the wind booming like air blowing across the lip of a bottle.

"We felt as if we were being followed, but that might have been paranoia. But then paranoia turned into reality as the tiny movement we'd detected at the end of the tunnel, a shape that bounced off the mirror-bright walls, coalesced into the advancing outline of yeti. And there was something else, a noise reverberating at regular intervals like the thunder of a massive gong, followed by the nerve-racking scraping of claws against the solid ice walls.

"My blood was suddenly deafening in my ears as I strained to hear the noise again, which was getting closer.

"Gerber and I exchanged a glance, staring at each other as though we knew we were encountering a new and deadly species, but then he moved quickly, using a flamethrower first to sterilize the corridor ahead, letting loose incinerating blasts at regular intervals, the ice walls melting and then reforming as an opaque pavement beneath our feet. The creature ahead disappeared with remarkable speed, like a frightened snake.

"The storm troopers shouldered their equipment as we escaped into the open, where the wild wind cut us like knives.

* * *

"Somehow we managed to retrace our original course down through the canopy of trees, and presently stopped in a small clearing, a dark patch stretching between coniferous trees and glistening black rock. The waterfall was as grey as fog in the distance, and the light spray tasted of rock and dirty snow. A heavy mist was upon us. I was breathing heavily. Then, remembering the camera, I quickly located it and retrieved it.

"What, if anything, it contained would have to wait, because just then we heard more movement from a place close by, but higher, as if something had followed us from the plateau. Then it was nearer still, almost upon us. The troopers stared at each other, uncertain, seeing nothing. They recoiled slightly and clutched in desperation at their guns as if they were a type of magic wand that could be used to protect them against witches and demons.

"Then the whistle noise turned into a mighty roar. We were being hunted. And out of the shifting insubstantial mist, there leapt the sudden presentment of a monster.

"A huge creature of broken branches, rolling stones, and waterfall mud burst into view like a monstrous paw. It reared higher than any bear and seemed twice the size of any man. Its teeth were yellow, exposed with rancorous intent.

"A gun was fired instantly.

"It was unclear whether the bullet hit the target, but it did not seem to hinder the beast in any way, which attacked immediately, with the speed of a man avoiding a snake, turning the first storm trooper upside down and whirling him around with embedded claws locked like metal bars across his chest. The monster was so efficient that there wasn't even time for a scream, just the spurting of blood and a slumped human form on the ground.

"It threw another down, crushing the head against rock, twisting and breaking limbs like straw. Incredibly the yeti then opened its mouth to its fullest capacity, tore a huge section out of the midriff of one of the troopers, and began eating him, throwing back its head to consume chunk after chunk of human flesh as an alligator might consume a zebra trying to cross an African river.

"This giant creature was unstoppable and overpowering. The dogs, tied here but now let free of their harnesses, amazingly backed away, snarling, but then Gerber shouted orders at them. They tried to attack but were made pulp within a series of effortless blows, their crushed bodies still faintly twitching as they tried in vain to stand. They jerked and writhed with maniacal ferocity, issuing forth a shrill piercing noise before becoming silent, and their blood viscous in the earth. "Gun fire was splayed in the direction of the yeti in near continuous fashion. Holding human flame rife close for the final confrontation, taking careful aim.

"The first bullet caught the yeti in its hind leg. It squealed in pain, temporarily knocked backwards by the impact, but then it scrambled up, still yelping but ready to kill anything that endangered it further.

"Rising on two legs the size of temple pillars, it spun in pain, whistled like a broken flute, and then moved with remarkable speed towards me, as fast as any wolf emerging from the moonlit darkness, accelerating with extraordinary efficiency. I fired my pistol, the small internal stirrings of metal ending not in a roar but in a click, like that of a cigarette lighter which won't give a flame.

"The creature hurled itself at me, reaching out a lunging clawed hand that struck me a mighty blow and ripped through my thigh muscle with talons that could tear metal. I screamed with every sinew of my being and struggled for a moment to see through the fog of pain and nausea, thrashing wildly as I did so on the ground. Blood sprayed like crimson water from tiny springs in my leg.

"Alexandru fired this time. The shot went wild. Everyone seemed to be yelling simultaneously, no longer calm and controlled. The voice in my own skull screamed at me. *Get out now!*

"The yeti did not attack me again but instead limped in a circle, as though confused by the rich scent to it's of its own blood.

When another shot missed the target a third time, the creature couched and exposed its jaundice teeth, sniffing at the air continuously.

"We were unable to get to the armoured vehicle carrier, where we had additional supplies of ammunition. A rudimentary calculation estimated that Alexandru had a single bullet left. This one hit the target in the face. After several moments, once the massive beast had fallen, Gerber swapped his rifle for a flamethrower and opened fire at it. There was an immediate stench of burning fur and flesh, followed by the sound of the splattering of the creature's monstrous guts as magma-red blood sprayed from its wounds. Slowly, the flooding of oxygen through its cells and the pulsing of its life ceased…its last movement was to turn completely on its back like a dying dragonfly.

"Despite the pain and the blood pouring down my leg, I inspected the creature nervously and saw that, as well as the destruction of the torso, the yeti's head had been blown half away. Somehow, we had to find a way to get it back to the temple. Gerber for once agreed with me and looked down the forest slopes. 'We just push it,' he said. 'Gravity will help us. Then we follow it down, pushing it again until it rolls into our campsite.' He paused before saying: 'How we get it onto the back of the vehicle I don't know, but we'll deal with that problem when we get there.'

"We reached our campsite, gaining fresh reserves of bullets and grenades. Our collective eyes urgently scanned the landscape around the personnel carriers for any movement, the storm troopers spreading out quickly in order to cover as much ground as possible without putting too much distance between one another, as that might lead to the possibility of someone being picked off. My eyes became as alert as any soldier's as I checked out the holes in the walls of the forest – into every shadowed, dark satin corner.

"Evening fog was swirling between the trees, creating grey ghosts between the tall trunks. The adrenaline was evidently flowing in Gerber, whose eyes were wide – the eyes of war! He prowled the area, his movements predatory and exaggerated.

"The yeti lay dead and mutilated at our feet, having been kicked and shoved downhill, falling between trees and dense forestation. We knew from what we'd seen in Shambhala that the yetis tried to protect and keep secret their dead and were therefore not going to accept this theft of one of their own without a battle. That said, they were not invulnerable and could be killed by bullets and flamethrowers. That is the one thing that my expedition had proved – they were as mortal as anything that had ever walked, flown, or swam across the face of the earth. They were not a supernatural being of any kind, merely one with a massive instinct for survival and extreme power and cunning.

"Gerber, thinking he heard something from inside the tent, launched a lion-like gout of flame which raged and slashed across the face of the textile structure, rapidly illuminating the general vicinity, until the canvas disintegrated into Titian-red ash, floating on the wind like dirty snow. As the tent disintegrated, we saw that all that was inside was the now charred remains of a mountain fox.

"Standing within the middle of a knot of troops, we heard high whistles in the darkness of the forest, most closely to our left beyond the armoured vehicles. Again I knew I was safer surrounded by armed men who were trained to defend a location and defeat an enemy. It may or may not have proven to be true in the long run, but it was, at that point in time, a comforting thought.

"Down two storm troopers, my legs exploding into violent motion, we got into the six-wheeled armoured carrier as large branches were snapping around us in the undergrowth. I found an empty pocket and filled it with a grenade. I wasn't a soldier, but I knew how to pull out a pin and throw one!

"The vibration from the engine was enough to shock me back into the real world. I had lost a lot of blood, but I made a tourniquet from a swastika flag, which I pulled so tight that I nearly passed out with the pain. At the same time, I could feel that the flow of blood was mostly curtailed.

"I was no longer fearful – and there wasn't time to panic anyway. There were far too many other things to concentrate on, including my oxygen deprived breathing. With enhanced strength, the result of fear-induced adrenalin and desperate energy, we somehow dragged and lifted the yeti into the back area of the vehicle. It took the full effort of every one of us. Alexandru slammed the vehicle into gear, wheels spinning on damp ground as we lurched forward, momentarily skidding and leaving a vast trail of exhaust smoke.

"As we accelerated, a distant glistening shape like a runaway train was battering its way through the undergrowth in the ruddy mist behind us. Fast and ferocious, it lunged at the back of the vehicle. For a moment we seemed halted by a monstrous force, but then the creature failed to hold on, nor could it keep up with us as we picked up speed.

"We negotiated our way out of the difficult terrain, hitting the dirt road back to Salween and Lhasa.

"The dark enveloped us as we neared the temple gates; the wind had picked up and blown away most of the green tinted fog. Our vehicle's powerful arc lights illuminated the wind-scoured walls of the temple. The heavy wheels threw up sheets of icy water as the vehicle rumbled through potholes on the track near the cemetery.

"The makeshift tourniquet on my thigh was still working, but needing medical assistance of some kind urgently, I knew that Kano would arrange this for me once safely back inside the temple.

"But the yetis had tracked us from Shambhala.

"Gerber's men laid down a murderous arc of fire and Alexandru threw three grenades in quick succession, the triple boom sounding like a massive gong being struck. One of the grenades, we could clearly see, set yeti fur on fire. Despite this, it was apparent that the creatures had no fear of us.

"However, the rain of bullets and explosions did stop them from coming any closer. They were shuffling around in an agitated state. I was sure that at some point they would drop on all fours like bears, but they never did. After a while, seeming to give up hope, they wandered away into the dark distance, but there was no saying when they would be back.

"We sped in through the gates like an ingot shot from a cannon, and as quickly as we could we chained and padlocked the gates behind us. Monstrous shapes appeared suddenly within the diffused mist.

"I was immediately taken up to my bed chamber. In need of urgent medical attention, I received ancient Tibetan medical treatment. Firstly, a mix of plants, herb extracts, and nettles were mashed into a pulp, smeared thickly over the wound, and then strapped in place against my thigh. The pain of this concoction was unbearable, but I knew it was a good pain, one of healing and not of illness or infection.

"Secondly, I was told to eat a strange soup, which was not unpleasant smelling but was certainly pungent and very thick, like eating a very rich-tasting porridge. This natural medication was remarkable and kept me half-way comfortable, but it also blurred my vision, making my eyes water and slowing my responses and reactions for a number of days. I wouldn't have chosen to have slept so much, but my body knew what I needed more than I did, and the medication offered no alternative.

"Whilst I slept, unbeknownst to me, the cross given to me by the Sky Woman was placed beneath my pillow.

"Many days later, when I was fit enough to get out of bed and walk, I went to work on the yeti corpse, which had been packed in ice so as to preserve it. At close range, it defied facile description. There was something both of the bear and the ape about its general appearance, but it could not have been mistaken for either. It appeared to be covered in two distinct kinds of hair, the first type being the reddish hair which gave it its characteristic colour, forming a tight, close fur against the body. This mingled with the second type, long and loose straight hairs which gave off a slightly greyish tinge as the light caught them. The shoulders sloped sharply down to a powerful chest. Seen in profile, the back of the head was a straight line from the crown into the shoulders.

"But one thing was certain: this creature was not mythical. For many years in Europe, the gorilla was believed to have been invented in fiction, before a French explorer shot one in the 1920s and its existence was finally accepted.

"I had brought state-of-the-art equipment for scientific analysis with me on the expedition. Once I had completed the six basic nucleon tests that Dr Mengele had recommended to me, I knew I had to return home to Germany as soon as I felt well enough to travel.

"The tests were perfectly clear: the yeti's genetic code was exactly that of a humanoid, simply stunted in intellectual development for over several million years before we developed from them. They were probably our oldest descendants.

"And I remembered something that I'd learned from both the Sky Woman and Kano," that, through human history, the yeti appears as a damned spirit, a thieving monster, or a protector of monasteries and mountains. It is omnipresent. I found it particularly interesting that in depictions of the cosmos, the yeti is described as way ahead of animals but only slightly below humans.

"But there was also one last think, this yeti was definitely female – and pregnant! I removed the foetus and packed it in separate ice to try to preserve it for further experiments."

* * *

"I needed to recover from both the physical and mental effects of the yeti attack, and to come to terms both with what I had seen in the ice caverns of Shambhala and the nature of my experiments.

"The following months passed slowly.

"On my last night in Tibet, I looked up at the mountains somewhere between dusk and midnight. There was no longer any blue to be seen. The sun was dispersed into a great patch of cream that would soon be hidden completely, and the temple walls rose out of the encroaching charcoal curtain as a new moon prepared itself to be born to throw the black mountains into sharp shadows on the slopes.

"Somewhere in the sky the thunder grumbled like the sound of machines in the earth.

"I shook Kano's hand with great sincerity and hugged young Tenzin, who had been saved from experiencing the war-like carnival of our return from the plateau. I told the boy that I had simply fallen down a rocky slope and that this was how I had damaged my leg.

"I thanked them both genuinely for all their help and support.

"As I climbed into the vehicle, a meadow was visible beyond the trees, green stalks splattered with the brightness of bluebells. And before me was a mountain range shimmering on the horizon, a frozen tidal wave, its glacial peaks towering into puffy cotton-wool clouds, resembling crests of waves.

"The vehicle moved forward. I was on my way back to Berlin."

Chapter 16

Schröder's Story, Part IV

End of the Master Race Quest

Schröder stood up and peered out of the window of Goeth's villa, taking in the secluded gardens of Auschwitz. The last vestiges of the setting sun were disappearing over the horizon before him, the copper hues giving way to purple. The moon was a silver disc in the east and Venus burned brightly above the trees.

He heard a faint beating of wings and, looking up, saw an owl, soft and white against the sky; then it grew distant and was gone, having risen and vanished into the thin mist which hung across the dismal, cramped shed-like structures of Auschwitz. From the house, the camp area could be seen whole. There was a rural stretch graced with a churchyard folded between two tiny hillocks.

Turning away from the window, leaving the ghost of his reflection there, Schröder caught sight of a document left on an adjoining sideboard, classified "Top Secret Edict". Past caring about protocol, he peered at the first page of the document, which was illuminated in a bright circle of light from a nearby lamp. It was advising Auschwitz-Birkenau, or at least the extermination wing, to expect a shipment of thirty-one hundred reject prisoners from Płaszóow and saying that cattle trucks had been arranged to transport them, which would run up the spur to the main gate of Auschwitz. The next line chilled his soul: "These prisoners are for Sonderbehandlung." *Sonderbehandlung* was a compound term that would become famous in later years. Even though it was a medieval Teutonic word used in children's fairy stories, it would become synonymous with Nazidom. It means special treatment, which in SS parlance was code for "liquidate upon arrival".

Schröder felt a sudden and overwhelming sense of nausea.

Himmler studied him sharply, before pouring more cognac into a slim crystal glass. "So the yeti *does* exist," he said in a wondrous way, pretending he hadn't noticed Schröder reading the document. "Your story was told remarkably, Hans, as elegant as a Shakespearean sonnet."

Schröder faced him sharply. "There are many vanished creatures and, with them, monstrous legends that owe nothing to reality. The yeti is in neither category. They are beasts of a vast scale and are the most deadly species on earth." He paused. "I have, as you asked, discovered the yeti's zoological blueprint. The myth is somehow truer than truth itself. I have taken wild conjecture and turned it into solid reality."

There was a flow like a current of energy in the air as all eyes turned in his direction."And, as they are linked genetically to humans, they are also cannibals?" Himmler asked, his mind drifting into unfathomable possibilities.

Goeth overheard this and barked a short laugh, a fierce, humourless sound.

"It's a shame you couldn't have brought one back alive, Hans, as there would be plenty of food for it here. We could even fatten the yeti up a bit first by giving them more than thin soup." He tittered heartlessly. His look was colder than the coldest stone, his smile like the tightening of a wire. He had the natural capacity to make normal people feel disgust.

But then Goeth seemed suddenly pre-occupied, like a man who has remembered in the middle of dinner some urgent business detail that he should have cleared up earlier that afternoon and which now called out to him from the darkness of his demonic mentality. He turned his attention away.

Again Schröder could feel a charge animating the air. He realised that Kano was right in that the universe was a machine, and humankind's infinitesimal place within it was as nothing more than a cog. Schröder felt a deep depression mark his soul. The world was moulded out of blood, and this war was swollen on the amplitude of time.

"On another matter," Himmler said in a sullen, earnest voice, the conversation taking on a new intimacy, "we are losing the war on the Eastern Front, and the English and Americans are advancing in surges from the west. Despite Goebbels' latest propaganda message, it is only a matter of time before we are lost. We have a year, at best." He said this last in a business-like tone of sadness. A sour smile moved only one corner of his mouth as his customary zeal and sparkle evaporated. For the first time, Schröder saw the real person beneath the meticulously constructed façade.

Schröder frowned and spoke thoughtfully as if he were not there. "I understand," he said, not feeling as blithe as he sounded and unable to restrain a tremor from twitching at his lips as Himmler continued even more softly.

"Hitler has a great mind, but it has grown cancerous, half bacterium and half magic." For a moment his face was dusky with blood, but the smile stayed where it was. He stood in silence a while, seemingly in a state of confused emotions, and then, very suddenly, he buried his face in his hands as if harbouring monstrous thoughts.

"Hitler's promise of a better future has not been a limitless rope. It has been a piece of elastic. The harder we go forward, the more fiercely we are jerked back to our original position. We no longer have the luxury of self-deceit. Our vision of deliverance is futile now."

A collapsed look creased his face. He seemed suddenly smaller, older.

"The world will not forgive the human savagery of our death factories," he said, "and it is not illusory. The killing process is entering its last furious days. Save yourself before it is too late. Whatever you may or may not have done, you will be deemed to have been duplicitous, and you will be accused of crimes of the most indefensible kind. The world will not distinguish between guilt and duty, Hans. However," he said, with a fleeting look of humour, "Adolf thanks you for the *Iron Man* artefact."

Schröder offered a bitter smile in return, thinking, but not voicing, that although the war was lost, the SS system had become more implacable. Schröder looked in a state of exalted desperation and moral disgust, characteristic of many who had worked inside the system, but not always for it, positively dependent on his myopia.

"The hour of honour makes it our duty to watch and keep order," Himmler said sternly then. His speech weaved from issue to issue, exhausting some ideas, returning tangentially to others, before he reached the epicentre of its temerity. "We are defeated, and not even the yeti could save us." He laughed outwardly now with an underlining sense of resignation.

Downing the last of his cognac and standing, Himmler clicked his heels in the traditional Nazi manner and saluted. "I am tired of mysteries," he said. Then the men all shook hands, after which Himmler left.

The next time Schröder would see Himmler would be at the Nuremburg trials in 1946 when, after being arrested, Schröder would have an eye open to the option of suicide for the first time.

Chapter 17

Palace of Justice, Nuremberg,

Bavaria, January 1946

Hans Schröder accepted the small capsule from the guard as his cell door was slammed in his face with a solemn boom.

Schröder waited for the sound of receding steps to become faint, and then he turned to look through the iron-barred window, his hands gripping the bars tightly. The rain had fallen all day and was still falling, the dank drizzle seeming not so much to fall as coagulate from the clouds straight into the air.

In the courtyard of the Palace of Justice, the green leaves were being beaten off the trees by the steady downpour and were drifting about in the puddles. Now and then there would come a gust of wind so that the trees moaned and tossed their arms imploringly, although they had been rooted in the soil long enough to know better. Darkness had fallen early; indeed there had seemed little light all day, so that the process was slow and imperceptible. But when it was complete, the darkness was intense beyond the street lights. And the rain still fell through it.

There was a sudden sound of blown water dashing over the panes like gravel.

Schröder began to pace to and fro across the small stone floor of the cell, grasping the Sky Woman's cross in his hand and thinking, What distinguishes man from the rest of creation may be no more than the simple fact of his capacity to look at the facts and draw a logical conclusion from them. He meditated on this for a moment before resuming his pacing.

In the world's spotlight, literally, he had given evidence that day at the war crimes trial, the likes of which would never be seen again. He had felt like an insect under a microscope – and the world had heard of his Tibetan tale and its lunatic Nazi inspired objectives.

He was drained and in need of an end to it all. He considered for the last time the prospect of spending the rest of his life in prison, even if he escaped execution, and then presently he lay back on the single bunk in his cell and pulled a thin blanket up to his neck to cover himself. The darkness and loneliness gave him plenty of time to think. He held up the small capsule in his right hand and, following a hectic stare of concentration, placed it carefully in his mouth, producing enough saliva to be able to swallow it whole, without the need to bite down.

He peered momentarily at the stars, which glimmered in a cold slice of night. A crescent moon was drawn in chalk, blotted out occasionally by rain clouds as they moved slowly across the moon's smiling face.

As the cyanide entered his blood stream, he felt a strange cloudiness in his stomach. With this came a dream of confidence.

Schröder thought about Tibet for the last time and how the night sky there was a negative image of its daytime beauty, midnight blue with clouds swirling like spilled black ink in water. In the summer days in Tibet, the clouds are so brilliant above the mountains, such pure white, that even the palest of skies is the darker of the two.

His thoughts turned to his time at the temple, and then his mind delved deeper into previously impassable mental territory, lightening him until he thought he would float. He was in a private tormented dreamscape, adding curiosity to the origins of life, his nature and his final status within God's great order of things. The yeti adventure had haunted his dreams and was now fixed there indelibly.

He inhaled forcibly, coughed, and inhaled again. And then the fear returned, in every corpuscle of his blood, lightening him until he thought he would float. The fear was as sensual and lovely as any pleasure he had known, the intermingling emotions enhancing his mindscape. Terror possessed and summoned him, enveloping him like a poisonous cloud.

During the comatose state, between sleep and nightmare, he saw himself climbing the high plateau that never turns green, the dream continuing with vivid scenes of the ice caverns, the trapped little girl whom Gerber killed, the violent yeti attack on their descent, and the inherent evil that had been seen in the Tibetan chemo since time immemorial.

The fleeting nature of such remembrances filled Schröder with a strange hypnotic and dreamlike sense of joy, the images falling like cooling rain on his heart. A great lightness took the place of grief in his sub-conscious, and the constellations looked down upon him through the little barred window, as he drank in the chill of the night air with pleasure.

As gentle as the fall of a dying breeze, his terror arced and was gone, the jewelled cross lying low across his chest like a conquered spirit. His last thoughts were of the temple fortress jutting half-way into the sky, and then of Kano and Tenzin.

A shadow of pain seemed to pass across his face, before the arteries of his brain and heart hardened with the honeyed poison – at which point everything faded from his mind forever.

Storytellers die, but true stories survive the passage of time.

Schröder's story would be one of those that survived.

* * *

High on the tableland, the pink underlay of rock, which belonged to a prehistoric epoch of geological time, lay horizontally, seeming to have been lifted and smoothed.

The creatures that inhabited this land were of the same epoch. They were neither man nor woman, but distant ancestors of a humanoid race from the depths of ages and antiquity, untouched by the practices of men, not affected when the earth had changes of mood and casually wiped out species upon species. The chemo hovered on the brink of extinction but somehow had survived the passage of time, undamaged and almost unnoticed.

They were as old as the mountains, a dim racial remembrance of long-lost prehistoric monsters, with cunning, instinctive brains and skilled hands, the germ of the modern day ogre, imbued with human characteristics.

The foothill forests were like the bent knee of a giant whose leg, tufted with trees and bushes, interrupted the glimmering sill of

311

the waterfall and whose ungainly feet were splayed out in the endless forest, lost within the blackness.

The sky over the Himalayas was in terrible darkness. The wind howled, and the jagged peaks, wintry and vast, gleamed like fangs. A crackle of pale lightning ignited the blizzard; the sky was momentarily lit with a satin blue. It was beyond nature's legislation, the epitome of magic.

Above the trees and parallel to the line of darkness, everlasting Everest knifed up into the sky with dreadful majesty.

A ruined king in the wilderness of ice.

Chapter 18

An Old Beginning

Lhasa Temple, 2020

Seventy-Three Years Later

A cold wind shrieked in the mountains and turned the trees into apparitions. In the temple courtyard, the monkey cages rocked back and forth. The surface of the great lake was turbulent, and swept mini waves onto the pathways on both sides.

From a high courtyard window, Deng watched with cold bright eyes as the first coaches filled with tourists pulled in through the gates and parked outside the grand reception. As the tourists began to disembark, he could hear the chattering of excited voices rising in the air. The temple workers started to unpack the luggage holds.

The room behind him was dark as he held up a silver candle holder, the flame seeming to leap and expand, to reach the gleam of oranges, yellows, and golds that met his reflection wherever he glanced in the room.

Nobody looked up in his direction, but if they had, they would have seen a traditionally dressed Tibetan man staring down at them with a fixed grin on his face. He wore a purple cloak

313

attached to both shoulders and cut from the finest Tibetan linen. The scarlet tunic was short and slit at the sides.

The wind, which only broke in puffs and draughts, moving into the room through the shutters, tossed the thin light of the candle in a myriad directions.

Deng pulled the corner of his cloak across his face to hide the smile, appalled and secretly gratified by his genuine distaste for humanity and the violent mess they had made of themselves. Perhaps a more ancient *Homo sapiens* species could still prevail. Perhaps the perdition and damnation of modern life could still be achieved.

The past was a forbidden land, and its people's trials were nearing an end. In future times, when gravity had mastered the mountains, humbling them to no more than pebble and crumb, everyone, including him and the whole species, would be in that hour glass called "now".

The moonbeams lifted the blackness of the sky to a deep blue, the silvery beams brilliant against the navy sky.

Deng paused and looked at his own reflection in the window, noticing the power in his eyes, as reckless as a mountain storm. His stare was painful and piercing with a blinding teal light. Yet they were also beautiful eyes, like an ancient building with ivy gripping the peeling walls in a timeless hug.

The eyes were not soulless or lifeless. Instead, they were like two pristine stones of onyx that lit up and glowed emerald when touched by the candle light, lines and dots forming in the irises as ancient and modern humanoids, intimate enemies bound by blood, fought in an eternal struggle for dominance within him.

To be continued …

Closing Quotations

Robin Coningham claimed to have found the origins of the unicorn myth in a wall etching on the Chilean-Argentinean border at Patagonia. Depicted since antiquity in the ancient seals of the Inca Valley civilizations, the unicorn legend spread into Greek mythology and European folklore. Research found it to be a long-extinct species of Patagonian forest pony, resembling a giant goat with a long horn and cloven hooves, known locally as the *Huemul*. Coningham was also a well-known explorer in Africa, South America, and the West Indies, examining the voodoo rites in the jungle glades, and then the blood-smoked pyramids of Mexico.

On his deathbed, Coningham said: "I am also a firm believer in the yeti legend and regret that I had never had the chance to prove its true origins and authenticity." Virtually the last words he uttered expressed his hope that "somebody, one day, would be able to comprehend and explain this timeless Himalayan King Kong, and place it within the correct order of things."

Robin Coningham, British archaeologist, explorer, and historian. Discoverer of the sky disc in the Cypress Jewell Tree expedition of 1972.

"Tibetan Buddhism is too great to be inquired after and too powerful to be learned. I am part of the myth myself. It is not just Hindoo Gods that reached the Himalayas. There are other beliefs, customs and fears that endure in Tibet along the roof of the world. Divinity exists in ancient human form, passed from successor to successor and species to species."

Geduin Druppa, First Dalai Lama, speaking of the era of fragmentation.

Quoted from the Tibetan book of the dead, fifth century AD.

Lightning Source UK Ltd.
Milton Keynes UK
UKOW05f2154160617

303535UK00001B/92/P

9 781524 681852